D0125387

U·X·L
COMPLETE
LIFE
SCIENCE
RESOURCE

U·X·L
COMPLETE
LIFE
SCIENCE
RESOURCE

volume THREE: O-Z

LEONARD C. BRUNO
JULIE CARNAGIE, EDITOR

U·X·L®

AN IMPRINT OF THE GALE GROUP
DETROIT · SAN FRANCISCO · LONDON
BOSTON · WOODBRIDGE, CT

U·X·L Complete Life Science Resource

LEONARD C. BRUNO

Staff

Julie L. Carnagie, *U·X·L Senior Editor*

Carol DeKane Nagel, *U·X·L Managing Editor*

Meggin Condino, *Senior Market Analyst*

Margaret Chamberlain, *Permissions Specialist*

Randy Bassett, *Image Database Supervisor*

Robert Duncan, *Imaging Specialist*

Pamela A. Reed, *Image Coordinator*

Robyn V. Young, *Senior Image Editor*

Michelle DiMercurio, *Art Director*

Evi Seoud, *Assistant Manager, Composition Purchasing and Electronic Prepress*

Mary Beth Trimper, *Manager, Composition and Electronic Prepress*

Rita Wimberley, *Senior Buyer*

Dorothy Maki, *Manufacturing Manager*

GGS Information Services, Inc., *Typesetting*

Bruno, Leonard C.

U·X·L complete life science resource / Leonard C. Bruno; Julie L. Carnagie, editor.
p. cm.
Includes bibliographical references.
Contents: v. 1. A-E v. 2. F-N v. 3. O-Z.
ISBN 0-7876-4851-5 (set) ISBN 0-7876-4852-3 (vol. 1) ISBN 0-7876-4854-X (vol. 2)
1. Life sciences Juvenile literature. [1. Life sciences Encyclopedias.] I. Carnagie, Julie. II. Title.

QH309.2.B78 2001   00-56376

Table of Contents

Contents

Contents

Reader's Guide

U·X·L Complete Life Science Resource explores the fascinating world of the life sciences by providing readers with comprehensive and easy-to-use information. The three-volume set features 240 alphabetically arranged entries, which explain the theories, concepts, discoveries, and developments frequently studied by today's students, including: cells and simple organisms, diversity and adaptation, human body systems and life cycles, the human genome, plants, animals, and classification, populations and ecosystems, and reproduction and heredity.

The three-volume set includes a timeline of scientific discoveries, a "Further Information" section, and research and activity section. It also contains 180 black-and-white illustrations that help to bring the text to life, sidebars containing short biographies of scientists, a "Words to Know" section, and a cumulative index providing easy access to the subjects, theories, and people discussed throughout *U·X·L Complete Life Science Resource.*

Acknowledgments

Special thanks are due for the invaluable comments and suggestions provided by the *U·X·L Complete Life Science Resource* advisors:

- Don Curry, Science Teacher, Silverado High School, Las Vegas, Nevada

- Barbara Ibach, Librarian, Northville High School, Northville, Michigan

- Joel Jones, Branch Manager, Kansas City Public Library, Kansas City, Missouri

- Nina Levine, Media Specialist, Blue Mountain Middle School, Peekskill, New York

Comments and Suggestions

We welcome your comments on this work as well as your suggestions for topics to be featured in future editions of *U·X·L Complete Life Science Resource*. Please write: Editors, *U·X·L Complete Life Science Resource,* U·X·L, 27500 Drake Rd., Farmington Hills, MI 48331-3535; call toll-free: 1-800-877-4253; fax: 248-699-8097; or send e-mail via www.galegroup.com.

Introduction

U·X·L Complete Life Science Resource is organized and written in a manner to emphasize clarity and usefulness. Produced with grades seven through twelve in mind, it therefore reflects topics that are currently found in most textbooks on the life sciences. Most of these alphabetically arranged topics could be described as important concepts and theories in the life sciences. Other topics are more specific, but still important, sub-categories or segments of a larger concept.

Life science is another, perhaps broader, term for biology. Both simply mean the scientific study of life. All of the essays included in *U·X·L Complete Life Science Resource* can be considered as variations on the simple theme that because something is alive it is very different from something that is not. In some way all of these essays explore and describe the many different aspects of what are considered to be the major characteristics or signs of life. Living things use energy and are organized in a certain way; they react, respond, grow, and develop; they change and adapt; they reproduce and they die. Despite this impressive list, the phenomenon that is called life is so complex, awe-inspiring, and even incomprehensible that our knowledge of it is really only just beginning.

This work is an attempt to provide students with simple explanations of what are obviously very complex ideas. The essays are intended to provide basic, introductory information. The chosen topics broadly cover all aspects of the life sciences. The biographical sidebars touch upon most of the major achievers and contributors in the life sciences and all relate in some way to a particular essay. Finally, the citations listed in the "For Further Information" section include not only materials that were used by the author as sources, but other books that the ambitious and curious student of the life sciences might wish to consult.

Timeline of Significant Developments in the Life Sciences

c. 50,000 B.C. *Homo sapiens sapiens* emerges as a conscious observer of nature.

c. 10,000 B.C. Humans begin the transition from hunting and gathering to settled agriculture, beginning the Neolithic Revolution.

c. 1800 B.C. Process of fermentation is first understood and controlled by the Egyptians.

c. 350 B.C. Greek philosopher Aristotle (384–322 B.C.) first attempts to classify animals, considers nature of reproduction and inheritance, and basically founds the science of biology.

A.D. 1543 Flemish anatomist Andreas Vesalius (1514–1564) publishes *Seven Books on the Construction of the Human Body* which corrects many misconceptions regarding the human body and founds modern anatomy.

1615 The modern study of animal metabolism is founded by Italian physician, Santorio Santorio (1561–1636), who publishes *De Statica Medicina* in which he is the first to apply measurement and physics to the study of processes within the human body.

12,000 B.C.	3,000 B.C.	552
The dog is domesticated from the wolf	The world's population reaches 100,000	Buddhism reaches Japan

| 15,000 B.C. | 7,500 B.C. | A.D. I | 1,000 |

1628 The first accurate description of human blood circulation is offered by English physician William Harvey (1578–1657), who also founds modern physiology.

1665 English physicist Robert Hooke (1635–1703) coins the word "cell" and develops the first drawing of a cell after observing a sliver of cork under a microscope.

1669 Entomology, or the study of insects, is founded by Dutch naturalist Jan Swammerdam (1637–1680), who begins the first major study of insect microanatomy and classification.

1677 Dutch biologist and microscopist Anton van Leeuwenhoek (1632–1723) is the first to observe and describe spermatozoa (sperm). He later goes on to describe different types of bacteria and protozoa.

1727 English botanist Stephen Hales (1677–1761) studies plant nutrition and measures water absorbed by roots and released by leaves. He states that the plants convert something in the air into food, and that light is a necessary part of this process, which later becomes known as photosynthesis.

1735 Considered the father of modern taxonomy, Swedish botanist Carl Linnaeus (1707–1778) creates the first scientific system for classifying animals and plants. His system of binomial nomenclature establishes generic and specific names.

1779 Dutch physician Jan Ingenhousz (1739–1799) shows that carbon dioxide is taken in and oxygen is given off by plants during photosynthesis. He also states that sunlight is necessary for this process.

1802 The word "biology" is coined by French naturalist Jean-Baptiste Lamarck (1744–1829) to describe the new science of living things. He later proposes the first scientific, but flawed, theory of evolution.

1650	1710	1770
England's first coffee house opens	The first copyright law is established in Britain	The Boston Massacre occurs

1620   1680   1740   1800

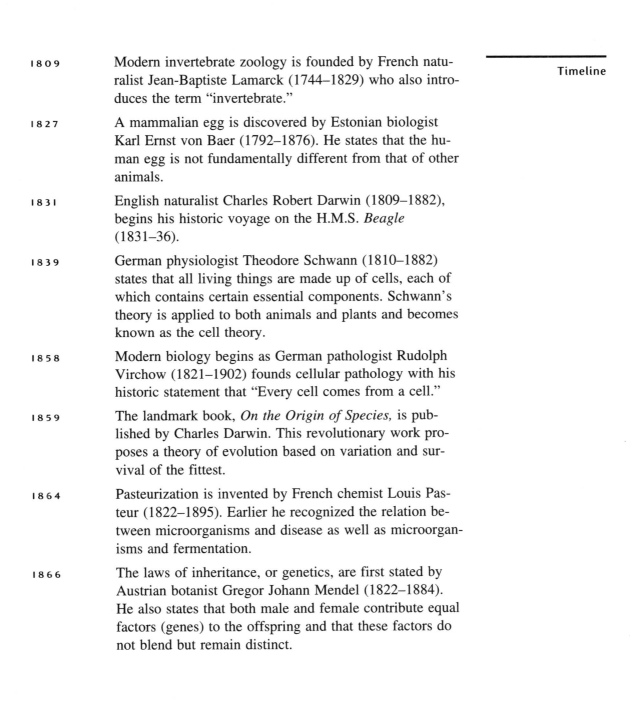

1809   Modern invertebrate zoology is founded by French naturalist Jean-Baptiste Lamarck (1744–1829) who also introduces the term "invertebrate."

1827   A mammalian egg is discovered by Estonian biologist Karl Ernst von Baer (1792–1876). He states that the human egg is not fundamentally different from that of other animals.

1831   English naturalist Charles Robert Darwin (1809–1882), begins his historic voyage on the H.M.S. *Beagle* (1831–36).

1839   German physiologist Theodore Schwann (1810–1882) states that all living things are made up of cells, each of which contains certain essential components. Schwann's theory is applied to both animals and plants and becomes known as the cell theory.

1858   Modern biology begins as German pathologist Rudolph Virchow (1821–1902) founds cellular pathology with his historic statement that "Every cell comes from a cell."

1859   The landmark book, *On the Origin of Species,* is published by Charles Darwin. This revolutionary work proposes a theory of evolution based on variation and survival of the fittest.

1864   Pasteurization is invented by French chemist Louis Pasteur (1822–1895). Earlier he recognized the relation between microorganisms and disease as well as microorganisms and fermentation.

1866   The laws of inheritance, or genetics, are first stated by Austrian botanist Gregor Johann Mendel (1822–1884). He also states that both male and female contribute equal factors (genes) to the offspring and that these factors do not blend but remain distinct.

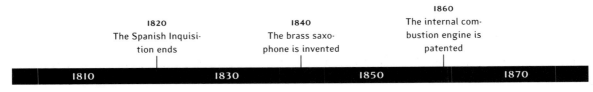

1820
The Spanish Inquisition ends

1840
The brass saxophone is invented

1860
The internal combustion engine is patented

1810   1830   1850   1870

1873	Italian histologist Camillo Golgi (1843–1926) devises a way to stain tissue samples with inorganic dye and applies this new method to nerve tissues.
1882	German bacteriologist Robert Koch (1843–1910) establishes the classic method of preserving, documenting, and studying bacteria.
1882	German anatomist Walther Flemming (1843–1905) becomes the first to observe and describe mitosis or splitting of chromosomes, the structure in the cell that carries the cell's genetic material.
1900	Different types of human blood are discovered by Austrian American physician Karl Landsteiner (1868–1943), who names them A, B, AB, and O.
1901	Spanish histologist Santiago Ramon y Cajal (1852–1911) demonstrates that the neuron is the basis of the nervous system.
1902	Hormones are first named and understood by English physiologists Ernest H. Starling (1866–1927) and William H. Bayliss (1860–1924), who describe them as chemicals that stimulate an organ from a distance.
1905	English biochemist Frederick Gowland Hopkins (1861–1947) provides proof that "essential amino acids" cannot be manufactured by the body and must be obtained from food.
1907	Russian physiologist Ivan Pavlov (1849–1936) conducts pioneering studies on inborn reflexes and the conditioning of animals.
1910	American geneticist Thomas Hunt Morgan (1866–1945) works with the fruit fly *Drosophila* and establishes the chromosome theory of inheritance. This theory states that chromosomes are composed of discrete entities called genes that are the actual carriers of specific traits.

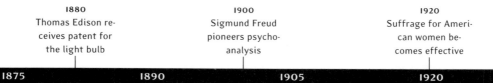

1880	1900	1920
Thomas Edison receives patent for the light bulb	Sigmund Freud pioneers psychoanalysis	Suffrage for American women becomes effective

1875	1890	1905	1920

1912	English biochemist Frederick Gowland Hopkins (1861–1947) proves that "accessory substances," later called vitamins, are essential for health and growth.
1932	German biochemist Hans Krebs (1900–1981) discovers that glucose (sugar) is broken down in a chain of reactions that comes to be called the Krebs cycle.
1953	The double helix structure of deoxyribonucleic acid (DNA) is discovered by American biochemist James Dewey Watson (1928–) and English biochemist Francis Harry Compton Crick (1916–). Their model explains how DNA transmits hereditary traits in living organisms, and forms the basis for all genetic discoveries that follow. This is considered one of the greatest of all scientific discoveries.
1961	Messenger ribonucleic acid (mRNA), which transfers genetic information to the ribosomes where proteins are made, is discovered by French biologists Jacques Lucien Monod (1910–1976) and Francois Jacob (1920–).
1978	The first "test tube" baby is born in England. Physicians remove an egg from the mother's ovary, fertilize it with the father's sperm in a petri dish, and reimplant it in the mother's uterus.
1982	A gene from one mammal (a rat growth hormone gene) functions for the first time in another mammal (a mouse). As a result, the mouse grows to twice its normal size.
1983	American biologist Lynn Margulis (1938–) discovers that cells with nuclei can be formed by the synthesis of non-nucleated cells (those without a nucleus, like bacteria).
1987	Genetically engineered plants are first developed.

1935
Adolf Hitler creates
the *Lüftwaffe*

1955
British Prime Minister Winston
Churchill resigns

1975
Microsoft is
founded

1925   1945   1965   1985

1990 The Human Genome Project is established in Washington, D.C., as an international team of scientists announces a plan to compile a "map" of human genes.

1991 The gender of a mouse is changed at the embryo stage.

1992 The United Nations Conference on Environment and Development is held in Brazil and is attended by delegates from 178 countries, most of whom agree to combat global warming and to preserve biodiversity.

1995 The first complete sequencing of an organism's genetic make up is achieved by the Institute for Genomic Research in the United States. The institute uses an unconventional technique to sequence all 1,800,000 base pairs that make up the chromosome of a certain bacterium.

1997 The first successful cloning of an adult mammal is achieved by Scottish embryologist Ian Wilmut (1944–), who clones a lamb named Dolly from a cell taken from the mammary gland of a sheep.

1998 The first completed genome of an animal, a roundworm, is achieved by a British and American team. The genetic map shows the 97,000,000 genetic letters in correct sequence, taken from the worm's 19,900 genes.

1999 Danish researchers find what they believe is evidence of the oldest life on Earth—fossilized plankton from 3,700,000,000 years ago.

2000 Gene therapy succeeds unequivocally for the first time as doctors in France add working genes to three infants who could not develop their own complete immune systems.

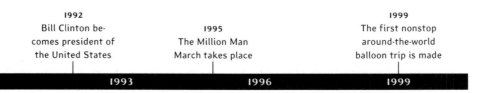

1992 Bill Clinton becomes president of the United States	1995 The Million Man March takes place	1999 The first nonstop around-the-world balloon trip is made
1990	1993	1996	1999

Words to Know

A

Abiotic: The nonliving part of the environment.

Absorption: The process by which dissolved substances pass through a cell's membrane.

Acid: A solution that produces a burning sensation on the skin and has a sour taste.

Acid rain: Rain that has been made strongly acidic by pollutants in the atmosphere.

Acquired characteristics: Traits that are developed by an organism during its lifetime; they cannot be inherited by offspring.

Active transport: In cells, the transfer of a substance across a membrane from a region of low concentration to an area of high concentration; requires the use of energy.

Adaptation: Any change that makes a species or an individual better suited to its environment or way of life.

Adrenalin: A hormone released by the body as a result of fear, anger, or intense emotion that prepares the body for action.

Aerobic respiration: A process that requires oxygen in which food is broken down to release energy.

AIDS: A disease caused by a virus that disables the immune system.

Algae: A group of plantlike organisms that make their own food and live wherever there is water, light, and a supply of minerals.

Allele: An alternate version of the same gene.

Alternation of generations: The life cycle of a plant in which asexual stages alternate with sexual stages.

Amino acids: The building blocks of proteins.

Amoeba: A single-celled organism that has no fixed shape.

Amphibians: A group of vertebrates that spend part of their life on land and part in water; includes frogs, toads, and salamanders.

Anaerobic respiration: A stage in the breaking down of food to release energy that takes place in the absence of oxygen.

Anaphase: The stage during mitosis when chromatids separate and move to the cell poles.

Angiosperms: Flowering plants that produce seeds inside of their fruit.

Anther: The male part of a flower that contains pollen; a saclike container at the tip of the stamen.

Antibiotics: A naturally occurring chemical that kills or inhibits the growth of bacteria.

Antibody: A protein made by the body that locks on, or marks, a particular type of antigen so that it can be destroyed by other cells.

Antigen: Any foreign substance in the body that stimulates the immune system to action.

Arachnid: An invertebrate that has four pairs of jointed walking legs.

Arthropod: An invertebrate that has jointed legs and a segmented body.

Atom: The smallest particle of an element.

Autotroph: An organism, such as a green plant, that can make its own food from inorganic materials.

Auxins: A group of plant hormones that control the plant's growth and development.

Axon: A long, threadlike part of a neuron that conducts nerve impulses away from the cell.

B

Bacteria: A group of one-celled organisms so small they can only be seen with a microscope.

Binomial nomenclature: The system in which organisms are identified by a two-part Latin name; the first name is capitalized and identifies the genus; the second name identifies the species of that genus.

Biological community: A collection of all the different living things found in the same geographic area.

Biological diversity: A broad term that includes all forms of life and the ecological systems in which they live.

Biomass: The total amount of living matter in a given area.

Biome: A large geographical area characterized by distinct climate and soil and particular kinds of plants and animals.

Biosphere: All parts of Earth, extending both below and above its surface, in which organisms can survive.

Biotechnology: The alteration of cells or biological molecules for a specific purpose.

Bipedalism: Walking on two feet; a human characteristic.

Binary fission: A type of asexual reproduction that occurs by splitting into two more or less equal parts; bacteria usually reproduce by splitting in two.

Blood: A complex liquid that circulates throughout an animal's body and keeps the body's cells alive.

Blood type: A certain class or group of blood that has particular properties.

Brain: The control center of an organism's nervous system.

Breeding: The crossing of plants and animals to change the characteristics of an existing variety or to produce a new one.

Bud: A swelling or undeveloped shoot on a plant stem that is protected by scales.

C

Calorie: A unit of measure of the energy that can be obtained from a food; one calorie will raise the temperature of one kilogram of water by one degree Celsius.

Camouflage: Color or shape of an animal that allows it to blend in with its surroundings.

Carbohydrates: A group of naturally occurring compounds that are essential sources of energy for all living things.

Carbon cycle: The process in which carbon atoms are recycled over and over again on Earth.

Carbon dioxide: A major atmospheric gas.

Carbon monoxide: An odorless, tasteless, colorless, and poisonous gas.

Carnivores: A certain family of mammals that have specially shaped teeth and live by hunting.

Carpel: The female organ of a flower that contains its stigma, style, and ovary.

Cartilage: Smooth, flexible connective tissue found in the ear, the nose, and the joints.

Catalyst: A substance that increases the speed at which a chemical reaction occurs.

Cell: The building block of all living things

Cell theory: States that the cell is the basic building block of all life-forms and that all living things, whether plants or animals, consist of one or more cells.

Cellulose: A carbohydrate that plants use to form the walls of their cells.

Central nervous system: The brain and spinal cord of a vertebrate; it interprets messages and makes decisions involving action.

Centriole: A tiny structure found near the nucleus of most animal cells that plays an important role during cell division.

Cerebellum: The part of the brain that coordinates muscular coordination and balance; the second largest part of the human brain.

Cerebrum: The part of the brain that controls thinking, speech, memory, and voluntary actions; the largest part of the human brain.

Cetacean: A mammal that lives entirely in water and breathes air through lungs.

Chlorophyll: The green pigment or coloring matter in plant cells; it works by transferring the Sun's energy in photosynthesis.

Chloroplast: The energy-converting structures found in the cells of plants.

Chromatin: Ropelike fibers containing deoxyribonucleic acid (DNA) and proteins that are found in the cell nucleus and which contract into a chromosome just before cell division.

Chromosome: A coiled structure in the nucleus of a cell that carries the cell's deoxyribonucleic acid (DNA).

Cilia: Short, hairlike projections that can beat or wave back and forth; singular, cilium.

Classification: A method of organizing plants and animals into categories based on their appearance and the natural relationships between them.

Cleavage: Early cell division in an embryo; each cleavage approximately doubles the number of cells.

Cloning: A group of genetically identical cells descended from a single common ancestor.

Cnidarian: A simple invertebrate that lives in the water and has a digestive cavity with only one opening.

Cochlea: A coiled tube filled with fluid in the inner ear whose nerve endings transmit sound vibrations.

Community: All of the populations of different species living in a specific environment.

Conditioned reflex: A type of learned behavior in which the natural stimulus for a reflex act is substituted with a new stimulus.

Consumers: Animals that eat plants who are then eaten by other animals.

Cornea: The transparent front of the eyeball that is curved and partly focuses the light entering the eye.

Cranium: The dome-shaped, bony part of the skull that protects the brain; it consists of eight plates linked together by joints.

Crustacean: An invertebrate with several pairs of jointed legs and two pairs of antennae.

Cytoplasm: The contents of a cell, excluding its nucleus.

D

Daughter cells: The two new, identical cells that form after mitosis when a cell divides.

Decomposer: An organism, like bacteria and fungi, that feed upon dead organic matter and return inorganic materials back to the environment to be used again.

Dendrite: Any branching extension of a neuron that receives incoming signals.

Deoxyribonucleic acid (DNA): The genetic material that carries the code for all living things.

Differentiation: The specialized changes that occur in a cell as an embryo starts to develop.

Diffusion: The movement or spreading out of a substance from an area of high concentration to the area of lowest concentration.

Dominant trait: An inherited trait that masks or hides a recessive trait.

Double helix: The "spiral staircase" shape or structure of the deoxyribonucleic acid (DNA) molecule.

E

Ecosystem: A living community and its nonliving environment.

Ectoderm: In a developing embryo, the outermost layer of cells that eventually become part of the nerves and skin.

Ectotherm: A cold-blooded animal, like a fish or reptile, whose temperature changes with its surroundings.

Element: A pure substance that contains only one type of atom.

Endangered species: Any species of plant or animal that is threatened with extinction.

Endoderm: In a developing embryo, the innermost layer of cells that eventually become the organs and linings of the digestive, respiratory, and urinary systems.

Endoplasmic reticulum: A network of membranes or tubes in a cell through which materials move.

Endotherm: A warm-blooded animal, like a mammal or bird, whose metabolism keeps its body at a constant temperature.

Energy: The ability to do work.

Enzyme: A protein that acts as a catalyst and speeds up chemical reactions in living things.

Epidermis: The outer layer of an animal's skin; also the outer layer of cells on a leaf.

Eukaryote: An organism whose cells contain a well-defined nucleus that is bound by a membrane.

Eutrophication: A natural process that occurs in an aging lake or pond as it gradually builds up its concentration of plant nutrients.

Evolution: A scientific theory stating that species undergo genetic change over time and that all living things originated from simple organisms.

Exoskeleton: A tough exterior or outside skeleton that surrounds an animal's body.

Extinction: The dying out and permanent disappearance of a species.

F

Fermentation: A chemical process that breaks down carbohydrates and other organic materials and produces energy without using oxygen.

Fertilization: The union of male and female sex cells.

Fetus: A developing embryo in the human uterus that is at least two months old.

Flagella: Hairlike projections possessed by some cells that whip from side to side and help the cell move about; singular, flagellum.

Food chain: A sequence of relationships in which the flow of energy passes.

Food web: A network of relationships in which the flow of energy branches out in many directions.

Fossil: The preserved remains of a once-living organism.

Fruit: The mature or ripened ovary that contains a flower's seeds.

Fungi: A group of many-celled organisms that live by absorbing food and are neither plant nor animal.

G

Gaia hypothesis: The idea that Earth is a living organism and can regulate its own environment.

Gamete: Sex cells used in reproduction; the ovum or egg cell is the female gamete and the sperm cell is the male gamete.

Gastric juice: The digestive juice produced by the stomach; it contains weak hydrochloric acid and pepsin (which breaks down proteins).

Gene: The basic unit of heredity.

Genetic code: The information that tells a cell how to interpret the chemical information stored inside deoxyribonucleic acid (DNA).

Genetic disorder: Conditions that have some origin in a person's genetic makeup.

Genetic engineering: The deliberate alteration of a living thing's genetic material to change its characteristics.

Genetic theory: The idea that genes are the basic units in which characteristics are passed from one generation to the next.

Genetic therapy: The process of manipulating genetic material either to treat a disease or to change a physical characteristic.

Genotype: The genetic makeup of a cell or an individual organism; the sum total of all its genes.

Geolotic record: The history of Earth as recorded in the rocks that make up its crust.

Germination: The earliest stages of growth when a seed begins to transform itself into a living plant that has roots, stems, and leaves.

Gland: A group of cells that produce and secrete enzymes, hormones, and other chemicals in the body.

Golgi body: A collection of membranes inside a cell that packages and transports substances made by the cell.

Greenhouse effect: The name given to the trapping of heat in the lower atmosphere and the warming of Earth's surface that results.

Gymnosperm: Plants with seeds that are not protected by any type of covering.

H

Habitat: The distinct, local environment where a particular species lives.

Heart: A muscular pump that transports blood throughout the body.

Hemoglobin: A complex protein molecule in the red blood cells of vertebrates that carries oxygen molecules in the bloodstream.

Herbivore: Animals that eat only plants.

Herpetology: The scientific study of amphibians and reptiles.

Heterotroph: An organism, like an animal, that cannot make its own food and must obtain its nutrients be eating plants or other animals.

Hibernation: A special type of deep sleep that enables an animal to survive the extreme winter cold.

Homeostasis: The maintenance of stable internal conditions in a living thing.

Hominid: A family of primates that includes today's humans and their extinct direct ancestors.

Hormones: Chemical messengers found in both animals and plants.

Host: The organism on or in which a parasite lives.

Hybrid: The offspring of two different species of plant or animal.

Hypothesis: A possible answer to a scientific problem; it must be tested and proved by observation and experiment.

I

Ichthyology: The branch of zoology that deals with fish.

Immunization: A method of helping the body's natural immune system be able to resist a particular disease.

Inbreeding: The mating of organisms that are closely related or which share a common ancestry.

Instincts: A specific inborn behavior pattern that is inherited by all animal species.

Interphase: The stage during mitosis when cell division is complete.

Invertebrates: Any animal that lacks a backbone, such as paramecia, insects, and sea urchins.

Iris: The colored ring surrounding the pupil of the vertebrate eye; its muscles control the size of the pupil (and therefore the amount of light that enters).

K

Karyotype: A diagnostic tool used by physicians to examine the shape, number, and structure of a person's chromosomes when there is a reason to suspect that a chromosomal abnormality may exist.

L

Lactic acid: An organic compound found in the blood and muscles of animals during extreme exercise.

Larva: The name of the stage between hatching and adulthood in the life cycle of some invertebrates.

Lipids: A group of organic compounds that include fats, oils, and waxes.

Lysosome: Small, round bodies containing digestive enzymes that break down large food molecules into smaller ones.

M

Malnutrition: The physical state of overall poor health that can result from a lack of enough food to eat or from eating the wrong foods.

Mammals: A warm-blooded vertebrate with some hair that feeds milk to its young.

Medulla: The part of the brain just above the spinal cord that controls certain involuntary functions like breathing, heartbeat rate, sneezing, and vomiting; the smallest part of the brain.

Meiosis: A specialized form of cell division that takes place only in the reproductive cells.

Membrane: A thin barrier that separates a cell from its surroundings.

Mendelian laws of inheritance: A theory that states that characteristics are not inherited in a random way but instead follow predictable, mathematical patterns.

Mesoderm: In a developing embryo, the middle layer of cells that eventually become bone, muscle, blood, and reproductive organs.

Metabolism: All of the chemical processes that take place in an organism when it obtains and uses energy.

Metamorphosis: The extreme changes that some organisms go through when they pass from an egg to an adult.

Metaphase: The stage during mitosis when the chromosomes line up across the center of the spindle.

Microorganism: Any form of life too small to be seen without a microscope, such as bacteria, protozoans, and many algae; also called microbe.

Migration: The seasonal movement of an animal to a place that offers more favorable living conditions.

Mineral: An inorganic compound that living things need in small amounts, like potassium, sodium, and calcium.

Mitochondria: Specialized structures inside a cell that break down food and release energy.

Mitosis: The division of a cell nucleus to produce two identical cells.

Molars: Chewing teeth that grind or crush food; the back teeth in the jaws of mammals.

Molecule: A chemical unit consisting of two or more linked atoms.

Mollusk: A soft-bodied invertebrate that is often protected by a hard shell.

Molting: The shedding and discarding of the exoskeleton; some insects molt during metamorphosis, and snakes shed their outer skin in order to grow larger.

Monerans: A group of one-celled organisms that do not have a nucleus.

Mutation: A change in a gene that results in a new inherited trait.

N

Natural selection: The process of survival and reproduction of organisms that are best suited to their environment.

Neuron: An individual nerve cell; the basic unit of the nervous system.

Niche: The particular job or function that a living thing plays in the particular place it lives.

Nitrogen cycle: The stages in which the important gas nitrogen is converted and circulated from the nonliving world to the living world and back again.

Nucleic acid: A group of organic compounds that carry genetic information.

Nutrients: Substances a living thing needs to consume that are used for growth and energy; for humans they include fats, sugars, starches, proteins, minerals, and vitamins.

Nutrition: The process by which an organism obtains and uses raw materials from its environment in order to stay alive.

O

Omnivore: An animal that eats both plants and other animals.

Organ: A structural part of a plant or animal that carries out a certain function and is made up of two or more types of tissue.

Organelle: A tiny structure inside a cell that performs a particular function.

Organic compound: Substances that contain carbon.

Organism: Any complete, individual living thing.

Ornithology: The branch of zoology that deals with birds.

Osmosis: The movement of water from one solution to another through a membrane or barrier that separates the solutions.

Oviparous: Term describing an animal that lays or spawns eggs which then develop and hatch outside of the mother's body.

Ovoviparous: Term describing an animal whose young develop inside the mother's body, but who receive nourishment from a yolk and not from the mother.

Oxidation: An energy-releasing chemical reaction that occurs when a substance is combined with oxygen.

Ozone: A form of oxygen found naturally in the stratosphere or upper atmosphere that shields Earth from the Sun's harmful ultraviolet radiation.

P

Paleontology: The scientific study of the animals, plants, and other organisms that lived in prehistoric times.

Parasite: An organism that lives in or on another organism and benefits from the relationship.

Ph: A number used to measure the degree of acidity of a solution.

Phenotype: The outward appearance of an organism; the visible expression of its genotype.

Pheromones: Chemicals released by an animal that have some sort of effect on another animal.

Photosynthesis: The process by which plants use light energy to make food from simple chemicals.

Physiology: The study of how an organism and its body parts work or function normally.

Pistil: The female part of a flower made up of organs called carpels; located in the center of the flower, parts of it become fruit after fertilization.

Plankton: Tiny, free-floating organisms in a body of water.

Pollen: Dustlike grains produced by a flower's anthers that contain the male sex cells.

Pollution: The contamination of the natural environment by harmful substances that are produced by human activity.

Population: All the members of the same species that live together in a particular place.

Predator: An organism that lives by catching, killing, and eating another organism.

Primate: A type of mammal with flexible fingers and toes, forward-pointing eyes, and a well-developed brain.

Producer: A living thing, like a green plant, that makes its own food and forms the beginning of a food chain, since it is eaten by other species.

Prokaryote: An organism, like bacteria or blue-green algae, whose cells lack both a nucleus and any other membrane-bound organelles.

Prophase: The stage in mitosis when the chromosomes condense or, coil up, and the sister chromatids become visible.

Protein: The building blocks of all forms of life.

Protozoa: A group of single-celled organisms that live by taking in food.

Pseudopod: A temporary outgrowth or extension of the cytoplasm of an amoeba that allows it to slowly move.

R

Radioactive dating: A method of determining the approximate age of an old object by measuring the amount of a known radioactive element it contains.

Recessive trait: An inherited trait that may be present in an organism without showing itself. It is only expressed or seen when partnered by an identical recessive trait.

Reptiles: A cold-blooded vertebrate (animal with a backbone) with dry, scaly skin and which lays sealed eggs.

Respiration: A series of chemical reactions in which food is broken down to release energy.

Retina: The lining at the back of the eyeball that contains nerve endings or rods sensitive to light.

Rh factor: A certain blood type marker that each human blood type either has (Rh-positive) or does not have (Rh-negative).

Rhizome: A creeping underground plant stem that comes up through the soil and grows new stems.

Ribonucleic acid (RNA): An organic substance in living cells that plays an essential role in the construction of proteins and therefore in the transfer of genetic information.

Rods: Nerve endings or receptor cells in the retina of the eye that are sensitive to dim light but cannot identify colors.

S

Sap: A liquid inside a plant that is made up mainly of water and which transports dissolved substances throughout the plant.

Sedimentation: The settling of solid particles at the bottom of a body of water that are eventually squashed together by pressure to form rock.

Smooth muscle: Muscle that appears smooth under a microscope; they are involuntary muscles since they cannot be controlled.

Sponge: An invertebrate that lives underwater and survives by taking in water through a system of pores.

Spontaneous generation: The incorrect theory that nonliving material can give rise to living organisms.

Spore: Usually a single-celled structure with a tough coat that allows an organism, like bacteria or fungi, to reproduce asexually under the proper conditions.

Stamen: The male organ of a flower consisting of a filament and an anther in which the pollen grains are produced.

Stigma: The tip of a flower's pistil upon which pollen collects during pollination and fertilization.

Stimulus: Anything that causes a receptor or sensory nerve to react and carry a message.

Stomata: The pores in leaves that allow gases to enter and leave; singular, stoma.

Stress: A physical, psychological, or environmental disturbance of the well-being of an organism.

Striated muscle: Muscle that appears striped under a microscope; also called skeletal muscles, they are under the voluntary control of the brain.

Symbiosis: A relationship between two different species who benefit by living closely together.

Synapse: The space or gap between two neurons across which a nerve impulse or a signal is transmitted.

T

Taxonomy: The science of classifying living things.

Telophase: The near-final phase of mitosis in which the cytoplasm of the dividing cell separates two sets of chromosomes.

Territory: An area that an animal claims as its own and which it will defend against rivals.

Tissue: The name for a group of similar cells that have a common structure and function and which work together.

Toxins: Chemical substances that destroy life or impair the function of living tissue and organs.

Transpiration: Loss of water by evaporation through the stomata of the leaves of a plant.

Tropism: The growth of a plant in a certain manner or direction as a response to a particular stimulus, such as when a plant grows toward the light source.

V

Vacuole: A bubble-like space or cavity inside a cell that serves as a storage area.

Variation: The natural differences that occur between the individuals in any group of plants or animals; if inherited, these differences are the raw materials for evolution.

Vascular plants: Plants with specialized tissue that act as a pipeline for carrying the food and water they need.

Vegetative reproduction: The asexual production of new plants from roots, underground runners, stems, or leaves.

Vertebrates: Animals that have a backbone and a skull that surrounds a well-developed brain.

Virus: A package of chemicals that infects living cells.

Vitamins: Organic compounds found in food that all animals need in small amounts.

Viviparous: Term describing an animal whose embryos develop inside the body of the female and who receive their nourishment from her.

Z

Zygote: A fertilized egg cell; the product of fertilization formed by the union of an egg and sperm.

Research and Activity Ideas

Activity I: Studying an Ecosystem

Ecosystems are everywhere—your backyard, a nearby park, or even a single, rotting log. To study an ecosystem, you need only choose an individual natural community to observe and study and then begin to keep track of all of the interactions that occur among the living and nonliving parts of the ecosystem. Look carefully and study the entire ecosystem, deciding on what its natural boundaries are. Making a map or a drawing on graph paper of the complete site always helps. Next, you should classify the major biotic (living) and abiotic (nonliving) factors in the ecosystem and begin to observe the organisms that live there. Binoculars sometimes help to observe distant objects or to keep from interfering with the activity. A small magnifying glass is also useful for studying small creatures. You should also search for evidence of creatures that you do not see. A camera is also useful sometimes, especially when comparing the seasonal changes in an ecosystem. It is very important to keep a notebook of your observations, keeping track of any creatures you find and where you find them. You can learn more about your ecosystem by counting the different populations discovered there, as well as classifying them according to their ecosystem roles like producer, consumer, or decomposer. A diagram can then be made of the ecosystem's food web. You can search for evidence of competition as well as other types of relationships such as predator-prey or parasitism. You can even keep a record of changes such as plant or animal growth, the birth of offspring, or weather fluctuations. Finally, you can try to predict what might happen if some part of the ecosystem were disturbed or greatly changed. Ecosystems themselves are related to other ecosystems in many ways, and it is important to always realize that all the living and nonliving things on Earth are ultimately connected to one another.

Activity 2: Studying the Greenhouse Effect

The greenhouse effect is the name given to the natural trapping of heat in the lower atmosphere and the warming of Earth's surface that results. This global warming is a natural process that keeps our planet warm and hospitable to life. However, when this normal process is exaggerated or enhanced because of certain human activities, too much heat can be trapped and the increased warming could result in harmful climate changes.

The greenhouse effect can be produced by trying the following experiment. Using two trays filled with moist soil and some easy-to-grow seeds like beans, place a flat thermometer on the soil surface of each tray. After inserting tall wooden skewers in the four corners of one tray, cover it completely with plastic wrap and secure it with a large rubber band. Leave the other tray uncovered and place both trays outside where they are sheltered from the rain but exposed to the Sun. Record the temperature of each tray at the same time each day and note all the differences between the plants. The plastic-wrapped tray should be warmer and its seedling plants should grow larger. This is evidence of the beneficial aspects of the greenhouse effect. However, if the plastic wrap is left over the seedlings for too long they will overheat, wither, and die.

Activity 3: Studying Photosynthesis

If you have ever picked up a piece of wood that has been sitting on the grass for some time and noticed that the patch underneath has lost its greenness and appears yellow or whitish, you have witnessed the opposite of photosynthesis. Since a green plant cannot exist without sunlight, when it is left totally in the dark, the chlorophyll departs from its leaves and photosynthesis no longer takes place. The key role of sunlight can be easily demonstrated by germinating pea seeds and placing them in pots of soil. After placing some pots in a place where they will receive plenty of direct sunlight, place the other pots in a very dark area. After a week to ten days, compare the seedlings in the sunlight to those left in the dark. The root structure of both is especially interesting.

Another way of demonstrating the importance of sunlight to a plant is to pick a shrub, tree, or houseplant that has large individual leaves. Using aluminum foil or pieces of cardboard cut into distinct geometrical shapes that are small enough not to cover the entire leaf but large enough to cover at least half, paperclip each shape to a different leaf. After about a week, remove the shapes from the leaves and compare what you see now to those leaves that were not covered. The importance of sunlight will be dramatically noticeable.

Finally, as a way of demonstrating the exchange of gases (carbon dioxide and oxygen) that occurs during photosynthesis, place a large glass over some potted pea seedlings and place them in sunlight. In time, you will notice that some liquid has condensed on the inside of the glass. This condensation is water vapor that has been given off by the plant when it exchanges oxygen for the carbon dioxide it needs.

Activity 4: Studying Osmosis

In the life sciences, osmosis occurs at the cellular level. For example, in mammals it plays a key role in the kidneys, which filter urine from the blood. Plants also get the water they need through osmosis that occurs in their root hairs. Everyday examples of osmosis can be seen when we sprinkle sugar on a grapefruit cut in half. We notice that the surface becomes moist very quickly and a sweet syrup eventually forms on its top surface. Once the crystallized sugar is dissolved by the grapefruit juices and becomes a liquid, the water molecules will automatically move from where they are greater in number to where they are fewer, so the greater liquid in the grapefruit forms a syrup with the dissolved sugar. Placing a limp stalk of celery in water will restore much of its crispness and gives us another example of osmosis.

Osmosis occurs in plants and animals at the cellular level because their cell membranes are semipermeable (meaning that they will allow only molecules of a certain size or smaller to pass through them). Osmosis can be studied directly by observing how liquid moves through the membrane of an egg. This requires that you get at an egg's membrane by submerging a raw egg (still in its shell) completely inside a wide-mouth jar of vinegar. Record the egg's weight and size (length and diameter) before doing this. The acetic acid in the vinegar will eventually dissolve the shell because the shell is made of calcium carbonate or limestone which reacts with acid to produce carbon dioxide gas. You will observe this gas forming as bubbles on the surface. After about 72 hours, the shell should be dissolved but the egg will remain intact because of its transparent membrane.

After carefully removing the egg from the jar of vinegar, weigh and measure the egg again. You will notice that its proportions have increased. The egg has gotten larger because the water in the vinegar moved through the egg's membrane into the egg itself (because of the higher concentration of water in the vinegar than in the egg). The contents of the egg did not pass out of the membrane since the contents is too large.

The opposite of this activity can be performed using thick corn syrup instead of water. If the egg has its shell removed in the same manner as above but is then immersed for about 72 hours in a jar of syrup, you will find that the egg will have shrunken noticeably. This is because the water concentration of the syrup outside the egg is much less than that inside the egg, so the membrane allows water to move from the egg to the syrup.

Activity 5: Studying Inherited Traits

An inherited trait is a feature or characteristic of an organism that has been passed on to it in its genes. This transmission of the parents' traits to their offspring always follows certain principles or laws. The study of how these inherited traits are passed on is called genetics. Genetics influences everything about us, including the way we look, act, and feel, and some of our inherited traits are very noticeable. Besides these very obvious traits like hair and skin color, there are certain other traits that are less noticeable but very interesting. One of these is foot size. Another is free or attached earlobes. Still another is called "finger hair."

All of these are traits that are passed from parents to their offspring. You can collect data on any particular inherited characteristic and therefore learn more about how genetics works. You will need to collect data about each trait and develop a chart. Any of the above inherited traits can be analyzed. For example, there are generally two types of earlobes. They may be free, and therefore hang down below where the earlobe bottom joins the head, or they may be attached and have no curved bottom that appears to hang down freely. Foot length is simply the size of your own foot and is measured from the tip of the big toe to the back of the heel. The finger hair trait always appears in one of two forms. It is either there or it isn't. People who have the finger hair trait have some hair on the middle section of one or more fingers (which is the finger section between the two bendable joints of your finger).

In order to study one of these interesting traits like finger hair or type of earlobes, you should construct a table or chart that records data on the trait for as many of your family members as you wish. Although it is best to include a large sampling, such as starting with both sets of grandparents and working through any aunts, uncles, and cousins you can contact, even a small sample with only a few members can be helpful. Once you have determined the type of trait each family member has, you should draw your family's "pedigree" for that trait. This is simply a diagram of connected individuals that looks like any other genealogical diagram (which starts at the top with two parents and draws a line from them down to their offspring, and so on). You should use some sort of easily identifiable code or color to signify which individual has or does not have a certain trait. The standard coding technique for tracing the occurrence of a trait in a family is to represent males by squares and females by circles. Usually, a solid circle or square means that a person has the trait, while an empty square or circle shows they do not. In more elaborate pedigrees, a half-colored circle or square means that the person is a carrier but does not show the trait. Once you have done your pedigree, you may do the same for a friend's family and compare his or her family's distribution of the same trait. By comparing the two families' pedigrees for the same trait, you may be able to find certain general patterns of inheritance and to answer certain basic questions. For example, in studying the finger hair trait, you may be able to answer the question whether or not both parents must have finger hair for their offspring to also have it. You might also discover whether both parents having finger hair means that *every* offspring must show the same trait.

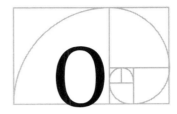

Oceans

Oceans are huge bodies of salt water that are extremely deep and which cover about 71 percent of Earth's surface. As the largest home for life on Earth, oceans contain a diverse set of environments that support a tremendous variety of animals and plants. All of the world's oceans are linked together, although they do not makeup one uniform environment.

Nearly three-quarters of Earth's surface is covered by oceans or seawater. To a scientist, an ocean is different from a sea. To qualify as a sea, a body of water must be large enough to have an effect on its environment, and usually be landlocked. An area is only considered an ocean if it is at least 6.562 feet (2,000 meters) deep. According to this, there are, therefore only six oceans: the Arctic, the North Atlantic, the South Atlantic, the North Pacific, the South Pacific, and the Indian Ocean.

All of the Earth's oceans are connected to one another, meaning that a person could actually go completely around the world and never touch land. All oceans are salty because seawater is made up of dissolved inorganic substances, of which sodium and chloride are the two largest, forming about 85 percent. Together, sodium and chloride form salt. All oceans also have tides (the regular rise and fall of their water level). These are caused mostly by the gravitational pull of the moon that moves around Earth. All oceans also have currents or a stream of water moving in one direction both at their surface and deeply below it. The currents usually are caused by the wind and the differences in water temperature. Oceans lose water by evaporation but regain it by precipitation (rain) and from rivers that drain into them.

PARTS OF AN OCEAN

The marine or ocean environment is divided into two major parts. The pelagic environment makes up all of the ocean water, and the benthic environment makes up the ocean floor. The pelagic environment is further subdivided into what are called provinces. The neritic province is from the shoreline out to open ocean of about 656.2 feet (200 meters) deep. The oceanic province is the ocean at a depth greater than 200 meters. No ocean is uniform in any of its features, and there are enormous differences between its several different zones. For example, in coastal areas close to shore, the primary producer, or the first level on the food chain (the transfer of energy in an ecosystem), is the phytoplankton (single-celled algae that live by photosynthesis). On the surface of the open ocean, however, the primary producers are the macroscopic algae, also known as seaweeds. Differences in the amount of light, as well as pressure and temperature, affect what will grow or thrive in which zone.

The coast of the Pacific Ocean in California. The oceans are the world's largest biomes and are home to the most fascinating plant and animals species. (Reproduced by permission of Field Mark Publications. Photograph by Robert J. Huffman.)

The Littoral Zone. Starting at the shoreline, or the littoral zone, where the land and ocean come together, high levels of light and nutrients make this a productive area. Since the water is so shallow, most organisms lie on or in the seabed, which may be rocky, sandy, or muddy. Rocky shores allow seaweeds to anchor themselves firmly and also provide protection for tiny animals.

The Continental Shelf. Extending outward from the littoral zone is the continental shelf, which is really just an underwater extension of the land. This area is by far the most productive part of any ocean. The ocean above the continental shelf, which extends from shore anywhere from 40 to 200 miles (64.4 to 321.8 kilometers), is fairly shallow compared to the rest of the ocean. It is usually in this shallower part of the shelf that tuna, porpoises, and sharks are found because that is where most of the fish they eat are found. The richness of the shelf is due to the light it receives as well as to the nutrients that rivers often pour into it. As the shelf gradually slopes away from shore, it eventually falls off rather sharply. This eventually leads to the abyssal zone that can reach an incredible depth of 7 miles (11.3 kilometers) in some places. Since light cannot penetrate below a depth of about 650 feet (198.1 meters), this depth is where the aphotic (no light) zone begins.

The Aphotic Zone. In such a deep ocean habitat, there is little life because there is no sunlight, the pressure is enormous, and the temperatures are constantly cold (barely above freezing). The few fish that do inhabit this dark zone have adaptations like huge jaws that allow them to swallow another fish whole and are often able to generate some light of their own. It was once believed that nothing could live below 1,800 feet (548.6 meters), but the fairly recent discovery of activity around the hydrothermal vents showed this not to be true. During the 1970s, new underwater technology allowed scientists to penetrate to great depths and they came upon "vent communities," or areas around underwater volcanoes that were teeming with life. This heated water was loaded with minerals that kept special bacteria as well as clams, crabs, and fish alive.

As with many other natural habitats, oceans also are threatened by humankind. Pollution of the oceans is usually a direct result of human activities, as oceans have long been a dumping ground for waste and land runoff. Recently, contamination from oil spills has become the most severe threat to their health. Overfishing also is becoming more of a threat. Human technology has created floating fish factories that in the long run may seriously endanger entire species. If something is not done to protect the oceans, people may soon lose the largest and most fascinating environment on Earth.

[*See also* **Biome; Water**]

Omnivore

An omnivore is an animal that eats both plants and other animals. Because of the wide variety in their diet, omnivores are adaptable to many different environments. They also can be found at several different levels on a food web (the connected network of producers, consumers, and decomposers).

Unlike carnivores who eat a diet almost completely of meat, and herbivores who eat only plants, omnivores are generalists when it comes to what they can and will eat. One of nature's principles is that animals' bodies are adapted to what they eat. Their systems are designed with their diet in mind. Therefore, carnivores, who must hunt and kill other animals in order to eat their flesh, are designed for those purposes. Their senses are sharp, they have deadly claws and teeth, and their digestive systems are prepared to process high-protein meat. On the other hand, herbivores do not have to track, catch, and kill their food. Since they eat only green plants, herbivores need only find and eat these plants. Their teeth are not sharp and pointed but are designed for grinding tough plant material. Herbivores' digestive systems are also specially built to break down cell walls made of cellulose (the main component of plant tissues) by containing microorganisms just for that purpose.

The name omnivore is taken from the Latin *omnis* meaning all, and *vorare* to eat or devour. According to this broad definition, humans are probably the most omnivorous of all animals, since they can eat almost anything. Besides classifying animals as omnivore, carnivore, or herbivore, biologists categorize the larger group of all living things as autotrophs or heterotrophs.

Besides humans, bears are probably the most common omnivore. These grizzly bears will eat both plants and animals. (©U.S. Fish & Wildlife Service. Photograph by Chris Servhenn.)

Autotrophs, like all plants and some bacteria, can make their own food. Heterotrophs (like animals) cannot make their own food and must eat plants or other animals. Autotrophs are considered to be producers since they are at the first level of the food chain (the series of stages energy goes through in the form of food). This is because the food they make supports all other life in the chain. Heterotrophs are considered to be consumers since they cannot make their own food and must eat others (plants or animals) to survive. Omnivores are also heterotrophs.

Unlike herbivores, who always are one level above the plants they eat, different omnivores can be found at different levels on the food chain at different times. Omnivores can be first-level consumers because they eat plants, but they can also be higher up since they also eat animals. For example, a bear will eat berries as well as a fish.

Many kinds of mammals are omnivores, such as humans, pigs, bears, apes, raccoons, and hedgehogs. Because of this varied diet, their digestive systems are not as specialized as others who eat only one type of food. Carnivores have a short digestive tract since their systems must break down easy-to-process protein. Herbivores, however, have elaborate and multichambered stomachs to process and reprocess the hard-to-breakdown cell walls of the plants they eat. Omnivores have intermediate digestive systems that can handle both meat and plants. It would seem that the varied food supply of omnivores gives them an advantage over other more specialized eaters.

[*See also* **Carnivore; Herbivore**]

Order

The term order is one of the seven major classification groups that biologists use to identify and categorize living things. These seven groups are hierarchical or range in order of size. Order is at the exact middle of the seven groups, located between class and family. The classification scheme for all living things is: kingdom, phylum, class, order, family, genus, and species.

Organisms in the same order are much closer to each other, genetically and on the evolutionary scale, than are those in the larger group called class. For example, although all animals in the class Mammalia produce milk for their young, those in the order Carnivora eat meat, while others in the order Insectivora eat insects. A house pet like a dog (Carnivora) is distinguished by its eating habits and preferences from a mole (Insectivora), although both are in the same class.

The order names of plant groups generally use the suffix -ales (e.g., Rosales), while the order names of animals usually end with an -a (e.g., Carnivora). In practical terms and in most scientific discussions, the order of an organism is seldom considered. Rather, the more specific terms of family, genus, and species are used.

[*See also* **Class; Classification; Family; Genus; Kingdom; Phylum; Species**]

Organ

An organ is a structural part of a plant or animal that carries out a certain function and is made up of two or more types of tissue. Each organ plays a key role in keeping the organism alive. A group of organs that work together to do a certain job is called an organ system.

Very often, a person's liver, heart, brain, and kidneys (among others) are referred to as internal organs, or vital organs. This is because they are usually inside the body (although some, like eyes, are not), and they are vital, or essential, to keeping us alive. The word vital can also mean living or alive. Plants also have many kinds of vital organs, such as leaves, stems, roots, and the various parts of a flower. However, whether in plants or animals, an organ is usually composed of two or more types of tissue that work together to do a particular job. For example, the heart is an organ whose job it is to pump blood throughout the body. It is made up of muscle tissue that contracts, nerve tissue that transmits impulses, connective tissue that binds it together, and epithelial tissue that lines its surfaces. Tissue is considered to be a group of similar cells that all do the same job. Some organs, like the heart, have only one job to do, while others, like the liver, may have many tasks to perform.

When a group of organs are linked together to perform a certain function, it is called an organ system. In large, complex animals, there are ten major organ systems that work together to make up the organism. The main organ systems of complex animals include the skeletal system, nervous system, circulatory system, respiratory system, muscular system, digestive system, excretory system, endocrine system, reproductive system, and integumentary system.

The skeletal system consists of bones and cartilage and helps support and protect the body. The nervous system consists of the brain, spinal cord, sense organs, and nerves. It collects, processes, and distributes information. The circulatory system includes the heart and blood vessels. It transports essential materials throughout the body. The respiratory system is made up of the lungs and air passageways. It supplies necessary oxygen while removing carbon dioxide (a major atmospheric gas). The muscular system consists of large, skeletal muscles that contract, as well as cardiac muscle and the smooth muscle. The digestive system includes the mouth, stomach, intestines and other organs that break down and absorb food. The excretory system consists of the kidneys, bladder, and other ducts, or tubes, that remove waste from the blood. The endocrine, or glandular, system consists of the thyroid, pituitary, mammary, and other glands. These glands release hormones (chemical messengers) into the circulatory system to regulate metabolic activities (all the body's chemical processes). The reproductive system is made up of the testes, ovaries, penis, vagina, and uterus. It passes on genes to its offspring. The integumentary system consists of the skin, hair, and nails that serve to protect the body and to regulate its temperature, as well as to receive stimuli.

The organs of a plant are its leaves, stems, roots, and the various parts of its flowers. A flower is actually an example of an organ system in a plant, since it is usually composed of stamens, pistils, petals, bracts, and receptacle. The stamens are its male reproductive organ, and are composed of anthers and filaments. The pistil is the female reproductive organ and consists of a stigma, style, and ovary.

[*See also* **Brain; Circulatory System; Digestive System; Endocrine System; Excretory System; Heart; Integumentary System; Muscular System; Nervous System; Reproductive System; Respiratory System; Sense Organ; Skeletal System**]

Organelle

An organelle is a tiny structure inside a cell that performs a particular function. Organelles are only found in eukaryotic cells (those with a distinct nucleus), and are not found in prokaryotic cells (those without a distinct nucleus). Both animal and plant contain many types of organelles (or "little organs").

Just as any organ has a specialized, particular function to perform as part of a larger system, so these "little organs" within a cell have certain tasks they perform. Organelles are bounded by a membrane and are run by the cell's control center, the nucleus (which itself is an organelle). Each organelle has a job to do that is crucial to maintaining the life of the cell and in most eukaryotic cells, organelles can be grouped into three categories according to their general function. The organelle that directs a cell's activities and holds the cell's genetic information is the nucleus.

Both plant and animal cells have a nucleus. It is the largest structure in animal cells and is separated from the rest of the cell's cytoplasm (jelly-like fluid) by a double membrane called a nuclear envelope.

Organelles also function in transport, synthesis (making things), storage, and recycling. In plant and animal cells, the organelles responsible for these activities are called the endoplasmic reticulum, ribosomes, Golgi bodies, and lysosomes. Plant cells also have organelles called vacuoles. The endoplasmic reticulum is a complex network of folded membranes that form tubes and transport, or move, materials to all parts of the cell. They are something like a pipeline. Ribosomes play an important role in the synthesis, or making of, proteins. Golgi bodies look like a stack of flattened pancakes. They put the finishing touches on proteins, and then sort the proteins and pack them for transport. Lysosomes are bags of enzymes that help a cell digest the food it takes in. Only plant cells have a large sac called a vacuole that they use for storage.

Other organelles function to produce energy. Called mitochondria and chloroplasts, these organelles are responsible for changing energy from one form to another. Mitochondria are found in both plant and animal cells and are called the powerhouses of the cell because these organelles break down a cell's food and release energy.

Although chloroplasts also produce energy for cell, they are a little different than mitochondria for two reasons. First, chloroplasts are not found in animal cells, they are only found in plant cells. Second, unlike animals that must take food into their bodies, plants can make their own food from which they obtain their energy. Plants create this food using small, green organelles called chloroplasts that capture the energy in sunlight. Chloroplasts use this trapped radiant energy of the Sun and turn it into chemical energy for use or storage. When the plant is ready to use the energy, the mitochondria take over and release the stored energy.

[*See also* **Chloroplasts; Endoplasmic Reticulum; Golgi Bodies; Lysosomes; Mitochondria; Nucleus; Ribosomes**]

Organic Compounds

Organic compounds are substances that contain carbon (a nonmetallic element that occurs in all plants and animals). All living things have an essential dependence on organic compounds, since carbon occurs in almost every chemical compound found in living things. There are four main types of organic compounds in living things: carbohydrates, proteins, lipids, and nucleic acids.

An organic compound is a combination of carbon and almost any other element. Because of its unique atomic structure (the way a single atom of carbon is built), a carbon atom is able to link up with as many as four other atoms of another element. Since it can also link up with other carbon atoms and form long, stable chains, the variety of combinations carbon can form with other elements is almost limitless. Scientists have already identified more than 1,000,000 organic compounds.

Until the nineteenth century, it was commonly believed that organic compounds only could be produced by something that was living. In those days, it was thought that some sort of "vital force" existed only in living things, and that it was this force that made living things uniquely capable of producing organic compounds. Two hundred years ago, organic meant "vital," or "living." Therefore, in the past, an organic compound was the tissue or the remains of a living thing, while an inorganic compound was something lifeless like a rock or the waters of the earth.

In 1828 the German chemist Friedrich Wohler (1800–1882) changed all of this thinking. That year, he quite unintentionally produced urea, an organic substance formed naturally in the bodies of mammals, in his laboratory using strictly inorganic substances. Starting with this laboratory breakthrough, science eventually came to recognize that no "vital force" was necessary for a substance to be considered an organic compound. Eventually, it was learned that what was important was molecular structure, or the way the atoms arranged themselves into molecules. This led to the modern definition of what became the study of organic chemistry—the chemistry of carbon compounds.

Today, it is known that all living things are not only organic compounds, but that they also are critically dependent on organic compounds. Specifically, foods are all organic compounds since they are made up of carbohydrates, fats, and proteins. Materials such as the cotton and wool in clothing, the petroleum for cars and factories, and all synthetic (man-made) drugs and plastics are organic compounds. Finally, the very chemistry that carries our genetic information—nucleic acids—are complex organic compounds made up of small molecules called nucleotides.

Interestingly, the word organic has been taking on more of its much older (and less precise) meaning, as people now speak positively of the benefits of "organic gardening," "organic food," and "organic vitamins." This use of the term organic suggests that some sort of mysterious "vital" force is at work in these compounds that gives them special qualities that synthetic products do not have. While an organic tomato harvested from a small farm may taste much better than one grown commercially and picked green, from a chemical standpoint, however, they are identical.

Organism

An organism is any complete, individual living thing. As a living thing, an organism necessarily has certain attributes or displays certain characteristics that make it different from a nonliving thing. The things that organisms must do to maintain life are called life processes.

Although both living and nonliving things are made up of many of the same types of atoms (the building blocks of an element that come together to form a molecule), there are drastic differences between the two in terms of how energy is used and how materials are organized. A bacterium living in a cow's gut is an organism, as is a worm or a tree—but a rock or a fire is not. Despite how dissimilar organisms can often appear, they exhibit certain features that are common to all. Knowing these life characteristics allows us to determine whether something is alive (and therefore is an organism) or not.

METABOLIC ACTIVITY

All organisms share the characteristics of taking in materials and releasing waste. Plants take in carbon dioxide and water and use sunlight to make food. Animals eat plants or other animals to take in nutrients or food. Plants give off oxygen and animals give off carbon dioxide and other waste materials. After taking in materials, all organisms show some form of metabolic activity. This means that organisms are able to break down materials and release the energy these materials contain. They can store this energy or use it to fuel their life processes. An organism can also build more of itself and grow or increase its size. It can repair itself and grow new and larger cells.

Organisms pass through their own life cycles. These cycles include a series of changes called development. All organisms also use part of their energy to produce more of their own kind. Reproduction is another characteristic of life. Every organism is itself the product of reproduction. This means that every organism is the offspring of one or more parent organisms. An individual organism can also be terminated or its life processes stopped permanently. If this happens because of an outside cause, then something has killed the organism. Whether or not it is killed, every organism still goes out of existence because of death. Death is therefore a characteristic of life.

INTERNAL ORGANIZATION AND HOMEOSTASIS

There are other characteristics of life important to organisms. All organisms show a capacity for internal organization. They are not a random jumble of cells, but are instead very organized internally and externally. Each organism has its own individual form of organization, so that a worm has a characteristic pattern that is quite different from a shrub. Another characteristic of organisms is their reactions, or responses to changes in their environment or surroundings. Animals often respond by movement, but nonmoving plants respond as well. A typical example of a plant responding to its environment is a potato plant forming an overwintering tuber (an underground bulb) as the days get shorter, or an onion plant forming bulbs during the long, hot days of summer. Organisms also react to their environment by making internal adjustments called homeostasis. Through homeostasis, organisms adjust their internal environment so that they maintain balanced or stable conditions. Organisms instinctively work at keeping things in control and constant. In terms of their behavior, all organisms have some degree of adaptive potential, which means that they can adjust to environmental changes over both the short term and the long term. This long-term adjustment occurs through the process of evolution (the changes an organism goes through over generations). A final characteristic of organisms is that their cells all contain deoxyribonucleic acid (DNA), which carries the genetic information specific to each organism. This DNA is carried in almost every cell within an organism and contains the instructions for reproducing traits that are to be inherited, or passed on, from parent to offspring.

An organism displays all of these traits or life processes. A nonliving thing may show some. For example, a fire can move, consume or take in materials, and give off a gas, or an automobile engine takes in materials and gives off a waste product. However, no nonliving thing can show all of them as an organisms does.

BASIC NEEDS

Organisms also have certain basic needs that must be met if they are to continue to live. Given the great variety of living things, those essential needs can be generalized by the following four requirements: energy, water, appropriate gases, and proper temperature. Organisms also share one common trait that is perhaps the most basic. All organisms are made up of one or more cells. Therefore, each organism shares the cell as the basic unit of life. Thus, a single-celled algae is as much an organism as a human being made up of trillion of cells.

[*See also* **Homeostasis; Metabolism**]

Ornithology

Ornithology is the branch of zoology that deals with birds. It includes the study of the development, anatomy (structure), physiology (function), behavior, classification, genetics, and ecology of birds, among other things. Scientists believe that they know more about birds than any other group of organisms.

Named after the Greek word for birds, ornithology is the scientific study of birds. The Greek philosopher, Aristotle (384–322 B.C.), was very interested in all aspects of biology and wrote a great deal on birds. He listed about 40 species and described their habits, migration (movement from one place to another), and relationship to the environment. Many consider the thirteenth-century emperor, Frederick II (1194–1250), as the first real ornithologist because of his book, *On the Art of Hunting with Birds.* Although Frederick II was a falconer and wrote his book about using falcons to catch prey, his work was also a serious, scientific account of the habits and the structure of many types of birds. Most books written on birds during his time focused on the practical aspects of birds, such as falconry or game-bird management. However, the fifteenth-century discovery of the Americas eventually gave students of the natural world a huge number of new and sometimes wildly different and exotic birds to describe and understand. By the 1750s, birds were included in all classification systems, and by the end of the next century, their place in the world's evolutionary history was becoming understood. However, until about 1900, most bird studies still were concerned only with classifying and describing them. Soon after the beginning of the twentieth century, universities began to grant degrees in ornithology, and professional ornithologists came on the scene. As a result, the twentieth century saw an emphasis on further understanding bird anatomy and behavior as well as their role in the overall balance of life (ecology).

There are nearly 9,000 species of birds, and ornithologists have decided that what most distinguishes an organism as a bird is not its ability to fly, but rather its feathers. Birds are vertebrates (animals with a backbone) that have feathers covering their body, and have forelimbs that are modified into wings. They are endothermic (warm-blooded; maintain an internal temperature despite their environment) and many parts of their bodies have adapted to their ability to fly. For example, they have large, powerful breast muscles, a streamlined shape, and hollow bones (since weight is a critical factor in flying). Birds lay eggs, have an extremely active life cycle, and use song and sounds for many different reasons, such as a warning, to mark territory, and to show dominance or attract a mate. Birds are very diverse. There are 27 orders of birds in the class Aves, divided into about 166 families that contain about 9,000 species. Some migrate extremely long distances, while others stay in the same habitat. They can vary in size from the 300-pound (136.2-kilogram) ostrich to the 0.08-ounce (2.27-gram) hummingbird. Some, like the Arctic tern, stay in the air for weeks at a time, while others, like the penguin, are entirely flightless.

Although traditionally a great deal of information about birds has been obtained by simple field observations, ornithology has put available technology to greater use with such techniques as banding. This technique of putting a ring or band on a bird's leg has been practiced for a long time, but now it has become a major way of obtaining information about bird movements since it is used with sensitive radar equipment. Ornithologists are also able to study bird calls in natural environment since they now have high quality, portable sound equipment.

One thing that makes ornithology different from almost every other branch of the life sciences is the fact that amateurs have regularly made major contributions to the field. Many a nonscientist who has only a passion for birds and plenty of time has been able to learn a great deal about birds and actually discovered things unknown to science. The best

The banding of an ovenbird. This banding technique is a major way of obtaining information about bird movements. (Reproduced by permission of Field Mark Publications. Photograph by Robert J. Huffman.)

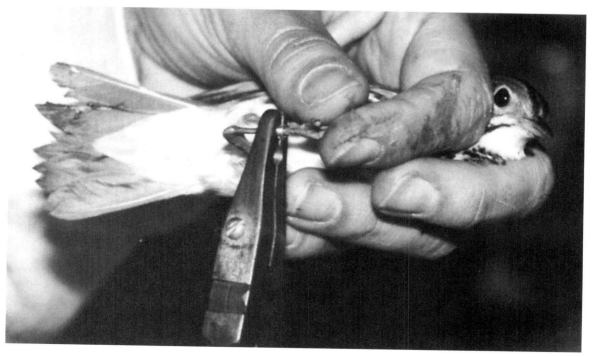

known amateur may be the American artist John James Audubon (1785–1851), whose four-volume *The Birds of America* (1827–38) is a monument to art and science. More recently, the best work on the life history of the song sparrow was done by a housewife and mother of five, Margaret M. Nice.

Today, ornithologists are necessarily concerned with environmental conditions that affect birds since birds seem especially sensitive to pollution and climate changes. Because of this, the more ornithologists learn about birds, the more knowledge they gain about our own environment. It is significant that the environmentalist Rachel Carson chose to focus on the lack of birdsong (*Silent Spring*) as a tangible example of the disappearance of certain bird species due to pollution. She showed how, in many ways, birds are a sentinel species for humans, meaning that they are the first to suffer when the environment becomes degraded.

[*See also* **Birds**]

Osmosis

Osmosis is the movement of water from one solution to another through a membrane or barrier that separates the solutions. Osmosis is a natural process that takes place whenever the proper conditions arise. It occurs when solutions of different strengths are separated by a barrier whose pores will only let molecules of a certain size pass through. Water moves from the weaker solution to the stronger solution in order to make both solutions of equal strength. Osmosis occurs in both animals and plants.

One of the characteristics of nature is that it always tries to equalize situations, to bring things into balance, or to make extremes more similar. This characteristic leads to a phenomenon known as diffusion in which a substance will always spread from an area where it is highly concentrated to one of lesser concentration. Osmosis is a variation of diffusion and might be described as diffusion involving a solution and a barrier. Osmosis necessarily involves liquids called solutions. A solution is a liquid with something dissolved in it. If a teaspoon of sugar is stirred into a glass of pure water until it dissolves, a solution is made. If that container of sugar water is somehow arranged so that only a permeable barrier (one with holes the size of water molecules) comes between it and another container of pure water, after a few hours the pure water will have moved through the barrier and into the sugar solution. The water moved into the sugar solution because water molecules are smaller than sugar molecules. Therefore, only the water molecules are able to move and equalize the solutions. This passage or movement stops when the osmotic pressure is reached, or the equalization of pressure on both sides of the barrier. Equal pressure means that the solution concentrations on both sides of the barrier are no longer high and low but the same.

In the life sciences, osmosis occurs at the cellular level. Since animals have watery body fluids that contain a variety of dissolved salts, osmosis is necessary to keep their salt and water levels constant. Osmosis plays a key role in the kidneys of mammals since these organs filter urine from the blood, reabsorb water and nutrients, and secrete wastes. Plants obtain the water they need through osmosis that occurs at their root hairs. Root hairs contain more dissolved substances (such as sugar and salts) than there are in the soil. Because of this difference in the solution concentration between the outside and the inside of the plant, water is able to pass through the root hair cells and into the roots by osmosis. Osmosis also helps a plant stay upright and stiff. Osmosis is an ideal method of moving small amounts of water slowly, whether in a plant or an animal, since it does not require the use of any energy or tubelike transport systems.

Two illustrations showing how osmosis equalizes the concentration of a liquid. (Illustration by Hans & Cassidy. Courtesy of Gale Research.)

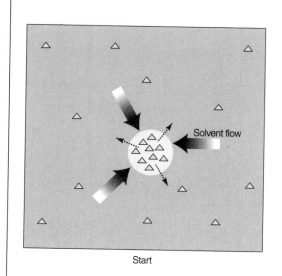

Solvent flow

Start

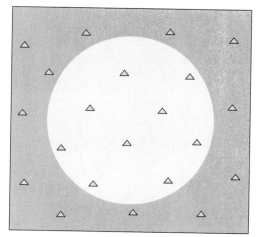

End

Ozone

Ozone gas is a form of oxygen found naturally in the stratosphere or upper atmosphere that shields Earth from the Sun's harmful ultraviolet radiation. Ozone is also found in the lower atmosphere as a man-made pollutant best known as smog. In recent years, it was discovered that certain synthetic gases are destroying Earth's stratospheric ozone shield.

Ozone is a natural component of Earth's upper atmosphere and is essential to the continuance of life on this planet. It is located between 6 and 28 miles (9.7 and 45.1 kilometers) above Earth. As a high-energy form of oxygen, it is formed naturally in the air both by the electrical charges given off during lightning and by high intensity, short wavelength light. Without this ozone layer absorbing the Sun's ultraviolet radiation, living things on Earth's surface could not survive. Many scientists believe that life on Earth could not have evolved without this protective ozone shield because direct penetration of the atmosphere by solar radiation would make Earth unlivable. Besides suffering life-threatening radiation burns and cancer, all aboveground organisms would eventually experience severe genetic damage. Although beneficial in the atmosphere, at ground level ozone is a bad-smelling, colorless gas that is poisonous and usually formed by pollutants people put into the air. Ozone at this level does not shield life from harmful radiation and is instead a major component of urban smog and a threat to all living things. Ground-level ozone, therefore, has only bad effects. Because smog can cause shortness of breath, chest pain, coughing nausea, and respiratory congestion in some people, many large cities have established "Ozone Action Day" campaigns to educate citizens how to reduce ground-level ozone and to warn them when to avoid strenuous outdoor activities.

OZONE DEPLETION

What might be considered good ozone is the gas found naturally high up in the atmosphere around Earth. It was this layer of ozone that was discovered in the late 1970s to be getting thinner. Further research revealed a severely thin spot, which some called a hole, in the ozone layer over Antarctica. By the mid-1980s, monitoring by satellites and high-altitude planes revealed that ozone levels over Antarctica had declined about 50 percent. Scientists argue that such a dramatic decrease could be related to increases in human skin cancers as well as cataracts and a weakening of the body's immune system. The decline in the ozone layer might also contribute to crop failures and a reduction in phytoplankton, which forms the basis of a major food web (the connected network of producers, consumers, and decomposers).

Many scientists argue that there is extensive evidence that a group of synthetic chemicals called chlorofluorocarbons (CFCs) are the primary cause of ozone reduction. While certain natural events like volcanoes and surges in solar activity certainly affect the ozone layer, the argument against CFCs as the primary human-influenced cause is very strong. CFCs are compounds of chlorine, fluorine, and carbon. They are odorless, invisible, and otherwise harmless gases that were put to so many uses that they were thought to be miracle compounds. CFCs were widely used as propellants in aerosol spray cans, although they soon came to be used regularly as coolants in refrigerators and air conditioners. Finally, CFCs proved useful in making Styrofoam cups and packaging materials. With all this use of CFCs, molecules of the gases were released, spreading upwards into the stratosphere where they took part in an unusual and ultimately dangerous set of chemical reactions.

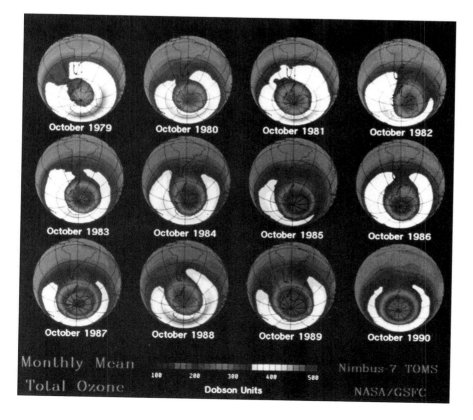

A series of NASA photos depicting ozone depletion over the South Pole from October 1979 to October 1990. (Reproduced by permission of the U.S. National Aeronautics and Space Administrations (NASA).)

When a molecule of CFC absorbs ultraviolet radiation, it releases a chlorine atom. This atom then reacts with the ozone (O_3) to form an oxygen molecule (O_2) and a chlorine monoxide molecule. At this stage, a molecule of ozone has already been converted into oxygen. The cycle then continues, as the chlorine monoxide reacts with a free oxygen atom and releases yet another atom, which in turn attacks another molecule of ozone. It has been estimated that each chlorine atom released from a CFC reaction can convert as many as 10,000 molecules of ozone to oxygen. Since ozone reduction is greatest when the atmosphere is at its coldest, the extreme atmospheric conditions of the Antarctic region provide excellent conditions for these reactions to occur, thus accounting for the "ozone hole" found there.

During the 1990s, ozone depletion was shown to be happening seasonally over populated areas. This led to a decision by the United States government and several European governments to begin phasing out the production and use of CFCs by the year 2000. There is some evidence that the buildup of CFCs is declining since then, but unfortunately, the amount of highly stable CFCs already pumped into the atmosphere will remain for a century doing their destructive work. However, some comfort can be taken in the knowledge that not only are humans no longer contributing to the problem, but that an amazingly small amount of ozone in the stratosphere still can screen out more than 95 percent of the Sun's ultraviolet radiation.

[*See also* **Pollution**]

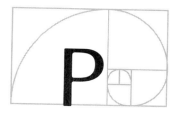

Paleontology

Paleontology is the scientific study of the animals, plants, and other organisms that lived in prehistoric times. It largely involves the study of fossil remains. The fossil record enables paleontologists to reconstruct what type of life existed at various periods in Earth's long history.

Paleontology has often been described simply as the scientific study of fossils. Fossils are the remains of once-living plants or animals that were preserved in rock or other material. Fossils are found in sedimentary rock, or rock that started out as wet sand or mud. Fossilization occurs if an animal or plant dies and is quickly covered with a sediment like mud. Although its soft body parts usually decay, the harder parts (like teeth and bone) are sometimes preserved by petrifaction. This means that its organic material is replaced over millions of years by minerals that turn it into rock. By studying this evidence of the ancient past, paleontologists can reconstruct an account of what kind of life existed in various periods of Earth's history. This, in turn, allows them to go further and try to establish a record of how all the animals and plants that make up today's biosphere (part of Earth that contains life) evolved from their earliest beginnings. In this way, paleontology has often been able to provide actual evidence to support the theory of evolution (the process by which living things change over generations). Paleontology also has its practical aspects and sometimes helps in locating deposits of oil and natural gas. This is not surprising since these "fossil fuels" are often found in the same location as the fossils themselves.

Paleontology combines the skills of geology with that of biology. Geology is essential, since a paleontologist would be lost if he or she had no knowledge of the type of rock where fossils are typically found. The paleontologist also needs to be able to know the ages of different rocks (which indicate the age of the fossils found in those rocks). Biology helps paleontologists figure out how the ancient plants and animals that they discover may have actually lived. Although the word "paleontology" does not have an especially scientific meaning—literally, it means "a discourse on ancient beings"—in practice it has been able to scientifically establish the evolutionary development of life. Paleontology tells us when minor or major extinctions occurred, and sometimes why they happened. Paleontology helps recreate these ancient environments and explains why the plants and animals that lived then were built the way they were.

Like geology (the study of the history of Earth), paleontology is a fairly young science. Before it was established, geologists had no way of determining the relative ages of rocks. By comparing fossils of organisms that lived for a short time, geologists were able to put together a chronology or time line of Earth's history. Serious paleontological research dates back to the early 1800s, and is based on the work of two men born the same year. In England, the geologist William Smith (1769–1839) established the principle of stratigraphy—that the deeper layers of the earth were deposited earlier and were thus older than the layers closer to the surface. This would hold true for the fossils contained in those layers. Based on his theory, Smith was able to arrange fossils in terms of their age. The French anatomist, Georges Cuvier (1769–1832), was so skilled in animal anatomy (their body structure), that he was able to reconstruct a complete animal from an incomplete collection of bones. It was Cuvier who brought the new science of classification (the scientific way of identifying and grouping living things) to fossils. By grouping animals according to their skeletons or internal structure, instead of their outer form or how they looked, Cuvier eventually laid the basis for evolution despite his disagreement with that theory. Modern scientists were eventually able to show that the oldest fossils were in fact ones that differed from the more recent fossils and even more so from living animals.

Modern paleontology uses several advanced dating techniques and has become, like many other branches in the life sciences, more specialized. The study of fossil plants is called paleobotany; that of fossil communities is paleoecology; that of extremely small fossils is micropaleontology; and that branch concerned with the study of fossil spores and pollen is called palynology. Altogether, these branches of paleontology seek to learn the history of life on Earth.

[*See also* **Dinosaurs; Fossil; Geologic Record; Radioactive Dating**]

Parasite

A parasite is an organism that lives in or on another organism and benefits from the relationship. Most parasites harm their host organisms in some way and often cause disease in plants and animals. There are many different forms of parasitism.

SYMBIOSIS

True parasites do not simply benefit at the expense of another organism, since that is also what a predator does (it benefits by killing and eating another organism). Instead, a parasite relies completely on the organism (called the host) it lives on or in for its nutrients. If the host dies, the parasite dies. Parasitism is a form of symbiosis, which is described as some type of relationship between two different species. There are three types of symbiosis: commensalism, mutualism, and parasitism.

Commensalism. In commensalism, a relationship exists in which one of the participants benefits but the other is neither helped nor harmed. The Spanish moss is an example of a commensalism parasite. It seems to live off certain host trees, but is not a parasite since it harmlessly attaches itself to branches while getting its nutrients not from the tree but from the decaying leaves at the base of the tree.

Mutualism. In mutualism, both members in the relationship benefit. Sometimes, neither can live without the other. A good example are the microorganisms that live in the gut of herbivores (plant-eaters) like cows. The cow could not digest its plant diet without these tiny organisms in its digestive tract, and the microorganisms themselves could not get the food they need from anywhere but the cow's gut.

Parasitism. In parasitism, however, the relationship not only benefits one partner much more than the other, but it benefits that partner at the expense of the other. Nearly every animal and plant is a host or home to some form of parasite, and many parasites have evolved ways to minimize the damage they do to their host since if they quickly kill their host, they will die also.

TYPES OF PARASITES

A parasite can be a single-celled organism, like a protozoan, or a complex arthropod, like a tick. Protozoans usually cause diseases directly, while arthropods usually function as "vectors" and cause disease indirectly. For example, the mosquito that carries the parasite that causes yellow fever is described as the vector since the mosquito transfers the parasite to the host when the mosquito bites it. The mosquito's action allows the parasite to enter the host's system.

Parasites also can be divided into those that live inside the host (endoparasite), and those that live outside or on the surface of the host (ectoparasite). For instance, the endoparasite that causes malaria lives in the liver and red blood cells of a human being, whereas a flea is an ectoparasite because it lives off its host's blood while remaining only on the host's outer surface or skin. A flea is actually a temporary ectoparasite, since it does not remain permanently attached to its host, but leaves after feeding and will later jump off to bite another host.

Many parasites are host-specific, which means that they can only live on or in a certain host. The adult beef tapeworm is such a parasite since it can only live in the large intestine of a human being. Other parasites can make hosts of any type of animal. Certain parasites only can live off plants. A good example is the well-known Dutch elm disease that is caused by a parasitic fungus that feeds off living elm wood and destroys its internal transport systems that carry the nutrients the wood needs to survive.

RESPONSES TO PARASITES

When a host is invaded by a parasite, it often attempts to fight back. The human immune system reacts defensively to try to rid itself of invading parasites. The fever, chills, and sweating associated with malaria are the body's attempts to destroy the parasite. Since the death of the host means that the parasite also dies, some parasites have evolved ways to live off their hosts without killing them too quickly. However, if the parasite has not developed these ways, and the host is unable to adapt mechanisms of its own to fight back, an entire species may be killed off. This happened when the American chestnut tree was suddenly invaded by a parasitic fungus from Europe. The tree is almost extinct now.

An orange infested with parasites. This type parasite is not beneficial since it causes crop damage leading to a possible shortage of food and financial hardships for farmers. (Reproduced by permission of Dr. Edward Ross.)

Parasites are not some low form of life that dumbly live off a higher form. Rather, they are highly adapted and adaptable organisms that are genetically programmed to know when, how, and what to attack (and when not to). They may communicate with one another and even compete or avoid competing. While some parasites can only live a parasitic existence (and are called obligate parasites), others are more flexible and can provide for some of their own needs. It is important to remember, however, that some parasites are beneficial and vital to both plant and animal life.

[*See also* **Arthropod; Protozoa; Symbiosis**]

pH

pH is a number used to measure the degree of acidity of a solution. It is used on a pH scale that ranges from 0 to 14, with the difference between each number being a factor of 10. In the life sciences, as well as in chemistry, many chemical reactions depend on the pH of a solution. pH is also used to analyze body secretions, to test soil suitability, and for industrial purposes.

pH refers to the amount of acid in a substance. The letters are said to have come from the French for "hydrogen power," meaning how many

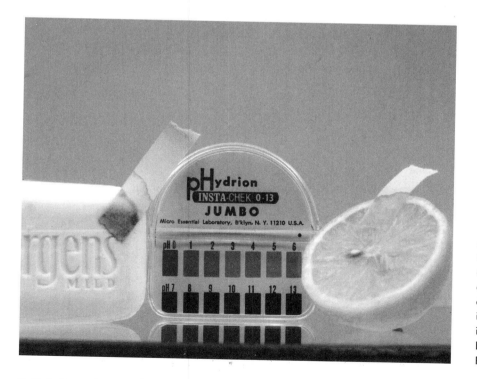

A litmus paper experiment demonstrating the pH of a bar of soap and an orange. Litmus paper is a common pH indicator. (Reproduced by permission of Phototake.)

hydrogen atoms are concentrated in a solution. The lowercase p means its "power," or its logarithmic value. This means that each time a number is raised to another power (from a 2 to a 3), it increases by a factor of 10. Another explanation for pH is that it stands for "potential of hydrogen." Either way, it is known that the pH symbol was first used by the Danish chemist, Soren Sorenson (1868–1939), in 1909. He used the pH symbol on what he called a Sorenson scale.

Today, however, it is called a pH scale, and it is a 0 to 14 scale that tells us exactly how acidic a substance is. This scale uses as a reference point the number 7 which is the midpoint between the scale's two extremes of 0 and 14. A pH of 7 is considered to be neutral—or neither acid nor its opposite, base. Acids and bases are two types or classes of biological compounds. They affect every living cell as well as the habitats of organisms.

The pH of a solution can be measured with an electronic pH meter or by various paper or liquid indicators. These change color depending on the pH of the mixture. A pH meter will give a digital readout, or number, indicating the pH of a solution. A treated paper indicator turns darker pink for more acid and darker blue for more base. The paper color is checked against a standard chart that indicates the pH number. The scale itself tells the exact degree of acid in a solution. Starting with the lowest number, the strongest acid, a pH of 0, would be concentrated nitric acid. Following that, in approximate values, stomach acid has a pH of 1, lemon juice 2, vinegar 3, fresh tomatoes 4, black coffee 5, and peas 6. Distilled water is neutral and has a pH of 7.

After this, the base part of the scale begins. Baking soda has a pH of 8, borax 9, ammonia 10, lime 12, oven cleaner 13, and lye 14. Since these values are logarithmic, the difference between each one is a factor of 10. Thus a solution of pH 5 is 10 times more acidic than a solution of pH 6. In the living world, almost all biological processes take place in a pH environment between 6 and 8. There are, however, a few exceptions such as digestive acids that are extremely powerful (with a pH of 1). Many organisms have built-in regulators that act as buffers and either soak up or join with small amounts of excess acid or base.

[*See also* **Acid and Base**]

Pheromone

Pheromones are chemicals released by an animal that have some sort of effect on another animal. They are used to communicate or pass a signal to another animal. They will provoke either an immediate response or a more generalized and longer-lasting one. Both types are intended to affect or to modify the behavior of another animal.

Unlike hormones, which are described as chemical messengers *inside* the body of an animal, pheromones are part of the exocrine system. This system releases chemical signals *outside* the body. Hormones are used internally and are one way an organism's body systems communicate and cooperate. Pheromones are exactly the opposite. Although they are chemical signals, they are used only outside of the body and are intended to communicate something to another animal. While hormones have as their object certain "target cells" inside the body that they seek out for a response, pheromones have other organisms as their target.

In terms of the amount of energy an organism uses by communicating this way, a chemical communication system is highly efficient. The animal usually uses substances that it already produces as waste or debris. Like hormones, pheromones are powerful and are highly effective in small amounts. Another reason that animals use pheromones or chemical signals is that these convey stable and simple signals. The message they contain is easily understood and often remains around for quite some time. Chemicals can also carry information in the dark.

Pheromones are usually intended only for other animals of the same species. They are often released by animals into their environment in the form of urine or sweat. They may also be passed from one animal to another by glands in the skin. Pheromones are classified in two major categories: primers or signalers (also called releasers).

PRIMING PHEROMONES

Priming pheromones are not used often. These cause a long-term response in the body of another animal that later influences how it behaves. An example of this is a female moth who releases an airborne chemical mixture. The mixture causes male moths of her species who are downwind to fly toward her (sometimes from as far away as 4 miles [6.44 meters]). As a result, the male moths change their behavior and keep flying upwind until they reach the female.

SIGNALING PHEROMONES

The more common signaling pheromones result in an immediate response, such as fear or aggression. An animal leaving its scent markers on its territory is an example of the use of signaling pheromones. Aside from these broad categories of pheromones, pheromones can also be grouped according to the type of behavior they provoke and by the role they play for a certain species.

BEHAVIORAL PHEROMONES

Pheromones can stimulate or deter (stop or prevent) a certain behavioral response such as egg-laying. Pheromones can also attract an animal to seek out the source of the chemical as some males do when they are get the scent of a female who is ready to mate. Other pheromones can repel or warn animals away from the source (as a territorial urine marker would do). Pheromones can serve as sexual or courtship chemicals to attract mates. Aggregation pheromones serve to attract other members of the species to the same spot, as when ants lay down a chemical trail for other ants to guide them to a food source.

Animals that are social and live in groups may release pheromones for defensive purposes in order to alert the band to some danger. Territorial, or marking, pheromones serve to communicate the boundaries of an animal's territory to others and to warn others to keep out. Finally, pheromones are an important means of regulating the behavior of individuals in a group. Studies have shown that when the odor of a male mouse is introduced among a group of female mice, the female's reproductive cycles become synchronized. It also is thought that humans release pheromones, but that they are mostly unaware of them.

[*See also* **Excretory System**]

An experiment where pheromones are placed in a pouch to attract insects. Pheromones are usually used to communicate with another animal of the same species. (Reproduced by permission of Photo Researchers, Inc.)

Photosynthesis

Photosynthesis is the process by which plants use light energy to make food from simple chemicals. Photosynthesis is vital to all life on Earth since all food comes from this process, either directly or indirectly. People not only eat green plants and their fruit and grains, but they also eat the animals that feed on the green plants.

The word photosynthesis means "putting together with light," and perfectly describes a process by which a plant converts carbon dioxide and water into food by using light. The miracle of photosynthesis is that it captures light energy and converts it into chemical energy that can be used by organisms. Photosynthesis occurs inside the leaf of a plant at the cellular level. Plant cells contain chloroplasts. These chloroplasts contain a green pigment called chlorophyll. The flat leaf, acting as a solar collector, allows the light to strike the chlorophyll, which is stimulated to absorb it. In the chloroplasts, the light reacts with carbon dioxide (that the plant breathes in through microscopic holes in its leaves called stomata) and with water (that the plant takes in through its roots). During a series of complicated reactions, the water molecules are broken down into hydrogen and oxygen, and the hydrogen combines with carbon dioxide to produce glucose, a simple sugar that is used as a building block for starch and other complex carbohydrates. The excess oxygen is later released through the stomata into the atmosphere. The plants use the glucose as food. What they do not use they convert to starch for storage and to build cells walls.

If all life on Earth depends on photosynthesis, then all life really begins with what makes photosynthesis work—light. Sunlight is the energy that travels from the Sun. It arrives on Earth in waves of different lengths, and those lengths give it

A chart showing the stages of photosynthesis and how each stage is related. (Reproduced by permission of McGraw-Hill, Inc.)

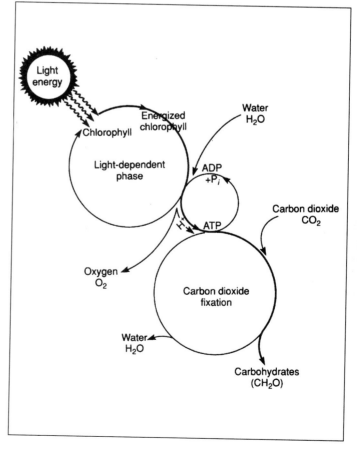

JAN INGENHOUSZ

Dutch plant physiologist (a person who studies how an organism and its body parts work or function normally) Jan Ingenhousz (1730-1799) discovered photosynthesis and plant respiration. He demonstrated that plants use sunlight and carbon dioxide (atmospheric gas) to make their own food, and that they give off oxygen as a by-product. He was the first to indicate the close connection between animals and plants and to show how much animals depended on green plants.

Jan Ingenhousz was born in Breda, The Netherlands, where he received his basic education. He then attended the University of Louvain and later the University of Leyden. After receiving his medical degree, he worked at a private practice in Breda, but left for England when his father died in 1765. While at work in a hospital there, he became an expert in the new technique of smallpox inoculation. This was a hazardous occupation since he administered a live virus instead of today's weakened vaccine. However, his treatments were so effective that he was called to Vienna, Austria, to inoculate the royal family. He was then appointed court physician and given a lifetime income. This allowed him to pursue his research, and in 1779, after seven years in Vienna, he returned to England where he would remain for the remainder of his life.

It was also that year that he began experiments that led to his discovery of photosynthesis, the process by which plants convert sunlight into food. Ingenhousz found that green plants take in carbon dioxide and give off

its different colors. As a combination of different wavelengths, sunlight is really a mixture of violet, blue, green, yellow, orange, and red light. These wavelengths can be observed by passing sunlight through a prism. Chlorophyll is extremely efficient and absorbs red, orange, and blue light, allowing only green light to pass through. This is what makes a leaf look green. When chlorophyll absorbs the Sun's light, the first part of photosynthesis begins as light energy splits up water molecules (hydrogen and oxygen). This process is called photolysis and produces energy-carrying molecules called adenosine triphosphate (ATP). In the second part of photosynthesis, energy from ATP and other energy carriers remove oxygen from carbon dioxide, allowing the carbon and hydrogen to combine and form glucose.

It has taken scientists hundreds of years to understand what happens during photosynthesis. Beginning in the early seventeenth century, the work of Flemish physician Jan Baptist van Helmont (1577–1644), and oxygen, but they do this only in the presence of sunlight. In the dark, he found that the opposite happens, and like animals, they absorb oxygen and give off carbon dioxide. This is called respiration. This was the first recognition that sunlight played a key role in the life of plants. Ingenhousz also proved that only the actual, visible light and not the Sun's heat, was necessary for photosynthesis to work. Others had been experimenting with air at this time, and the work of English chemist, Joseph Priestley (1733–1804), showed that a candle flame burning in a closed container eventually would go out. He also found that small animals placed in a similar space eventually died since all the oxygen was consumed and only carbon dioxide was left. Ingenhousz realized that since plants give off oxygen, which is essential to animal life, and then took in the carbon dioxide that animals breathed out as a waste product, there was a fundamental connection between plants and animals that no one before had realized. To Ingenhousz, photosynthesis meant that animals and plants are totally dependent on one another. We now know that photosynthesis is the key to all life on Earth since it provides food, either directly (for plants) or indirectly (for animals that eat the plants or eat other animals that have eaten plants) for virtually every living thing. For Ingenhousz, plants "purified" the air and "revitalized" it. His 1779 book detailed his plant discoveries and laid the foundation for the continued study of photosynthesis. Ingenhousz also broke new ground in physics and chemistry. For example, he improved phosphorous matches, invented a hydrogen-fueled lighter, and mixed an explosive propellant for firing pistols.

later the English botanist (a person specializing in the study of plants) Stephen Hales (1677–1761), demonstrated that plants needed air and water to grow. In the eighteenth century, chemists began to identify individual gases, and in 1779, the Dutch physician, Jan Ingenhousz (1730–1799), showed that plants take in carbon dioxide and release oxygen when light shines on them. By the 1880s, the German physiologist (a person specializing the study of the processes of living things), Theodor Wilhelm Engelmann (1843–1909), showed that the light reactions that capture solar energy and convert it into chemical energy occur in chloroplasts. It was not until the twentieth century, however, that scientists began to fully understand the complex biochemistry of photosynthesis.

Photosynthesis is a key part of a cycle that not only maintains life on Earth but keeps Earth's levels of carbon dioxide and oxygen in balance. Plants convert carbon dioxide into food and oxygen, which animals "burn" in a process called respiration (combining food with oxygen to release energy). Respiration is therefore the opposite or reverse of photosynthesis. In respiration, oxygen is used up and carbon dioxide and water are given off (which plants use to start photosynthesis again).

[*See also* **Carbon Dioxide; Carbohydrates; Chloroplast; Light; Plant Anatomy; Plant Hormones; Plants**]

Phototropism

Phototropism is the term used to describe a plant's response to light. When we notice that a potted plant on a windowsill has turned its leaves toward the light, we are witnessing phototropism. This is but one form of tropism or plant "behavior." A tropism is a phenomenon in which a plant grows in response to some outside stimulus.

Although plants cannot move in the manner of other organisms, plants are living things and, therefore, are sensitive to external stimuli. Their reactions to the many different outside forces they meet sometimes give the impression that they have indeed moved. Although plants usually appear motionless unless they are moved by the wind, they are in fact growing

Phototropism is plants' response to the direction and amount of light they receive. The seedling at the left received light on only one side, while the plant in the center received no light, and the plant on the right was grown in normal, all-around light. (Reproduced by permission of Photo Researchers, Inc. Photograph by Nigel Cattlin.)

much of the time and responding to a variety of environmental stimuli. When a plant's reactions to a stimulus result directly in any type of plant growth, botanists call this phenomenon a tropism. Tropisms can be positive or negative. A positive tropism means that the plant begins to grow toward the outside stimulus. Negative tropism means that it grows away from the source.

When a plant responds to a light source by growing in the direction of that source, it is called positive phototropism. (*Photo* means light in Latin.) There are many other forms of tropisms, but all must involve plant growth as a response. Chemotropism is a plant's response to chemicals; thigmotropism is its response to being touched; geotropism is its response to the force of gravity. Since all tropisms can be positive or negative, the growth of a seed's roots downward into the soil is positive geotropism (in the direction of the source) but also negative phototropism (away from the light). The upward growth of the new shoot is the reverse (positive phototropism and negative geotropism).

Plants have evolved tropism in order to maximize a particular function and therefore be better able to compete, survive, and reproduce. When a plant grows toward the light (positive phototropism), it can grow more rapidly and if necessary, out-compete its neighbor for scarce resources. An obvious example of tropism is hydrotropism in which a plant during a drought will make its root system grow away from its natural, gravity-pulled downward course and off in a direction containing life-sustaining water. Tropisms are one means that plants have to battle for their survival.

The actual mechanism by which a tropism (stimulus/growth) occurs could be described as uneven growth. Specifically, when a stem or root moves toward or away from an outside stimulus, it must grow in a curve. It achieves this "curved" growth by having the outside of the curve grow faster than the inside. This is caused by the plant hormone called auxin. According to what type of specialized tissue is receiving the stimulus (such as a root or a stem), a larger amount of auxin moves from the growing tip and down one side than moves down the other. Since auxins come from the tip, when a plant wants to move toward the light it sends an unequal amount of auxin down its sides. More auxin goes to the shaded side and less to the sunny side, meaning that the shaded side grows more than the sunny side and the plant therefore grows in a curve toward the light source.

[*See also* **Light; Plants**]

Phylum

The term phylum is one of the seven major classification groups that biologists use to identify and categorize living things. These seven groups are hierarchical or range in order of size. Phylum is the second largest and is located between kingdom and class. The classification scheme for all living things is: kingdom, phylum, class, order, family, genus, and species.

The category phylum is fairly broad, and members of the same phylum can be very different and have only basic similarities. Organisms in the same phylum, however, are presumed to have a common evolutionary ancestry. To determine an organism's place in a particular phylum, biologists study it to find similarities and differences between it and other organisms within the kingdom. An example within the animal kingdom is Chordata, which contains all vertebrates (animals with a backbone). Fish, amphibians, reptiles, birds, and mammals all belong to the phylum Chordata. However, invertebrates (no backbone) of the animal kingdom, like snails, clams, and octopus, belong to the phylum Mollusca. Others, like insects and crabs, belong to the phylum Arthropoda. The animal kingdom can be divided into twenty or more phyla.

Within the plant kingdom, the term "division" is used instead of phylum. Examples of some divisions include Coniferophyta (cone-bearing plants such as pine trees) and Anthophyta (plants that have flowers able to develop into seeds). Altogether, there are ten divisions (or phyla) in the plant kingdom.

[*See also* **Class; Classification; Family; Genus; Kingdom; Order; Species**]

Physiology

Physiology is the study of how an organism and its body parts work or function normally. It is closely related to anatomy, which studies an organism's structure. There are different types of physiology, such as human physiology, plant physiology, and comparative physiology.

As a branch of biology that studies exactly how the different processes in living things work, physiology seeks to answer a more difficult question than its counterpart anatomy. Where anatomy wants to know how things are built, shaped, and how they fit together, physiology wants to know how something functions. For example, how does human lung tissue work? How can a seal survive underwater for ten minutes without taking a breath? How do camels survive so long without water? These and many other questions have been asked by people ever since they started to wonder about the natural world. In order to answer them, physiology must examine an organism's functions at several different structural levels.

At the simplest or chemical level, physiology studies atoms and molecules. The cellular level is next and focuses on cells, which are the smallest units of a living thing. In complex organisms like humans, groups of similar cells form tissues, resulting in the tissue level. An organ is composed of two or more tissue types that perform a certain function, and it is at the organ level that really complex functions take place. Organs that work together to accomplish a common purpose form an organ system. Together, all the organ systems make up the living body or the complete organism. This is the highest structural level, and each of the levels has its own physiology (functions). It is difficult if not impossible to study the body's functions without some knowledge of how it is built and organized (anatomy). Studying physiology without an understanding of anatomy would be like trying to understand how a car's engine works without having any idea what an engine looks like.

HISTORY OF PHYSIOLOGY

Physiology is thought to have first developed in the Greek Hippocratic school of medicine (before 350 B.C.). Around the same time, the Greek philosopher Aristotle (384–322 B.C.) stated that every part of the body is made for a purpose, and, therefore, that the function (physiology) of something can be figured out by learning its structure (anatomy). The publication that marks the beginning of modern physiology, *On the Movement of the Heart and Blood in Animals,* was published by the English physician, William Harvey (1578–1657), in 1628.

For nearly the next three centuries, physiology was closely associated with anatomy, and it was not until the nineteenth century that it became recognized as a separate discipline. By the middle of that century, discoveries suggesting the unity of all life (as well as the functions of all living things) led to the development of general physiology. This branch seeks to learn the physiological functions that are common to all living things. Comparative physiology is similar and tries to find the evolutionary connections between living things. One of the fundamental concepts of both is the notion of "homeostasis." This is the ability of an organism to function under very different conditions. Put another way, it is the ability of an organism to maintain an internal environment that compensates or corrects for changes that take place in its external environment. It is

ARISTOTLE

Greek philosopher (a person who studies the source and nature of human knowledge) and naturalist Aristotle (384 B.C.–322 B.C.) is considered not only the greatest philosopher who ever lived but also the father of biology. His great interest in the natural world led him to closely observe living things and to classify them according to a system. He taught the world that true knowledge could be obtained by observation and experience.

Aristotle was born in Stagira, Macedonia, then a Greek colony north of Greece. His father was physician to the Macedonian king, Amyntas II. It is said that Aristotle lost both parents at an early age and was brought up by a family friend. At age seventeen, he traveled to Athens and joined Plato's Academy. Plato (c. 427 B.C.–c. 347 B.C.) was one of the greatest philosophers of all time, and Aristotle became his best pupil. When Plato died, Aristotle began a journey to various parts of the Greek world and was able to pursue his long-held interest in the natural world. The study of animals was his first love, and he began to systematically learn as much as could about them. However, in 342 B.C. he was called to Macedon by the new king, Philip II, the son of Amyntas II, to become tutor to his own young son named Alexander II (later called Alexander the Great). Aristotle schooled the young man for about six years until Alexander became king when Philip II was assassinated. When the new king began his own conquering campaigns, he no longer needed a tutor, and Aristotle returned to Athens. There he founded his own school he called the Lyceum, where he would do his research and give lectures. When Alexander II died in 323 B.C., however, Aristotle moved to his mother's hometown called Chalcis, where he died the next year.

important to the survival of any organism that it be able to adapt quickly to its environment while at the same time keeping its internal functions and systems in a steady or balanced state. Control is another concept that is very important to physiologists. It is related to homeostasis and might be described as the way in which an organism's different systems communicate with and influence each other.

HUMAN PHYSIOLOGY

Human physiology is the branch that studies how the human body and its parts work or function. Among the major functional systems studied are the integumentary system (the skin), the skeletal system (the framework), the muscular system (causing movement), the nervous system (control), the endocrine system (glandular control), the circulatory system

Aristotle wrote on many subjects, from logic (the principles of reasoning) and ethics (the general nature of morality), to politics and biology. However, of all of his scientific writings, most consider his work in biology to be the most successful. To begin with, he was one of the first to look at animals in a scientific way. Always a careful observer, he eventually began to place all of the known animals in to some sort of order. This is called classification. After studying, observing, and even dissecting (cutting apart for anatomical study) them, Aristotle arranged more than 500 animals according to their physical similarities and tried to understand the relationships between them. Always an excellent observer, he noticed, for example, that dolphins give birth to live young, so he put them in with all of the land beasts (now known as mammals) despite the fact that they were considered fishes. He also dissected a great many animals and wrote about the complex stomach of cattle. His work on the developing embryo of the chick showed that this early phase of life was equally worthy of study. In his writings on biology, he first taught that the form of natural objects is determined by their purpose. This, he said, leads to the conclusion that the structures of organisms are determined by the functions they are supposed to serve. He also hinted at an idea of evolution (the process by which living things change over generations) because he arranged living things in a lower-to-higher order that suggested a sort of chain of progress.

While known today for his ethical and political writings, it was Aristotle who showed the earliest "natural philosophers," or scientists, that experience, observation, and experiment are necessary when one investigates the natural world. He regularly stressed the importance of theory being based on facts. For this and his regular observations, not to mention his love of the natural world, he is rightly called the father of biology.

(transport and delivery), the respiratory system (oxygen supply), the digestive system (breakdown and absorption of food), the urinary system (eliminating waste), and the reproductive system (to produce offspring). These highly organized and complex systems work together and contribute to what are called the necessary life functions. These are: movement (actively getting around), responsiveness (sensing and reacting to stimuli), digestion (breaking down food so it can be absorbed), metabolism (all the chemical reactions in cells), excretion (removing waste), reproduction (producing new life), and growth (increasing in size). Taken together, these are the internal processes and functions that maintain life, the study of which is physiology.

While human physiology is of great value to medicine, plant physiology is most useful to agriculture and forestry. However, whether the type of physiology studied is that of plants or animals, it is important to know how a living organism works normally or is supposed to function, since only then can one determine if something is wrong and what might be done to correct the problem. Without the knowledge of anatomy, physiology would not be as useful as it now.

[*See also* **Brain; Circulatory System; Digestive System; Endocrine System; Excretory System; Heart; Integumentary System; Muscular System; Nervous System; Reproductive System; Respiratory System; Skeletal System**]

Piltdown Man

Piltdown man is the name given to the "fossil" bones found in England that turned out to be the greatest hoax in the history of science. When discovered in 1912, these remains were claimed to provide evidence of the missing link between apes and humans. It was not until the 1950s, however, that scientists were able to prove that Piltdown man was a complete fake.

Around 1900, science knew that Neanderthal man was an extinct form of *Homo sapiens* who was similar to modern humans. Many scientists then believed that, according to evolutionary theory (the belief that all living things change over generations), since man evolved from apes, there must be some link or in-between stage that came between this Neanderthal and the apes themselves. Scientists, therefore, assumed that the next great discovery would be this "missing link." Although most paleoanthropologists (scientists who study fossils to try to discover how humans evolved) thought that if this link were found it would be in Africa or Asia, in 1912 it was suddenly found at a dig on Piltdown Common in Sussex, England. An amateur archaeologist (one who studies the material remains of past cultures) named Charles Dawson supposedly stumbled upon nine fossilized pieces of a skull, as well as a jawbone and molars. When he put them together, it appeared that he had discovered actual evidence of the "missing link" between apes and humans.

What Dawson's discovery showed was a complete skull that was literally half man and half ape. Its upper skull was definitely human, since it had the high brow typical of intelligent humans. Its lower part was surely that of an ape since it had both a protruding jaw (jutting out) and a receding chin. Besides the bones themselves, Dawson found crude flint (a substance used to make fire) and bone tools along with the bones of other, long-extinct animals. Piltdown man was soon hailed as evidence of evolution's missing link, and this new fossil, dated at about 200,000 years old, was given the scientific name *Eoanthropus dawsoni,* meaning "dawn man of Dawson."

During the next thirty-five years, many hominid (human-like species) fossils were found in other parts of the world, but none ever came close to matching the features that Piltdown man displayed. This gave many a scientist a reason for doubting the find, and in 1948, testing began on Piltdown man that used new dating techniques. When preliminary results suggested that the bones were of very recent origin, they were tested again each time a new dating method was invented. By the time the new and highly reliable carbon-14 method was used in 1959 to confirm those conclusions, it was apparent to all that Piltdown man was a deliberate forgery. The jaw belonged to an orangutan that probably was killed in the Middle Ages (500–1450), and the cranium was human, but only slightly older than the jaw. Someone also had deliberately filed the molar teeth to make them look old and used, and someone had purposely stained the fragments. Eventually, no one could dispute the fact that the entire discovery had been planted, and that one or more persons had decided to make their own "missing link." Since then, the strangest and most unexplainable piece of paleontology has been resolved, and Piltdown man is now regarded only as a hoax that fooled people for forty years. Conclusive proof

Four busts of prehistoric man's evolution (from left to right): *Pithecanthropus erectus,* "Piltdown" man (which was a hoax put over on the scientific community; its fossils turned out to be modern-day human skull combined with an orangutan jawbone), Neanderthal man, Cro-Magnon man, and modern man. (Reproduced by Corbis-Bettmann.)

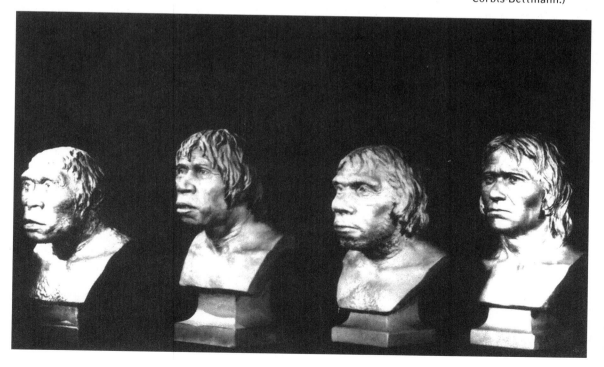

of who planned and carried out the hoax was never obtained, and despite several books about Piltdown man, no one has ever been able to absolutely link one or more persons to this deception.

The Piltdown man was beneficial to science in two ways, however. First was the fact that new methods of dating were demonstrated and proven in the field. Second, it forced scientists to become more rigorous and demanding when confronted with sudden, new discoveries.

[*See also* **Evolution; Evolution, Evidence of; Evolutionary Theory; Human Evolution**]

Plant Anatomy

Plant anatomy is the study of the shape, structure, and size of plants. As a part of botany (the study of plants), plant anatomy focuses on the structural or body parts and systems that make up a plant. A typical plant body consists of three major vegetative organs: the root, the stem, and the leaf, as well as a set of reproductive parts that include flowers, fruits, and seeds.

As a living thing, all of a plant's parts are made up of cells. Although plant cells have a flexible membrane like animal cells, a plant cell also has a strong wall made of cellulose that gives it a rigid shape. Unlike animal cells, plant cells also have chloroplasts that capture the Sun's light energy and convert it into food for itself. Like any complex living thing, a plant organizes a group of specialized cells into what are called tissues that perform a specific function. For example, plants therefore have epidermal tissue that forms a protective layer on its surface. They also have parenchyma tissue usually used to store energy. The "veins" or pipeline of a plant are made up of vascular tissue that distribute water, minerals, and nutrients throughout the plant. Combined tissues form organs that play an even more complex role.

THE ROOTS

A plant's roots, like the foundation of a skyscraper, help it to stay upright. They also absorb water and dissolved minerals from the ground and give the plant what it needs to make its own food. Most roots grow underground and move downward because of the influence of gravity, although the roots of some water plants float. Other root systems, like that of the English ivy, actually attach themselves to a vertical surface and allow the plant to climb. There are two main types of root systems: taproot and fibrous. Plants that have taproots grow a single, long root that penetrates straight down and firmly anchors the plant. Trees and dandelions have taproots that serve this function. Fibrous roots are shorter and more shallow and form a branching network. Grass has a fibrous root system that grows at a shallow level and in all directions. Inside a root are pipelines or veins that carry water and minerals to the rest of the plant. These pipes are concentrated in the center of the root, like the lead in the center of a pencil. At the end of each root is a cap that protects it as it pushes farther into the soil. Extending from the sides of the root, but further back from the root cap are root hairs. These hairs are the main water and oxygen absorbing parts of a plant. Materials enter and leave roots by two main processes: diffusion and osmosis. When molecules are distributed unequally, nature always seeks a balance and molecules will move from an area of high concentration to one of low concentration. When the cells of a root hair have little oxygen and the soil around the root hair has a lot, oxygen will move from the soil to the root automatically without the plant having to expend any energy. Osmosis is a similar situation (from high to low concentration), but it occurs when molecules, like those of water, move across a membrane that will not allow other materials to pass. Like diffusion, osmosis does not require the plant to use any energy.

THE STEMS

Plant stems perform two functions. They support the parts of the plant aboveground (usually the buds, leaves, and flowers), and they carry water and food from place to place within the plant itself. A stem is made up of an outer layer, the epidermis; an inner layer, the cortex; and a central zone called the pith. The stem of a green plant holds itself up by having thousands of cells lined up next to and on top of each other. As the cells take in water, they expand like a full balloon, and since their walls are elastic, they stretch very tight against each other and against the stem wall. It is their pressure that holds the stem up. A plant droops when its cells lack water and have begun to shrink. Woody plants, like trees, also contain a material called lignin that strengthen cell walls and make them more rigid. A plant's stem also functions as its circulatory system and uses what is called vascular tissue to form long tubes through which materials move from the roots to the leaves and from the leaves to the roots.

THE LEAVES

The leaf of a green plant manufactures food for plant growth and repair. A leaf is a highly specialized part of a plant since it is the place

STEPHEN HALES

English botanist (a person who studies plants) and physiologist (a person who studies how the many different processes going on inside a living thing actually work) Stephen Hales (1677–1761) is considered the founder of plant physiology. A pioneer in the study of blood circulation and blood pressure measurement, Hales applied the physics of his time to the problems of biology. In all of his experiments on plants and animals, he regularly emphasized the need for careful measurement of data.

Hales was born in Kent, England, and little is known of his life before he entered Cambridge University in 1696. There he studied science and religion, and in 1703 he was ordained in the church as a deacon (a clergyman just below a priest). In 1709 he became a clergyman at Teddington where he would remain for the rest of his life. At this time it was not unusual for a clergyman to also be a man of science, and Hales was able to do both well. It was at Teddington that Hales began to use some of the broad scientific education he had received and, in the spirit of English physicist and mathematician Isaac Newton (1642–1727), he tried to take what he knew of physics (the study of matter and energy) and apply it to biology.

Thus, in 1719, Hales began his first experiments on plants. Before this, he had done quite a bit of experimenting on animals and had achieved the first blood pressure measurements using a glass tube device of his own design. He also investigated the reflex actions in a frog whose head he had cut off, but after a while, Hales became in his own words, "discouraged by the disagreeableness of anatomical dissections." He therefore switched to plants

where photosynthesis takes place. In photosynthesis, the chlorophyll (green pigment) in the leaf absorbs energy from the Sun, combines it with water and minerals from the soil and carbon dioxide from the air, and produces the plant's food. Everything about a leaf is designed to intercept or capture sunlight. For example, a leaf is a flat structure with a large surface area and consists of a thin, flat blade called the lamina. The lamina is attached to a stalk called the petiole. The petiole is the leaf's main supporting rib and often branches into a network of veins. Leaves with only one blade are called simple, and those with two or more blades are called compound. Compound leaves often look like several small leaves attached to the same stalk. Leaves also grow in patterns to assure that they do not shade each other, and some plants have alternate leaves while others have leaves opposite each other. Leaves can control the amount of water they lose by opening or closing tiny slits called stomata (singular, stoma).

and carried over his blood-related experiments on animals to the study of the movement of sap in plants. Soon he was able to measure the force of a plant's sap flow just as he had measured blood pressure in animals. In his book, *Vegetable Staticks*, published in 1727, Hales described many of his discoveries concerning plant physiology. Hales detailed what he had learned concerning plant anatomy and what a plant does in order to survive and grow. He stated that plants take in part of the air and use it for food, that they need light for growth, and that they lose water mainly through their leaves. He showed that sap is under considerable pressure and that water flows in a plant in one direction only. He even calculated the actual velocity (its speed) of the sap and discovered that it differs according to the type of plant. As he did in his animal experiments, he investigated the role of water and air in an organism and explored all aspects of its growth.

Hales also had a very practical and even humanitarian side, and he was a pioneer in the field of public health. He used his knowledge of air and respiration to devise ventilators to remove "spent," or bad air (probably carbon dioxide), from closed spaces in hospitals, prisons, and merchant ships. He worked on ways to distill fresh water from seawater, and worked at water purification and food preservation. He even adapted a gauge from his plant experiments to measure the ocean depths. Besides all of the specific botanical knowledge and understanding he offered in his book on plant physiology, Hales' application of physics to biology and his emphasis on quantitative (measurable) experimentation provided an important model for those who were to follow.

FLOWERS AND SEEDS

The reproductive part of a seed-producing plant is called the flower. Flowers have male and female cells that produce a seed when they unite. The stamen is the male reproductive organ in a flower and contains the male cells (pollen) in its anther that grows at the tip of its long, narrow stalk. The pistil is the female reproductive organ and looks like a long-necked bottle. It has a round base containing the ovary, a slender tube or long neck called the style, and a flattened, sticky top called the stigma. Once a flower opens, its petals (which are a type of leaf) protect the sex organs and serve to help pollination (the transfer of pollen to the female parts) by attracting animals like bees and birds. When this happens, fertilization occurs and the ovaries become seeds.

Seeds have three main parts: the coat, the embryo, and the food storage tissue. The coat protects the embryo, which is the beginning of a plant and grows by using food stored in the seed. Most seeds are enclosed in fruit that can be dry like a ripe bean pod, or fleshy like an apple or a peach. Other plants, like fir trees, have naked or uncovered seeds that form on the upper side of the scales that make up a pine cone. All are designed to be scattered as far as possible from the parent plant to ensure the further survival of the species.

[*See also* **Botany; Photosyntheis; Plant Hormones; Plant Pathology; Plant Reproduction; Plants**]

Plant Hormones

Plant hormones are naturally occurring chemicals that influence plant development and growth. Often called plant growth regulators to distinguish them from animal hormones, they are similar to animal hormones in that they function as chemical messengers. There are three major groups of plant hormones, as well as two other hormones that do not fit in any group.

Plant hormones were developed by plants as one way of assuring their survival. Since a plant cannot move away from a threatening situation, it is important that it have an internal messenger system that ensures that the entire plant is able to react in a proper way to its environment. This role is filled by the messenger plant hormones.

HORMONE GROUPS

Besides influencing growth rate, plant hormones also control a plant's response to its environment. Like their animal counterparts, plant hormones are effective in small amounts and tend to be made in one place within the plant and transported somewhere else where they do their work. Unlike animal hormones, however, they are not produced by special glands nor do they only work on specialized target cells. Instead, plant hormones can have an effect on any part of the plant that produces them. Plant hormones were discovered in 1926 by the Dutch botanist (a person specializing in the study of plants), Frits W. Went (1903–1990), who isolated the first plant hormone, which he called "auxin." He chose this name from the Latin word meaning "to increase" since that word describes its result. Now known to be indoleacetic acid (IAA), this hormone is transported to the roots of young plants where it stimulates growth. Besides IAA, other growth-stimulating auxins besides IAA have been identified, and auxins are now considered to be one of the three major hormone groups.

In addition to auxins, there are two other major hormone groups: cytokinins and gibberellins. Cytokinins are an important group of plant hormones since they stimulate cell division and delay aging in older tissues. Cytokinins are thought to be produced in the tips of roots from where they travel upwards through the plant and stimulate branching rather than the lengthy growth promoted by auxins. Gibberellins are a chemically complex family of plant hormones that stimulate the growth of shoots (that part of a beginning plant that first pops out of a seed and reaches for the light). Gibberelins are important for plant embryos and seedlings, and stimulate the beginnings of root growth.

ABSCISIC ACID AND ETHYLENE

The other plant hormones that do not fall under any of the major three groups are abscisic acid and ethylene. While most plant hormones usually involve stimulating growth in one part or another, the hormone abscisic acid is actually an inhibitor since it turns off growth or development when conditions are not right for it. Sometimes certain environmental conditions, such as a drought, make water conservation a necessity. For a plant to survive in these conditions, it must slow down or stop its growth with the release of abscisic acid. Abscisic acid got its name because it was believed to play a key role in "abscission" or the seasonal loss of leaves. It is now know, however, that other hormones are more important in causing a tree to drop its leaves in autumn. Even though abscisic acid is not solely responsible for trees losing their leaves, it is extremely important given that the total lack of this hormone results in the inability of a plant's embryos to stop growing inside their seeds. Without abscisic acid premature eruption of a shoot through the seed coat may occur at a time and place where the seedling may not be able to grow.

The final and possibly best-known plant hormone, ethylene, plays a major role in the ripening of fruit. Ethylene is an unusual plant hormone in that it is released outside the plant and into the atmosphere. One plant is therefore able to influence its neighbors. It is ethylene gas that explains the old saying, "One bad apple spoils the whole bunch." Since apples continue to release ethylene after they are picked, any wound in its skin will stimulate extra production of ethylene gas, which in turn speeds up the ripening or aging of any apples nearby.

COMMERCIAL USES FOR PLANT HORMONES

Greater understanding of plant hormones has led to their increased commercial use. Farmers and gardeners are now able to use certain hormones regularly to achieve desired effects. For example, a well-known use of ethylene is by farmers who use ethylene gas to ripen tomatoes that are mistakenly harvested while they are still green. Plant hormones have also been used for military purposes. An example is IAA, which if used in very high doses, can have the opposite effect of not only slowing down growth, but it also may prove poisonous to plants. This was the case when the United States used one of these auxin-related compounds during the Vietnam War (1954–75). Called "Agent Orange," this chemical spray caused a plant's leaves to dry and fall off, thus supposedly denying the military enemy any hiding places in the jungle. Unfortunately, a chemical by-product of Agent Orange is dioxin, a cancer-causing agent.

[*See also* **Botany; Plant Anatomy; Plant Pathology; Plant Reproduction; Plants**]

Plant Pathology

Plant pathology is the study of diseases, injuries, or other factors that affect the welfare of plants. It is mostly an applied science, meaning that it is studied with a specific, practical purpose in mind, usually of a commercial or economic nature. Also called phytopathology, it is studied by plant pathologists who try to understand and control the many factors that may affect a plant's health and productivity.

All species of plants are subject to disease that may be caused by infectious agents, poor environmental conditions, or the effects of parasites or predators. Unlike animals, there is sometimes no clear distinction between a healthy and an unhealthy plant, and plant pathologists generally describe a plant as diseased when it is regularly disturbed or badly affected by something outside itself. The actual cause might be a living, disease-carrying organism (called a pathogen) or unfavorable environmental conditions. If either factor results in a plant's biochemical or physiological (functions) systems being disturbed, the plant is considered diseased. As with animals, a plant's disease often shows itself in what are called symptoms, and it is therefore important to know how a certain plant looks and behaves in its normal, healthy state in order to recognize any symptoms of disease. Thus, plant pathologists must have knowledge of a plant's normal growth habits as well as the range of variability in the species—or what differences are normal.

CAUSES OF PLANT DISEASE

Plant pathologists divide plant diseases into categories. Infectious diseases include those caused by transmissible (capable of being spread) biological agents or pathogens such as bacteria, fungi, or viruses. Noninfectious disease (usually physiological or functional disorders in which something goes wrong with the way its major systems work) can be caused by environmental factors like nutrient deficiency, excess of minerals, a lack or an excess of moisture, soil temperature that is too high or low, a lack or an excess of light, a lack of oxygen, extreme soil acidity or alkalinity, and air pollution. Finally, noninfectious biological agents that harm plants by either eating them or living off them, called parasites, include such organisms as arthropods (like a mite, spider, or centipede), nematodes (roundworms), and other parasitic plants (like mistletoe that can only live off another plant). The most common causes of disease among plants grown commercially are pathogens (like bacteria), pests (like mites), and bad weather.

In treating plant diseases, the first thing a plant pathologist must do is to determine whether the diseases are caused by a pathogen or by a noninfectious factor in its environment. In many cases, a diseased plant shows obvious symptoms such as an unusual color change in its leaves or a loss of flowers, that immediately indicate its cause. A good example of disease symptoms are the bands of white on the foliage of pine trees caused by too much ozone in the air. Other times, identical symptoms can have very different causes.

A diseased phlox leaf covered by a powdery mildew. (Reproduced by Field Mark Publications. Photograph by Robert J. Huffman.)

Viruses. Among diseases classified as infectious diseases are those caused by a virus. A virus is an extremely small organism that cannot live or reproduce outside its host. A virus usually spreads easily and can severely damage or kill a plant. Viruses can be transmitted by insects feeding off a diseased plant or by a gardener's shears. Viral infections in plants are often called mosaics because of the blotchy appearance they cause. Viruses are extremely difficult to remove and it is often best to try to prevent infection from the start.

Bacteria. Bacteria (a group of one-celled organisms so small they can only be seen with a microscope) are essential to the life cycle on Earth and most are beneficial, but some attack and even destroy plants. Bacteria enter a plant through wounds or natural openings and can be spread by the wind. Like viral infections, bacterial diseases are often difficult to control. Bacteria cause a plant to wilt and even rot. For example, fire blight is a type of bacterial disease that makes an apple tree appear scorched.

Fungi. The greatest numbers of infectious plant diseases are caused by fungi (a group of many-celled organisms that live by absorbing food and are neither plant nor animal) that enter a plant through any openings, as do bacteria. Dutch elm disease is one of the best known fungal diseases. It killed millions of elms in the United States. Fungi cause diseases that are described by words like rust, smut, and mildew.

Parasites. Parasites also can be harmful to plants. For example, nematodes are parasitic worms too small to be seen with the naked eye that suck vital juices from a plant, causing major losses of fruit and vegetables. Other plants can be parasites as well. The mistletoe is a good example of a plant that invades the tissues of another and steals its nutrients. Other plants like strangleweed and witchweed stunt or kill their hosts by robbing them of water and food.

CONTROLLING PLANT DISEASES

Control of plant disease is usually a combination of several strategies, but it always begins by using healthy seeds. To combat actual pests, pathologists might use chemicals called toxicants that kill bacteria, fungi, or parasites. Seeds and soil can be treated chemically and leaves can also be sprayed. Without the widespread use of these chemicals, the successful commercial production of fruits and vegetables would probably not be possible. However, other less dangerous methods can be used, since strong chemicals can harm people as well as pests. Some of these strategies involve simply keeping anything infected away from other plants, properly rotating crops (not growing the same thing in the same location every season), pruning and burning diseased tissue, and ensuring that a plant's environment is the best it can be. Ideal disease control is best achieved by breeding plant varieties that can resist diseases on their own.

[*See also* **Botany; Plant Anatomy; Plant Reproduction; Plants; Pollution**]

Plant Reproduction

Plants reproduce either sexually or asexually. In sexual reproduction, two parents produce a genetically different individual. In asexual reproduction, a plant propagates (reproduces) itself and produces a genetically identical individual. Some plants reproduce both ways.

Sexual reproduction in plants requires separate male and female parts whose separate sex cells come together and fuse or unite. This unification produces a seed that if cultivated under the proper conditions, will grow into a unique offspring. In flowering seed plants or angiosperms, the reproductive parts are in the flowers. For humans, flowers may be simply a source of pleasure since they add color and fragrance to the world, but for plants they are complex and hardworking organs. Flowers vary in size, shape, and color, yet all have the same common structures. A flower's male reproductive parts, called stamens, consist of a filament or stalk and a pollen head called an anther. Its female parts, called carpels or pistils, consist of an ovary (where the seed eventually will develop), and a stalk or style at the end of which is a sticky flat top called a stigma, which will receive the pollen. The entire male part looks like an antennae with pads on their ends. The female parts resemble a long-necked, round-bottom bottle with a flat top.

POLLINATION

Before a flower can produce seeds, pollination must occur. This means that pollen (which contains the plant's male sex cells) has to somehow travel from its anthers to its stigma. While many plants have both male and female organs and can therefore easily pollinate themselves (self-pollination), this does not result in much genetic variety. Therefore, flowering plants have evolved several different methods and strategies to make sure that pollen is transferred from one plant to another (cross-pollination). Since plants cannot move on their own and accomplish this task, they require agents to do their work for them. The most common method is animal pollination in which a colorful, perfumed flower attracts an in-

An electron micrograph of the reproductive system of a flower. The bulbous carpel with the short-stalked female sigmas emerging from it is at lower center. The tip of the third stigma at the right is covered with pollen. The droplets in the bottom right and left corners are nectar to attract pollinating insects. (©Photographer, Science Source/Photo Researchers, Inc.)

sect, bird, or bat by producing a sugary liquid called nectar. In extracting the nectar from the flower, the animal picks up sticky pollen grains, which it then accidentally rubs onto another flower's stigma as it gets more nectar. This transfer of pollen is called pollination. Besides animals, the wind is another useful way of transferring pollen from one plant to another.

After a grain of pollen lands on the stigma of a suitable flower, the pollen begins to grow a thin tube that penetrates down the long neck or style of the female part and enters the embryo sac containing the ovary (female sex cells). The male cells travel down the tube and fertilize the egg or ovum. Soon a seed is formed, containing an embryo (the beginning of a new individual plant that has its own unique collection of genes), some stored food (the endosperm), and a protective coat (the testa). After a seed has developed, a plant's next job is to distribute the seed some distance from the parent plant, mainly to prevent its own habitat from becoming overcrowded. Plants that use animals to disperse their seeds often produce fruit that contain seeds. Fruit can be soft and juicy like a peach or hard and dry like a burr. Some fruit are eaten by animals that discard the seed somewhere else or have it pass through their system undigested. Other fruit have hooks or barbs that easily catch on to the fur of passing animals. Some seeds are mechanically dispersed by fruit that explode (like impatiens), while other seeds can float and use water to move about. When a seed falls into an environment where conditions are right for it, the seed takes in water and begins to grow. This beginning growth is called germination.

VEGETATIVE PROPAGATION

Plants can also produce more of their kind through asexual reproduction. Many perennial plants (plants that grow for several years) reproduce asexually by producing new parts that become entirely new plants. This form of asexual reproduction is called vegetative propagation. This method is favored by plants that live in especially harsh or severe conditions, such as those near a mountaintop, where the opportunity to attract animal pollinators is minimal or unreliable. The grass that grows on our lawns reproduces asexually by sending up new above-ground plants from its underground root system. The strawberry plant sometimes found as a weed in our lawns sends out runners along the ground that take root and produce a new plant while still attached to the parent plant. Strawberry plants can also reproduce by making seeds. Other plants can regenerate (regrow) parts from any plant parts that remain. Thus if we pull up a dandelion from our lawn but do not get the entire taproot and leave a piece underground, the plant will regrow new roots, stems, and leaves. Many plants with belowground tubers (stems), rhizomes (stems like roots), or bulbs (like tulips) can do the same and produce an entirely new plant. However, all of the plants produced by vegetative propagation are genetically identical to the parent plant. Farmers and gardeners use this technique to produce large numbers of desirable, identical plantlets. Nature, however, favors sexual over asexual reproduction since it prefers to have plants that vary genetically. Plants that are genetically identical can be susceptible to disease or a sudden climate change, and they can all be destroyed. If a species has genetic variety, though, some may be more resistant to disease or others may tolerate climate change and survive.

[See also **Botany; Plant Anatomy; Plant Hormones; Plants; Reproduction, Asexual; Reproduction, Sexual**]

Plants

A plant is a multicelled organism that makes its own food by photosynthesis. Although plants show a variety of form, function, and activity, all belong to the kingdom Plantae and generally are characterized by being immobile, or anchored, in soil, having strong woody tissues for support, and by being green and carrying on photosynthesis. Plants are essential to life on earth, especially human life, since they are at the beginning of the food chain and take in carbon dioxide (an atmospheric gas) and give off oxygen. Plants are also a source of medicine and useful materials. Botanists (people who study plants) have identified about 500,000 species of plants, although there are many undiscovered species yet to be classified.

The plant kingdom is one of the five main groupings of organisms; the four others being the monerans, protists, fungi, and animals. Although algae were long considered to be part of the plant kingdom, they are now regarded as being part of either the Moneran or Protista kingdom. Plants are found in virtually all land and water habitats and can range in size from tiny mosses to giant sequoia trees more than 300 feet (10.94 kilometers) tall. Whatever their size or habitat, all plants have the following characteristics: they are multicellular at some point in their life; they are eukaryotic (their cells have nuclei); they reproduce sexually (through the union of sperm and egg); they have chloroplasts (are the energy-converting structures) for photosynthesis; they have cell walls; they develop organs; and they have life cycles.

TYPES OF PLANTS

Although plants have all these things in common, scientists distinguish among the many different types of plants and classify plants as they do every other living thing. Therefore, in the kingdom Plantae, there are ten phyla or divisions of plants, each of which represents a number of classes, or more specific types. Most of these ten divisions can be grouped into five major types: seed plants, ferns, lycophytes, horsetails, and bryophytes.

Seed Plants. Seed plants are exactly what they sound like—plants that use seeds to reproduce. Plants that produce seeds that are enclosed in a protective case are called angiosperms. These include most of well-known plants like trees, wildflowers, and fruits and vegetables. Plants that produce seeds without any covering are called gymnosperms. Most gymnosperms produce their seeds in cones. Evergreens like firs and pine trees are a good example of gymnosperms.

Ferns. Ferns often vary greatly in size, but almost all grow in moist areas. Only their leaves, called fronds, grow above ground. The rest of the plant spreads out in stems that grow horizontally underground.

Lycophytes, Horsetails, and Bryophytes. Lycophytes are mostly mosses and have a single, central stem. Horsetails have tiny leaves and hollow, jointed stems that are scratchy. Bryophytes grow in shady areas and are a type of moss, but they do not have any vascular tissue or tubing that carries water throughout the plant. Sphagnum or peat moss is a good example of bryophytes.

PLANT ANATOMY

Despite the many types and divisions of plants, most of the common plants reproduce in one of two ways, have the same basic parts, and make their food the same way. Since the seed plants make up the largest single group of plants (around 250,000 species) and is the one most familiar, they will serve as a good example for plant anatomy. Nearly all these plants have three major body parts: roots, stems, and leaves.

Roots. A plant's roots anchor it in the soil and provide the plant with what it needs to grow by absorbing water and minerals. This underground root system also places a major restriction on plants since they are unable to move about and must cope with changing conditions instead of moving away as an animal would. Some plants use their roots to store food for the aboveground part of the plant to use, such as radishes and carrots. Others, like potatoes, are examples of plants with tubers, or a swollen underground stem, in which food is stored. As a plant grows in size, its root system must expand not only to feed it more, but also to simply hold it upright.

There are two main types of root systems: taproots and fibrous systems. A taproot is a large main root that grows straight down and has smaller, lateral roots growing off it. Carrots and dandelions have taproots, as do trees which sometimes send down an anchor as far as 15 feet below ground. Fibrous roots are all the same size and spread out horizontally not very far beneath the surface. Grass, wheat, and corn have fibrous roots. As roots grow, the tip of each slender branch is protected by a root cap as it pushed through the soil. Behind the cap are threadlike tubes, or root hairs, that spread out and increase a plant's ability to absorb what it needs from the soil. Some water plants have roots that float, while other plants like orchids have roots that attach themselves to the branches of another plant or tree.

Stems. The stem is that part of a plant that supports the plant's buds, leaves, and flowers. Although stems vary greatly in size and type, they all connect the roots to the leaves by a network of pipelines, and they also hold up the part of the plant that needs to reach for sunlight. Some stems are short and green, like those of lettuce that appear to have no stem at all, while others are woody and large like the trunk of a tree. Almost all plants grow by putting out buds from different parts of their stems. Terminal buds grow near the end or apex of a stem, while lateral buds grow where a leaf joins a stem. Buds are specialized and may grow into new branches, leaves, or flowers. Stems are made of vascular tissue that serve as the plant's pipeline, or tubing system, that performs two functions: one system (made of vascular tissue called xylem) is used mainly for transporting material from the roots to the leaves, and the other (made of tissue called phloem) is used for moving material from the leaves to the roots or other parts of the plant. The stringy strands of celery that get caught between our teeth are a good examples of a plant's vascular tissue.

Leaves. The leaves of a plant are where the really important and amazing work is done—making food. This food-making process in which green leaves change inorganic raw materials into organic nutrients is called photosynthesis. Photosynthesis involves a leaf's ability to trap light energy and convert it into chemical energy. As a solar collector, a leaf consists of a thin, flat blade that is attached to a stalk called a petiole. The blade is where photosynthesis takes place. The blade, also called the lamina, is made up of two layers of cells—the epidermis on the outer surface and the mesophyll on the inside—and is strengthened by a network of veins that also transport materials to and from the blade. The underside of a leaf has microscopic openings or pores called stomata (singular, stoma) that can open and close and allow oxygen to flow out and carbon dioxide to flow in. These pores also regulate the amount of water that a plant will lose.

Leaves are usually green because their cellular structures called chloroplasts contain the green pigment chlorophyll. It is chlorophyll that traps the Sun's energy and begins a four-step biochemical process of using carbon dioxide and water to produce a sugar called glucose and to release oxygen. The plant uses some of this food as fuel for itself, some to grow and repair, and some it stores. When a primary consumer eats a plant, it obtains the original light energy that was captured by the plant.

Leaves vary greatly in size and usually are arranged in definite patterns to make sure that each receives the most sunlight it can and does not shade its neighbor. Leaves also die during a process known as abscission (separation). As the days grow shorter in autumn, a layer of cells grows across the base of the petiole and stops the flow of food to it. This trapping of sugar in the leaf produces a bright red pigment called anthocyanin or a yellow pigment called carotene. In deciduous plants, all the leaves fall off at the same time, but in evergreen plants they are shed and replaced regularly, so the plant is never without leaves.

SEXUAL REPRODUCTION IN PLANTS

Plants reproduce either by sexual reproduction, in which a male sperm cell unites with a female egg cell to produce a unique individual plant, or by asexual reproduction, in which the plant divides itself up to produce an identical replica. A flower is the reproductive part of many plants, and it may contain the male or female reproductive structures or even both.

Flowers. Flowers have four main parts: the calyx, the corolla, the stamens, and the pistils. The calyx protects the petals (corolla), inside which are the stamens (the male reproductive part) and pistils (the female reproductive part). The purpose of a flower is to bring about pollination, which is the transfer of pollen (male sex cells) to the female parts. Insects, birds, bees, and even the wind play a role in pollination. When a pollen grain lands on a receptive pistil, fertilization takes place and an entirely new cell is formed that is the start of a seed. A seed containing an embryo of the new plant is often enclosed in something called a fruit.

Fruit. Whether fruit are hard and dry (like a walnut) or soft and juicy (like a raspberry), it is the plant's way of scattering its seeds as far as possible. Some fruit have burrs that cling to an animal's fur, while some fruit are capable of floating on water, and others can resist being digested as they pass through an animal's gut to be deposited somewhere else. By producing fruit that animals want to eat, plants are using animals to distribute their seeds and to make sure that they end up in a place where they may germinate or begin to grow. When conditions are right, the seed uses the water it receives and the food it has stored to send a root, or radicle, through its seed coat and into the soil, while a shoot (containing the beginnings of a stem, buds, leaves, and flowers) grows aboveground and toward the light. This begins a new plant.

ASEXUAL REPRODUCTION IN PLANTS

Plants can also spread asexually, usually by sending up new aboveground plants from an existing root system. Grass and strawberries grow this way, as do tulips. Many plants with tubers, like a dandelion or potato, will regenerate into a new plant if only a piece is left in the ground.

PLANTS ARE ESSENTIAL TO LIFE

Plants are basic to life on Earth. A world without plants would be a world humans could not recognize. Besides missing the beauty and pleasure that plants give, the world would be without any of the food the people and animals know and need. People would also be lacking the many medicines, shelter, and useful products that are based on plants. By capturing the energy of the Sun, plants make all other life on Earth possible.

[*See also* **Botany; Photosynthesis; Plant Anatomy; Plant Hormones; Plant Pathology; Plant Reproduction; Reproduction, Asexual; Reproduction, Sexual**]

Plasma Membrane

The plasma membrane is a thin, continuous sheet that separates all living cells from their environment. This membrane maintains conditions within the cell and allows certain things to pass in and out of the cell. It is strong and can repair itself if damaged.

Every living cell in every living thing, plant or animal, is surrounded by a plasma membrane. If cells did not have some sort of barrier to separate them from their fluid environment, they could not perform any functions. Their organelles (tiny structures that each have a job to do) would be floating around all over the place. More important, they would not be cells, since cells are separate units of living matter. It is the plasma membrane that makes cells a separate entity, or a self-contained unit of living matter.

The membrane is so thin that it was not proven to exist until the late twentieth-century invention of the super powerful electron microscope. Although incredibly thin, this delicate structure is very strong and even stretchable. It is made up of a double layer of molecules of a lipid (fats, oils, and waxes) that each have a head and a tail. Their tails point in toward the center of the cell and repel water. Their larger heads face outward and attract water.

Plasma membranes are selectively permeable. This means that they allow certain molecules to enter the cell through its pores while blocking the path of others. The plasma membrane is sometimes called the living gatekeeper. Although strong and flexible, it can be damaged. However, the plasma membrane has the ability to repair any breaks it may suffer. Although the plasma membrane is one of the few structures common to every living cell, the plasma membrane in a plant cell is not identical to what is called its cell wall. Animal cells do not have cell walls. They are found only in plant cells and are located outside the plasma membrane. Unlike the plasma membrane, the cell wall is made of tough cellulose (the main component of plant tissue). Fungi and bacteria also have cell walls, but they are not made of cellulose. Cells walls give plant cells a rigid shape, while the plasma membrane of animal cells give them the appearance of a tiny, jelly-filled bag.

[*See also* **Cell**]

Pollution

Pollution is the contamination of the natural environment by harmful substances that are produced by human activity. Pollution of Earth's air and water have become so widespread that the problem is now global and could threaten the biosphere (a life-supporting zone extending from Earth's crust into the atmosphere). Pollution by chemicals and nuclear material may have especially severe and long-lasting effects.

The term pollution can have several different meanings. Derived from the Latin *pollutus,* it suggests something that is made unclean or dirty. Today, the word pollution is almost always applied to the environment and usually has one of two meanings. The wider of the two suggests that pollution includes any unpleasant or unwanted environmental change, whatever its cause. According to this meaning, a natural event like a volcano can certainly cause pollution.

TYPES OF POLLUTION

In a narrower sense, pollution can be interpreted as any harmful environmental changes caused specifically by human activity. Human-caused pollution will be discussed here, since it not only poses the bigger threat today but is really the only type that humans can prevent. Pollution caused by human activities is extensive, since people produce an enormous variety of pollutants that eventually end up contaminating the air and the water that is so important to human life.

Air Pollution. Air pollution is sometimes the most obvious since at its worst, we can literally see the pollution in the sky. Air is polluted by the release of harmful gases and particles into the atmosphere. The gases given off by running an automobile are the major causes of today's air pollution. Although the United States has drastically improved its performance on auto emissions, the fact remains that although it has only 5 percent of the world's population, it accounts for 70 percent of the carbon monoxide (an odorless, tasteless, colorless, and poisonous gas) and 45 percent of the nitrous oxides (a poisonous gas) that are pumped into the atmosphere.

Heavy industry and power plants around the world also contribute to a steady stream of sulfur dioxide (toxic gas) released into the air. All of these gases are noxious or have harmful effects. Carbon monoxide increases the demands on the heart and reduces the blood's supply of oxygen to the tissues. Nitrogen oxides dissolve in water and form nitric acid, one of the components of acid rain. Sulfur oxides also combine with water to produce sulfuric acid. All of these air pollutants work to undermine humans' health, erode buildings, and kill green plants.

More alarmingly, what we are putting into the atmosphere may be changing the climate of the entire Earth. It has been argued that the accumulation of what are called "greenhouse gases," like carbon dioxide, methane, and chlorofluorocarbons (CFCs), have the effect of trapping the Sun's heat close to Earth. This can create a greenhouse effect that will lead to global warming, the results of which may be the melting of the polar ice cap (causing widespread flooding). Also, agricultural regions may become too hot and dry to grow crops. The protective ozone layer is also becoming thinner. This upper atmospheric layer shields Earth and its inhabitants from the harmful ultraviolet radiation contained in ordinary sunlight. When CFCs are released from our refrigerators, air conditioners, and spray cans, they react with the ultraviolet radiation and release chlorine atoms. These in turn destroy the oxygen molecules that make up the protective ozone layer.

Water Pollution. As important as air pollution is, the issue of water pollution is equally so. Clean water is as essential to life on Earth as is clean air, yet human activity has routinely polluted its sources of fresh water by allowing it to be contaminated by organic and industrial waste. Organic waste is mainly sewage, and even the best sewage treatments plants in the biggest cities cannot keep drinking water supplies from being contaminated. In fact, many larger cities get their drinking water from filtered and treated sewage water. Industrial pollution of water adds many dangerous inorganic (man-made) chemicals to our water supply. These chemicals may cause cancer and interfere with reproduction.

Pesticides and Nuclear Waste. In addition to the vast problems the world faces with air and water pollution, the pollution problems relating to pesticides (chemicals that kill insects) and nuclear power are also critically important. Ever since World War II (1939–45), increasingly pow-

This group of dead fish was killed by water pollution. Clean water is essential to life on Earth. (©U.S. Fish and Wildlife Service. Photograph by W. French.)

erful chemicals have been used to kill or control insects that are considered harmful to people or products. The first major success was the synthetic chemical DDT. Although able to kill any insect, DDT also was later found to infect fish and kill birds. It has since been found in the tissues of living things from the poles to the most remote forests. It sometimes can even be found in mother's milk. As a result of these harmful effects, the United States banned the use of DDT in 1972 and many other countries followed suit.

While the use of DDT has been banned in the United States and other countries, many other chemical pesticides (as well as herbicides and even fertilizers) used by commercial agriculture have been found to severely interfere with normal human and animal life processes, causing illness, mutations, and even death. However, as bad as these chemicals can be for living things, they have nowhere near the permanence found in radioactive materials. While nuclear power plants generate no air pollution, they result in the steady production of nuclear or radioactive waste. There is no known way of safely disposing of this near-permanent material which will remain radioactive for up to half a million years. The radioactive waste can result in cancers, birth defects, and death.

POLLUTION CONTROL

Beginning in the 1960s, a growing public and governmental awareness of the importance of the environment led to campaigns for laws and international agreements to curb pollution. In the United States alone, water quality has been improved (with dramatic reversals of "dead" lakes like Lake Erie), and air pollution has been reduced substantially. Recycling has also become a standard way of conserving resources. However, the world's pollution problems cannot be solved in only one country. All countries share the growing realization that the biosphere, or all the parts of Earth that make up the living world, includes everyone on Earth. For this reason, international cooperation is essential if Earth is to be restored to its natural and livable state.

[*See also* **Carbon Dioxide; Carbon Monoxide; Ozone**]

Polymer

A polymer is a chemical compound formed by the linking of many smaller molecules (particles) into a long chain. Polymers can be both natural and synthetic, and most living things are composed of natural polymers. Polymers can store energy and information and have structural uses as well.

In Greek, a polymer has many (*polys*) parts (*meros*). It is an organic compound or a natural substance containing carbon that is made up of many smaller repeating parts, or units, called monomers. Polymers play an important role in the chemistry of life, and without chemicals and chemical reactions, there would be no living things. Since they are compounds or are made up of many smaller units, polymers are also called macromolecules (meaning they are giant molecules). A polymer is also described as a "chain" molecule since the smaller units that make it up are linked together like a long chain. Polymers are so useful because although this chain has only a certain length, it can, like a piece of string, be tied and twisted and turned into all sorts of different shapes. Polymers combine flexibility with strength since their chains can be stretched several times their normal length without breaking. It is no surprise therefore that examples of substances composed of natural polymers would be starch, wool, and rubber.

Without polymers there would be no plants or trees since cellulose is a polymer. Plants use cellulose to build their cell walls, and trees use it to make their woody parts. Green plants also store their food as starch, which is a polymer. Proteins are another type of polymer, and wool is a variety of protein, as are the life-coding molecules of deoxyribonucleic acid (DNA) and ribonucleic acid (RNA). It could be said that life on Earth is based to a great degree on the existence, properties, and reactions of two classes of polymers—proteins and nucleic acids.

Aside from these organic forms of polymers, there are inorganic polymers and synthetic polymers. Since an organic compound is a chemical compound that contains carbon, an inorganic compound is one that does not have any carbon in it. Most of the inorganic polymers that are found in nature are typically very hard and strong. Many minerals, like diamond, quartz, and silica, are inorganic polymers. Synthetic polymers or polymers that are made by people can be organic (as with rubber that occurs both naturally and as a human-made product), or inorganic (like plastics and adhesives). Once chemists understood the process of polymerization or synthetic creation of polymers, they were able to produce everything from vinyl, polyurethanes, and silicones and to vary their properties in ways that exceeded even what nature could produce.

Population

The term population refers to all the members of the same species that live together in a particular place. This concept has proved very useful to

U·X·L Complete Life Science Resource

the life sciences since it has only two basic requirements. Its individual members must belong to the same species (and be able to mate and produce young), and they must also live in the same area at the same time. Ecologists refer to all of the animal and plant populations that live together and interact in a given environment as a community. This is a larger category than population.

Every ecosystem (living organisms and their environment) is composed of populations or groups of the same type of organisms. In any particular natural place, such as a forest or a lake, there are populations of certain animals (deer, earthworms, trout) along with certain plant populations (maple trees, spruce trees, honeysuckle) that thrive in the same place. Ecologists have decided to categorize these same-species groups, such as all of trout or all of the maple trees, that live in the same place as populations.

Population size is influenced by the interaction of two major factors: the rate that a population grows under ideal conditions and the rate at which certain external or environmental factors limit population growth. An example of population growth under ideal conditions would be placing a pair of fertile animals in a "new" habitat with no predators, no diseases, more than enough food, and a perfect climate. Since there are no external factors hindering the animals in any way, their population growth would be limited only by "intrinsic" or internal factors as how quickly they can produce young, how quickly their young become fertile, and how long they naturally live. Under these conditions, the maximum rate of population growth is limited only by the biology of the species. Ecologists know that any population growing at this unnatural rate would eventually reach what is called "carrying capacity," when external or environmental factors come into play.

Carrying capacity is described as the largest size of a particular population that can be supported by a particular environment. Once a population has reached a certain critical size (which is technically past its carrying capacity), it begins to feel the limitations of its habitat in terms of space and resources. When this limit is surpassed, the rate of population growth can only decline since individuals now have to compete with one another for living space and resources like food and water. Intense competition by itself can result in stress, which results in lower birth rates and increases mortality.

In the real world, populations of animals and plants change in size all the time. Some factors that put limits on a population include: low food supply, predators, bad weather, disease, competition, and human interference. Ecologists have developed mathematical models, called population dynamics, which are used to study and predict the condition of a population in an ecosystem. Ecologists base a model on the four major environmental factors that affect populations: birth rate (BR), immigration rate (IR), death rate (DR), and emigration rate (ER). Such a model states that P = BR - DR + IR - ER. Therefore, the change in population size (P) is equal to the birth rate less the death rate, plus the immigration rate (how many new members join the habitat) minus the emigration rate (how many old members leave the habitat). This statistical model is true of all populations, including humans.

Population studies are important if we are to understand how human activities affect the natural world. Being able not only to measure or count a single group of the same species in a particular ecosystem, but to be able to understand the dynamics of what forces make its numbers grow or decline, is especially valuable. Understanding a population also gives ecologists insight into the larger and more complex concept of communities.

[*See also* **Population Genetics; Population Growth and Control (Human)**]

Population Genetics

Population genetics is the statistical study of the natural differences found within a group of the same organisms. Instead of examining the genes of individuals, it looks at the dominant (the trait that first appears or is visibly expressed in the organism) and recessive (the trait that is present at the gene level but is masked and does not show itself in the organism) genes found within an entire population. Population genetics seeks to understand the factors that control which genes are expressed. It also creates mathematical models to try to predict which differences will be expressed and with what frequency.

In the life sciences, a population consists of all the individuals of the same species (all of the same kinds of organisms, like all the tigers) that live in a particular habitat at the same time. Scientists know that in any population, whether it be tigers or people, the individuals that make it up are all different. They may all be tigers, but each has individual and very recognizable traits.

Although some might think that all animals of the same species look exactly alike, it is known that once someone becomes familiar with a certain group of the same species, he or she can usually tell one from another. At first all black labrador retrievers look alike. After a closer look, it can be seen that there are very obvious and easily recognizable differences among them. It is known that it is mostly the individual's genetic inheritance that accounts for these minor differences. This means that the unique combination of dominant and recessive genes that the individual has inherited is responsible for all of its individual traits (color, size, abilities, and tendencies, to name only a few).

WHAT IS POPULATION GENETICS?

Population genetics is a tool used to study the genetic basis of evolution (the process by which gradual genetic change occurs over time to a group of living things), and it is helpful in allowing scientists to understand the relative importance of the many factors that influence evolution. It studies a given population's gene pool (which is the total of all of the genes available to a generation). Knowing what the gene pool consists of enables scientists to establish a sort of genetic base out of which future offspring will be composed. This assumes that over time, the population is made up of individuals that breed only with others of their species that live in the same habitat.

HARDY-WEINBERG LAW

Once the gene pool is established, scientists are able to use Mendel's laws of inheritance (concerning patterns of dominant and recessive genes) and predict what differences there will be among individuals in that population. Scientists are able to establish what are called gene frequencies, or percentages at which certain genes will be expressed. Scientists also have been able to establish a law that actually measures what changes will take place. Called the Hardy-Weinberg law, since it was proposed independently in 1906 by the English mathematician Godfrey H. Hardy (1877–1947), and the German physician Wilhelm Weinberg (1862–1937), this is a mathematical formula that has become the basis of population genetics. Using this formula (which only works perfectly when certain ideal conditions are met), scientists are able to describe a steady state called genetic equilibrium. In this state, gene frequencies stay the same and nothing changes unless some outside force intervenes.

Naturally, the real world, especially that involving human beings, is not perfect and there are many factors always at work that make conditions less than ideal. Chance events happen all the time. Reproduction does not always work and individuals leave populations while others may wander in. These are only a few potential variables. However, the Hardy-Weinberg formula is still useful and helps in being able to arrive at some relative frequencies, so it is still applies in some way to the real world.

WHY STUDY POPLUATION GENETICS?

By studying what makes individuals in the same population different, science is able to learn more about evolutionary change. Population genetics can also draw very useful conclusions. For example, when populations of interbreeding individuals are very small, they are highly susceptible to extinction by any number of chance events. This is because their interbreeding has not given them much genetic variation (differences). When something in their habitat changes, they may be unable to adapt quickly enough. Population genetics, therefore, is a valuable, if not always statistically perfect, tool for life scientists.

[*See also* **Dominant and Recessive Traits; Evolution; Genetics; Population**]

Population Growth and Control (Human)

The human population, or the number of people, on Earth has increased enormously during the past two centuries. Upon examining the reasons for this growth and the factors that could influence its continuance, it is not known whether Earth can sustain the great numbers of people predicted for the near future.

On October 12, 1999, the United Nations issued a population estimate that said the 6,000,000,000 mark had been reached. That figure is twice the population of 1960, a mere 40 years ago. Since the development of agriculture and the beginnings of settled human communities some 10,000 years ago, it took thousands of years for the human population to reach 1,000,000,000 around the year 1800. It took another 130 years to reach 2,000,000,000, but only 30 years to reach 3,000,000,000, 15 years to reach 4,000,000,000, 12 years to reach 5,000,000,000, and another 12 years to reach 6,000,000,000.

Today, the human population is growing at about 1.5 percent a year, or the equivalent of an additional 89,000,000 people a year. Every second five people are born and two people die, for a net gain of three people. The latest United Nations forecast for the year 2050 contains a projected low of 7,800,000,000 and a projected high of 12,500,000,000. However, if the world population continues to grow at its present rate, the high projection will be easily reached.

POPULATION HISTORY

The biological history of *Homo sapiens* (humans) extends back for more than 1,000,000 years. For almost all that time it consisted of a very small population that was barely staying alive by hunting and gathering. However, about 10,000 years ago, things began to change. People discovered primitive agriculture and began to domesticate a few plants and animals. With the discovery of the properties of metals and other technologies, the growth of the human population went from about 300,000,000 in the year A.D. 1 to about 500,000,000 in 1650. Around that time, the rate of population growth began to noticeably increase. High birth rates were accompanied by decreasing death rates due to better technologies for sanitation and medicine.

REASONS FOR POPULATION GROWTH

In 1800, the population reached 1,000,000,000. Yet in the past two centuries, its has skyrocketed to today's 6,000,000,000. There are three reasons why such unprecedented population growth has occurred. The first is the ability of the human species to adapt to new habitats. Early humans possessed the ability to learn and to remember, as well as the ability of being able to communicate what they knew to others. Humans have been able to use their technologies not only to disperse themselves virtually all over the globe, but to make their environment perfectly suitable for them if it is not naturally so. Today, people live in climates that might be considered extreme. They can live cooly in Phoenix, Arizona, in July; and they can play a professional football game indoors in Minnesota during a December blizzard. While most animals are "designed" to fit a certain habitat, humans have almost always made wherever they chose to live their habitat.

Humans have also been able to bypass what might have been natural limits on Earth's "carrying capacity." Carrying capacity is the maximum population that a habitat can support over a long period of time. However, humans have been able to increase that natural capacity by improvements in agriculture, as well as human use and management of natural resources. The use of

English economist Thomas R. Malthus was the first to draw attention to the fact that the human population could not keep growing indefinitely. (Reproduced by permission of Archive Photos, Inc.)

fertilizers, pesticides, and irrigation is only some examples of how Earth can be exploited more efficiently to support greater numbers.

The third and probably most significant reason why our population has exploded in the past 200 years is that many of the natural or built-in limits on growth were eventually limited themselves or even done away with. While death is still inevitable for every human born, the death rate has gone down dramatically. This means that more people are living longer than they used to. Until fairly recently, people died early and regularly from many conditions that were really preventable. Childhood was an especially dangerous time, as youngsters often died from malnutrition (the physical state of overall poor health), the flu, or diarrhea. Contagious diseases would spread rapidly and kill great numbers in epidemics, especially in crowded cities. Today, however, simple improvements in hygiene and sanitation have prevented millions of early deaths. Furthermore, medical victories over diseases like cholera, measles, polio, whooping cough, and tuberculosis were based on the development of vaccines, antibiotics, and other new drugs. As a result, these diseases are no longer a threat.

EFFECTS OF CONTINUED POPULATION GROWTH

In 1798 the English economist, Thomas R. Malthus (1766–1834), was the first to draw attention to the fact that the growth of the human population could not keep on indefinitely. He argued that the population would eventually outgrow its food supply and start to fall back because of famine, disease, or war. It may once have been argued that human ingenuity has been able to overcome any of Earth's natural limits to population growth, and that Malthus's theories no longer applied. However, many argue that if the growth of the human population does not stabilize at some point, we may unhappily discover that there is an actual limit to the carrying capacity of the planet.

No one knows how many humans Earth can support. Some scientists argue that we have already reached it, given the rate at which developed countries (as opposed to less developed or third world countries) consume available natural resources. A goal of all population planners is what is called zero population growth. This desirable situation represents stability in that it happens when the birth rate roughly equals the death rate. Presently, the people of Earth are nowhere near such a stable figure.

[*See also* **Population**]

Predation

Predation is the act of one animal hunting, killing, and eating another animal. A predator is an animal that survives by killing and eating other animals. Predation can be important in regulating the size of a prey species (the hunted animal). It is also a mechanism of evolution since it weeds out animals that are poorly adapted to being hunted, or to their environment, thus promoting adaptation by natural selection.

Predation can be coldly described as nature's "kill or be killed" approach to who survives in the wild and who does not. While there are some species of animals that have no natural enemies or are simply too difficult to catch and eat (such as a mature, healthy elephant), virtually all animals are at some point in their lives either predator or prey. All predators are heterotrophs, meaning that they cannot make their own food as plants (autotrophs) do, so they must consume another organism and digest it to obtain its energy. Many animals are herbivores (plant-eaters) and do not kill other animals to eat. They eat living plants that do not have to be hunted, caught, and killed before they can be consumed. Animals that exclusively eat plants are not considered preda-

Spiders, like this red-kneed tarantula, are successful predators because they are able to catch prey in the webs they spin. (Reproduced by permission of the Corbis Corporation.)

tors (although from a living plant's point of view, it could be said that the plant is being preyed upon). Carnivorous animals as well as omnivores are predators, since carnivores exclusively eat other animals, and omnivores eat both plants and animals, usually according to what is available.

Successful predation requires that a catch be made, and a catch can occur in a great variety of ways. Spiders spin webs to trap their prey; cats lie in wait for the proper moment to spring; hyenas stalk in groups and exhaust their prey; and humans use their technology to kill from a distance. Specialized predators usually go after a single species, while generalized predators will feed on a variety of other species. Predation is one of the ways in which nature selects who has done the best job of adapting to its environment and who will have the best chance to survive. In this way, predation can be said to be a mechanism or a means that nature employs to continue the important role of evolution.

Predators almost always select a meal that will give them more energy than they will use up to catch it. When faced with an opportunity to select an individual animal from a group to eat, predators will usually select the easiest to catch, such as the weakest, the slowest, or the youngest or oldest. Those animals that are poorly adapted will probably not survive and therefore not be able to pass on their poorly adapted traits to another generation. In the dynamic relationship between predator and prey, there is a continuing type of improvement that goes on in which the prey that survive pass on traits that make their offspring slightly better at avoiding being caught. On the other hand, predators that survive because they are excellent hunters will also pass on the good traits that made them better at catching prey. So in the long run, the seemingly cruel standards of the natural world use predation to improve the species.

In terms of entire populations in a certain habitat, predator and prey relationships often move along the same lines. Thus, when conditions favor a prey population—such as when field mice thrive during a good growing season and their population increases—the predator population will also be well fed and grow larger as its members grow strong and live longer. The opposite happens when populations drop. Finally, when the only predator of a certain species disappears (sometimes human intervention causes this to happen), prey populations will take off. The systematic killing of timber wolves and gray wolves in the American West has led to an increase in the number of rabbits and rodents that regularly served as their prey.

[See also **Evolution; Natural Selection; Survival of the Fittest**]

Opposite: A female pygmy chimpanzee with her young. Primates, like this chimpanzee, are the most highly developed group of animals. (Reproduced by permission of the World Wide Fund for Nature Photolibrary.)

Primate

A primate is a type of mammal with flexible fingers and toes, forward-pointing eyes, and a well-developed brain. Humans are primates, as are lemurs, monkeys, and apes. Except for humans, primates, are found in mostly tropical habitats. Primates are the most highly developed group in the animal kingdom.

Most primates either live in trees or have evolved from tree-dwelling ancestors. All are placental mammals meaning that before birth, their young are nourished by a structure in the mother's body called a placenta. There are about 180 species of primates, all which make up the order called Primata. This name comes from the Latin word *primus* meaning first, and the case can be made that primates are in may ways first among animals.

CHARACTERISTICS OF PRIMATES

Primates have many physical attributes that account for and contribute to their being considered in this manner. First, they have binocular vision, meaning that they use both eyes together. Because both eyes are located in the front of their faces and point forward rather than from the sides, they have sharp three-dimensional vision and good depth perception. Primates also have specially adapted hands for grasping things. Most have five flexible fingers on each hand and five flexible toes on each foot (with flattened nails on their ends instead of claws), as well as an opposable thumb. With a thumb that can be opposed to or that is able to touch the other fingers, primates can fully encircle or grasp something like a tree branch or a tool with their hand. They also can reach out and bring food to their mouth. Some primates are equally agile with their feet as well. All primates have large, well-developed and highly complex brains. Convolutions are folds in the brain that increase surface area and allow for a greater number of nerve cells. This brain enables chimpanzees to make and use tools and humans to reason and solve problems. Primates also have all four different kinds of teeth, meaning that they can eat all types of food. Primate teeth are less specialized for tearing and ripping and more useful for grinding and chewing a plant-based diet.

All primates also have a clavicle or collarbone that gives them a flexible shoulder whose joint allows free movement of the arm in all directions. Wrist and elbow joints are also highly mobile. Primates usually have only two mammae (or breasts), and give birth to one or sometimes two offspring per pregnancy. Compared to other mammals, their young are dependent for quite some time and take a long time to mature.

Primates are very social and exhibit the most complex behavior of all the mammals. They bond together in pairs of two, in larger family groups, or in even larger bands. In the larger groups, there is usually a leader or dominant male and a hierarchy after him. Communication is very important among primate species, and they use many visual signals as well as sounds to interact with one another. Primates regularly send each other messages, whether they are warnings of danger or calls for mating.

PROSIMIANS AND ANTHROPOIDS

Most biologists divide primates into two groups: prosimians and anthropoids. Prosimians are tree-dwelling, squirrel-like insect eaters including lemurs, lorises, and tarsiers. They were the first primates to evolve and are considered primitive compared with anthropoids. Most primates belong to the second group, the anthropoids. Monkeys, apes, and humans are all anthropoids. There are two types of monkeys who were probably split apart when the continents of South America and Africa drifted away from one another. New World monkeys are found in the tropical forests of Central and South America and include howler monkeys, capuchins, marmosets, and tamarins. Many of these monkeys are small and highly vocal. Old World monkeys are found in the tropics of Asia and Africa and include baboons, colobuses, and macaques. They are usually larger than their New World counterparts but have much shorter tails. Another way to tell them apart is by their noses. New World monkeys have flattened noses with widely set nostrils, while Old World monkeys have more definite noses and closely set nostrils.

HOMINOIDS

A separate and useful "superfamily" or extra grouping of primates, called hominoids, is often used by life scientists when they are discussing both apes and hominids. Hominids are humans and their direct ancestors of humans (meaning that humans are the only living species of hominid). Unlike other primates, hominoids have large heads and no tails. They also can move about on their back legs (although many apes cannot do this for a long distance). The ape family is made up of gibbons, who swing from tree to tree with their extra long arms, as well as orangutans, gorillas, and chimpanzees. These are humans' closest relatives in the animal kingdom, and they are able to see in color, move their lips, and even make a great number of facial expressions, all human-like actions. As for hominids, there is only one species living today, and that is *Homo sapiens* or human beings. While humans are the most intelligent species of primate (*Homo sapiens* means "wise human") gorillas are the largest and most powerful primate. Deoxyribonucleic acid (DNA) comparisons have shown that chimpanzees are the closest living relatives of human beings.

[*See also* **Homo sapiens**; **Human Evolution**; **Mammals**]

Protein

Proteins are the building blocks of all forms of life. As an organic compound (meaning that they are based on the element carbon) made up of amino acids (the building blocks of proteins), they are key to the major functions of growth and repair as well as to other important specialized functions. The human body makes proteins by following the coded instructions in its genes.

All living things are made up of cells, and the major ingredient of all cells is protein. As organic compounds, proteins play a major role in many of the functions that take place in living things. Proteins called structural proteins make up all of the parts, or building material, of a plant's or animal's body. They make up the walls of an organism's cells. In a human being, hair and fingernails are made of a structural protein called keratin, and tendons (linking muscle to bone) are made of a different structural protein called collagen. The enzymes, hormones, and antibodies in our bodies are all made of protein. Enzymes are essential to all of the chemical reactions that take place inside us; hormones are the body's chemical messengers; and antibodies help fight foreign substances or infection.

Proteins are made up of amino acids. Humans and most other animals require twenty separate types of amino acids in order to be able to make the many different types of proteins they need. Proteins are amino acids that are linked, or bonded, together like chains. Therefore, it is the order of the individual amino acids in the chain that make proteins different from one another. The twenty different amino acids form different proteins in a way similar to how the twenty-five different letters of the alphabet are used in different combinations to form different words.

Different proteins have different sequences of amino acids. The shape that these long protein chains eventually form has a great deal to do with the properties of a protein. Chains that form themselves into a springlike shape build a material that is flexible and can be stretched, while those that form a sheetlike structure are more rigid. An example often used to illustrate the former is the protein keratin that forms wool. Because keratin has a springlike structure, a length of wool can be stretched to nearly twice its original length. On the other hand, the natural fiber silk is composed of the protein called fibroin whose shape is not coiled. As a result, silk cannot be stretched to anywhere near the length that wool can.

Proteins have important structural uses. They are also a necessary part of an organism's diet. Of the twenty different amino acids commonly found in proteins, only ten can be made in cells. The other remaining ten amino acids (called "essential amino acids") must be obtained from food. Unless all these amino acids are obtained by eating various protein-based foods, the body will not have the necessary building blocks to form new protein molecules. The growth and repair of body cells could be harmed or even halted. Nutritionists have determined that these essential proteins can be obtained from meat, eggs, milk, cheese, and other foods usually derived from animals.

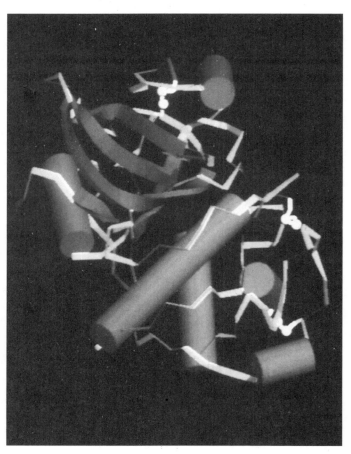

A computer graphic of a protein molecule found in fruit. This protein functions similar to human digestive enzymes that break down proteins in food. (©Photographer, Science Source/Photo Researchers, Inc.)

Finally, most proteins are species-specific, meaning that each species has slightly different proteins. Thus, the type of proteins found in the cells of a domestic house cat are different from those of a tiger. The farther apart two species are on the evolutionary ladder, the greater difference there will be in the proteins found in their cells.

[*See also* **Antibodies and Antigens; Amino Acids; Enzymes; Hormones; RNA**]

Protists

Protists are a group of single-celled organisms that make up the kingdom Protista. Although some protists behave like animals and others like plants, they are all organisms with a complex eukaryotic cell, or a cell that contains a nucleus and organelles (structures inside a cell that have a particular function). Protista is the most diverse of all the eukaryotic kingdoms, and its members range from free-floating plankton to deadly parasites that live in mammals.

There are so many different types of organisms that are classified as protists that biologists are not certain if they all share a common ances-

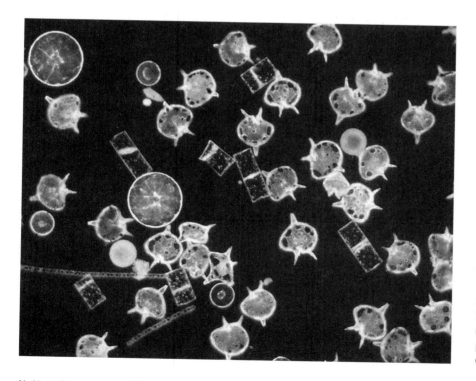

This diatom plankton is a good representative of the Protista kingdom. (Reproduced by permission of the Corbis Corporation.)

tor with higher life forms, or even if all known protists have evolved from the same ancestor. Recent studies suggest that even the name is not large enough, and that protist refers only to the microscopic members of this kingdom. Many leading scientists suggest that a more correct and inclusive name is Protoctist, since it includes every member of this kingdom from slime mold to huge brown kelp. However, one thing all scientists agree on is that protists are eukaryotes since they have at least one nucleus and many other little structures or cell organs called organelles. Further, all protists live in some form of a watery environment, even if that water is within the tissues of another organism. Protists do all the things that other living things can do—they eat, grow, excrete waste, and reproduce. Some are able to make their own food, as plants do. Some reproduce sexually (with male and female sex cells), while others reproduce asexually and simply divide into new identical parts.

TYPES OF PROTISTS

Recent studies indicate that there may be as many as 250,000 different species of protists. Despite these large numbers, all can be divided into three main types: animal-like, plantlike, and fungus-like cells. Many are familiar to us, such as slime molds, amoebas, red tide, pond scum, and green seaweeds, but many more are hardly known. For example, the protist known as *Trychonympha* lives inside the gut of termites and helps them digest and use the nutrients found in the wood they eat. Similarly, the stomachs of grazing animals contain countless protists without which they could not break down tough plant cells. Although they are single-celled organisms, protists are far from simple. Unlike multicelled organisms that have evolved specialized organs, some protists have evolved specialized structures, like hairs or a tail that allows them to move about.

Animal-like Protists. Many of the animal-like protists, called protozoans, cause disease in animals. For example, among the animal-like group known as flagellates (because they have a tail or flagellum that they use to propel themselves), the genus *Trypanosoma* causes African sleeping sickness in humans and their livestock. Other animal-like protists, like amoeba, live as parasites (organisms that live in or on another organism and benefit from the relationship) in animals and cause dysentery.

Fungus-like Protists. Some protists, such as the slime molds, have distinct fungus-like characteristics. Like a fungus, they disperse spores, but unlike fungus, these protists can also move about like an animal. One especially strange slime mold is actually a group of amoebas that get together when food is scarce and form a new being. Called a *plasmodium,* this sluglike creature oozes over surfaces leaving a visible track, and when it runs out of food, it grows upward into a "spore tower," dries out, and disperses its spores with the wind. Later, under proper conditions, the spores come to life as individual amoebas.

Plantlike Protists. The plantlike protists known as *Euglena* are usually recognized by anyone who has taken a biology class or seen an algae "bloom" on a lake. Some individual euglenoids have chloroplasts (energy-converting structures found in plant cells) and perform photosynthesis (the process by which plant use light energy to make food from simple compounds) the way plants do, yet also are able to eat food as animals do. Other plantlike protists called dinoflagellates have a pair of long, whiplike tails that they use to move about. Certain dinoflagellates live in warm seas where they give the surface a bright, bluish light, while others produce powerful toxins that can cause illness or death in animals that eat them.

Protists are among the strangest organisms on Earth, yet they play an important role. Many provide food for oysters, clams, snails and other ocean organisms that are important to humans. Many protists, called plankton, simply float on the water and provide food for shrimp and other aquatic animals. It is possible that without protists there would be no life on Earth at all since it is believed Earth's life-giving atmosphere is the result of billions of years of protists conducting photosynthesis and therefore producing oxygen.

[*See also* **Protozoa**]

Protozoa

Protozoa are a group of single-celled organisms that live by taking in food. As a major group in the kingdom Protista, protozoa are described as having animal-like—rather than plantlike—qualities, since they move about to find and eat their food. Since they are protists, protozoa are eukaryotes (they contain a nucleus).

GROUPS OF PROTOZOA

The word protozoa literally means "first animal," indicating that they are considered to be the early ancestor cells from which more complex, multicelled animals evolved. As animal-like protists, protozoa are divided into four phyla (one of the seven major classification groups that biologists use to identify and categorize living things) based mainly on how they move about.

CHARLES LOUIS ALPHONSE LAVERAN

French biologist Charles Laveran (1845–1922) discovered the parasite (an organism that lives in or on another organism and benefits from the relationship) that causes human malaria (a disease characterized by cycles of chills, fever, and sweating). This was the first time that a disease was shown to be caused by living animal cells called protozoa (a group of single-celled organisms that live by taking in food). His creative work not only led to understanding the disease and its transmission by certain species of mosquito but also directed many other researchers into this new field.

Charles Laveran was born in Paris, France, the son of a military doctor. When he was five years old, the family was transferred to Algeria. Returning to Paris at the age of eleven, Laveran eventually entered the same military medical school his father had attended and graduated in 1867. Continuing in his father's footsteps, he joined the military medical service and saw active duty during the Franco-Prussian War (1870–71). It was then that he saw how disease can ravage an army worse than any enemy. In 1878 he was sent to Algeria as his father had been, and it was there that he began a careful study of the disease malaria. Malaria was common in many parts of Algeria, and had affected humans for centuries, with no one able to do anything to prevent it. For a long time it was believed to be caused by *mal aria*, the Italian words for "bad air." During Laveran's time, it was thought that perhaps it had a bacterial cause since French chemist and microbiologist Louis Pasteur (1822–1895) was discovering more and more bacterial diseases.

Laveran went about his research in a careful, methodical way, and although he was limited by a primitive, low-powered microscope, he spent a great

Flagellates. The first group is the flagellates called Mastigophora, which move about by the use of one or more flagella (a whiplike tail). This phylum, also known as Zoomastigina, lives in a watery environment. Flagellates are very diverse since some live as parasites (organisms that live in or on other organisms and benefit from the relationship) and others as free-living organisms.

Sarcodina. The second group of protozoa are the members of the phylum Sarcodina, commonly known as amoeba. An amoeba is recognized because it has no particular, fixed shape. It has been described as looking formless like a bag of jelly. The reason for this is that the amoeba's single cell is surrounded by a plasma membrane and is constantly changing shape. It is this constant shape-changing that allows the amoeba to move. Amoeba can be found in all types of water and even in the soil.

deal of time examining blood samples from malaria patients both living and dead. Finally, in November 1880, he first observed under the microscope tiny circular and cylindrical bodies that had moving flagella or hair-like filaments. This, he knew, was no bacteria. Instead, he knew it was a living animal cell, a minute, single-celled creature called a protozoon (plural, protozoa). Once inside the human body, protozoa act like parasites. A parasite is a species that lives in or on another species at the expense of that species. In other words, the parasite thrives and the host gets sick or even dies. The particular protozoan parasite that Laveran discovered was later named plasmodium.

Laveran had a great deal of trouble, however, convincing a skeptical medical community of his protozoan discovery, and eventually it took the great Pasteur to agree with him before everyone was convinced. Laveran was able to study the cycle of malaria in the red blood cell and discovered exactly what goes on there. He found that the protozoa increased in size inside the red blood cell until they almost filled it, at which time they then divided and formed spores. When these spores were freed from the destroyed blood cell, they invaded healthy blood cells and continued to do the same thing. Laveran had a strong feeling that the malaria protozoa were nurtured and transmitted to humans by certain types of mosquito, but it remained for the English physician, Ronald Ross (1857-1932), to finally prove this in 1897. Laveran went on to study other protozoan diseases and eventually joined the Pasteur Institute devoting the rest of his life to the study of tropical diseases. For his discovery of the protozoa plasmodium, Laveran was awarded the 1907 Nobel Prize in Physiology and Medicine.

Some are parasites of humans and can cause fever, abdominal cramps, and diarrhea. There is also a species of shelled amoeba in which the organism's cytoplasm (jelly-like cell contents) is protected by a shell it has created out of its own mineral secretions. With names like foraminiferams, heliozoans, and radiolarians, the shells of these tiny water creatures represent some of the most intricate and beautiful designs of nature.

Sporozoa. The third group of protozoa belong to the phylum Sporozoa and are parasitic spore-formers. In their adult stage, they cannot move, but during another stage, they live in a host who transfers them to yet another organism who they infect. This is how the species *Plasmodium vivax* goes from a mosquito to a human and infects the latter with malaria. This particular protozoan kills between 2,000,000 and 4,000,000 people every year.

Ciliophora. Finally, the phylum Ciliophora makes up the fourth group of protozoa. These organisms are characterized by short, flexible, hair-like strands or filaments called cilia that cover their bodies. These move in a rhythmic, coordinated manner and are able to propel the protozoan through its liquid environment. Some species, like the *Paramecium,* have as many as 15,000 cilia per cell and can move very quickly. Ciliates are the most structurally complex of all the single-celled organisms on Earth, and although most ciliates reproduce asexually, some species conduct a complicated form of sexual reproduction called conjugation. Conjugation is similar to mating since one of the ciliates (the donor or "male") produces a small protein tube through which genes are transferred to the recipient or "female" when the cells are joined together. Although conjugation achieves gene mixing, it does not result in the production of an entirely new individual. Most ciliates are found in fresh and salt water and are fierce predators, eating bacteria and other small organisms.

Many protozoans serve as an essential food source for a wide range of animals. Therefore, they are very important to the ecological food web (the transfer of energy in an ecosystem) of higher organisms. Some are also used for medical purposes while others serve such practical uses as purification of sewage beds.

[*See also* **Protists**]

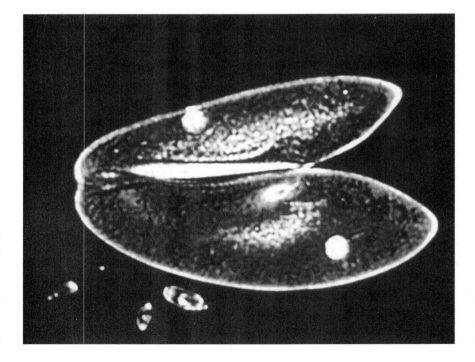

Protozoa are considered to be the early ancestors of more complex, multicelled animals. (Reproduced by permission of Photo Researchers, Inc.)

Punnett Square

A Punnett square is a diagram used to calculate inheritance patterns. Resembling a checkerboard, this device makes it possible to figure out the exact gene combinations that an offspring will inherit from its two parents.

Understanding the Punnett square, which is a handy tool for predicting results in genetics, first involves having knowledge of alleles (pronounced uh-LEELZ). Alleles have to do with genes, which are the carriers of the information that determines all of the traits or characteristics of an individual organism. Every human being receives 23 gene-carrying chromosomes (coiled structures in a cell's nucleus that carries genetic material) from each parent, resulting in a full set of 46 chromosomes (and some 100,000 genes). When these chromosomes pair up at fertilization to form a new and unique individual, they do so in a way that related chromosomes always pair off (since the same trait is also located in the same place on each chromosome). Since the new individual receives information from both parents concerning a single trait, it always has two sets of directions for that trait. This pair is called "alleles." When the two sets of instructions are the same (such as both coding for brown hair), they are called "homozygous." When they are different (such as one coding brown hair and the other coding red hair), they are called "heterozygous." An allele is therefore a single member that makes up a gene pair. Two alleles are a kind of partnership, and in some cases, one partner is stronger than the other. When this is the case, the stronger one is called the "dominant allele." The other one in this relationship is called the "recessive allele."

Ever since Austrian monk and botanist (a person who studies plants) Gregor Mendel (1822–1884) began experimenting with pea plants and their traits in the 1860s, the rule concerning dominance has been that when two organisms showing different traits are crossed (like a tall and a short pea plant), the trait that shows up or is expressed in the first generation is considered the dominant trait. Just as an athlete may dominate a game to the point where the opponent has no chance to do anything, so a dominant allele expresses itself and suppresses, or masks, the activity of the recessive allele for that trait. However, the recessive allele does not go away just because it is masked. It is still part of the organism's inherited package called its "genotype." The word "phenotype" is the opposite of genotype and describes only the visible characteristics.

Since Mendel stated what became known as the laws of inheritance, biologists have been able to use these principles to predict what will happen when organisms with specific traits are crossed. The easiest way to do this is with the diagram named for the English geneticist, Reginald Crundall Punnett (1875–1967). Punnett devised a square that he divided into four equal parts. Across the outside top of the square are the symbols for the alleles from the male parent. The allele symbols from the female parent are written outside the left-hand side of the square. A capital letter is used for the dominant allele and a small letter stands for a recessive allele. The inside four squares show all the ways in which these alleles can combine. The answers are achieved much like a multiplication problem with the answer in each box being the product (Ll) of one top allele (L) being multiplied by one side allele (l).

A Punnett square is most useful when the results of one gene are considered. Calculating for two genes can be a difficult and complicated process. A Punnett square does not tell how many offspring will be produced, but it does predict what the genotype (genetic makeup including masked traits) and the phenotype (visible traits) will be.

[*See also* **Gene; Genetics; Inherited Traits; Mendelian Laws of Inheritance**]

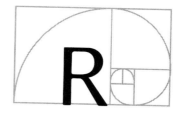

Radioactive Dating

Radioactive dating is a method of determining the approximate age of an old object by measuring the amount of a known radioactive element it contains. Rocks as well as fossil plants and animals can be dated by this process. It has given paleontologists (a person specializing in the study of fossils) as well as geologists (a person specializing in the study of the origin, history, and structure of Earth) a powerful way of dating ancient objects.

Until the discovery of radioactive dating, scientists had no way of approximating how old any part of Earth was. Once the principle behind this method was discovered, however, it became possible to gather reliable information about the age of Earth and its rocks and fossils. Radioactive dating was not possible until 1896, when the radioactive properties of uranium (a radioactive metallic element) were discovered by French physicist (a person specializing in the study of energy and matter), Antoine Henri Becquerel (1852–1908). When a substance is described as radioactive, it means that at the subatomic (relating to parts of an atom) level, some parts of it are unstable. When a substance is described as unstable, it means that it has a tendency to break down or decay. During this decay, one substance actually changes into another and radiation is released.

As long ago as 1907, the American chemist Bertram B. Boltwood (1870–1927) suggested that knowledge of radioactivity might be used to determine the age of Earth's crust. He suggested this because he knew that the end product of the decay of uranium was a form of lead. Since each radioactive element decays at a known rate, it can be thought of as a ticking clock. Boltwood explained that by studying a rock containing uranium, its age could be determined by measuring its amounts of uranium and lead. The more lead the rock contained, the older it was.

Although this was a major breakthrough, Boltwood's dating method made it possible to date only the oldest rocks. This is because uranium decayed or changed into lead at such a slow rate that it was not reliable for measuring the age of rocks that were younger than 10,000,000 years old. Another drawback was that uranium is not found in every rock. A later method that used rubidium (which changes into strontium) proved more useful because it is found in nearly all rocks, although it still was not useful for younger specimens. Perhaps the best method for rock dating is the potassium-argon method. This method proved useful to date rocks as young as 50,000 years old.

In 1947 another dating breakthrough occurred. The American chemist Willard F. Libby (1908–1980) discovered the radiocarbon method for determining the age of organic materials. Called the carbon-14 dating technique, this ingenious method used the simple knowledge that all living plants and animals contain carbon (a nonmetallic element that occurs in all plants and animals). Libby also knew that while most of this carbon is a common, stable form called carbon-12, a very small amount of the total carbon is radioactive carbon-14. All plants absorb carbon during photosynthesis (the process in which plants use light energy to create food), and animals absorb this carbon by eating plants or eating other animals that ate plants. Libby also found that as long as an organism remains alive, its supply of carbon-14 remains the same. However, once the organism dies, the supply stops and the carbon-14 in its body begins to decrease according to its own rate of decay. Libby realized that this could be a practical dating tool. He eventually designed a device that used Geiger counters (which measure radiation) to accurately measure the amount of carbon-14 left in an organic substance. Libby won the 1960 Nobel Prize in chemistry for his discovery. The discovery allowed him to correctly date a piece of wood from an Egyptian tomb that was known to be about 4,600 years old.

In the last 40 years, radiocarbon dating has been used on more than 100,000 samples in 80 different laboratories. Besides dating plant and animal life, this method has been used to verify the age of such different artifacts as the Dead Sea Scrolls (2,100 years), a charcoal sample from an ancient South Dakota campsite (7,000 years), and a pair of sandals from an Oregon cave (9,300 years). Improvements have raised its accuracy to nearly 70,000 years, with an uncertainty of plus-or-minus 10 percent.

[See also **Fossil; Paleontology**]

Rain Forest

Tropical rain forests are large areas that are warm and wet throughout the year, and whose tall evergreen trees are so dense they form a canopy. As the richest ecosystem (an area in which living things interact with each other and the environment) on Earth, rain forests support such a diversity of life that at least half of all the world's species of plants and animals live there. Rain forests also play a role in the world's climate, and are among the most fragile ecosystems.

Most rain forests are located in the central region of Earth, near the equator, where temperatures typically range between 73° and 87°F (22.78°C and 30.56°C). Most receive some rain almost every day, averaging more than 100 inches (254 centimeters) a year, and sometimes twice that much. This rain is soaked up from the soil by the lush plants and enormous trees that then return it to the air via transpiration. Transpiration occurs in all plants as they naturally lose water vapor through their leaves.

At least half of this water released by plants falls back down again onto the rain forest as rain. Since all tropical rain forests lie near the equator, daylight lasts 12 hours throughout the year, and the steady warmth of

The Amazonian rain forest, like all rain forests, is rich in plant and animal life. (Reproduced by permission of Conservation International. Photograph by R.A. Mettermeier.)

the land heats the air above it, causing it to rise and release its moisture (rain). Everything growing below is always green and flowers regularly.

LAYERS OF A RAIN FOREST

The largest rain forest is the Amazon in South America, and it is typical of what is called a tropical rain forest, as opposed to a temperate rain forest which is located in a cooler climate. A tropical rain forest like the Amazon is a complex system that can be divided into different horizontal layers (like floors in an apartment building). As with an apartment building, there are different things going on at different levels.

Forming the topmost layer are the tallest of the rain forest's trees. Able to sometimes grow as high as a football field is long, these giants are scattered throughout the forest. The next level or layer is called the canopy, because it shades everything below. This green roof is created by a dense thicket of trees that stand between 60 and 150 feet (18.29 and 45.72 meters) high and whose branches and leaves are so close together that they form an umbrella over the rest of the forest below. These trees grow so tightly that rainfall reaches the ground only by running down the tree trunks or the stems of other plants. The canopy is alive with animal life as well, such as iguanas, tree frogs, monkeys, and bats.

The next section is called the understory and includes smaller trees, ferns, vines and palms, and smaller bushes. Since the canopy traps and holds much of the heat and moisture, the understory is extremely hot and humid. It also does not have many flowering plants because of the lack of direct sunlight. The bottom level, or the forest floor, is covered with shade-loving mosses, herbs, and fungi, as well as dead plants and animals. The forest floor receives only 2 percent of the sunlight needed for photosynthesis (the process by which plants use light energy to make food). Dead material on the forest floor decomposes very quickly, thus providing nutrients to the soil and everything that grows in it. Masses of insects and the animals that feed on them, like the anteater, also live on the forest floor. Many of these animals, like bats, mice and rats, and porcupines, are nocturnal or active only at night. Some, like monkeys and apes, are busy during the day, while still others, like large cats and wild dogs, are most active at dusk and dawn.

PLANT LIFE IN THE RAIN FOREST

No other biome (a particular type of large geographic region) on Earth can match the tropical rain forest for its diversity of plant and animal species. All of these species, however, have the same thing in common. As rain forest dwellers, they all have adapted in many ways to life in this special ecosystem. One example of plant adaptation is a tree's buttresses or "prop roots" that spread out above ground and help support the tree in the shallow, unstable soil of the forest floor. Other trees often grow stilt roots or "air roots" which grow out from its trunk as high up as 10 to 12 feet (3.0 to 3.66 meters) and help spread the weight of the tree over a wider area.

Leaf structure is also highly adapted. Some leaves have what are called "drip tips"—a special shape that helps rainwater and condensation run off easily. This allows the leaf to breathe better. Other plants called epiphytes grow on or in trees and never actually touch the soil.

ANIMAL LIFE IN THE RAIN FOREST

Animal life in the rain forest is equally adapted and strange and fascinating. The vast majority of all species are insects, although there are twice as many mammals and birds in its tropical environment as there are in temperate zones. South America is especially rich in birds, bats, and fishes. Rain forest species often have spectacular shapes, colors, or sizes. These include the huge-billed toucan, the brilliantly colored American butterfly with a wingspan of nearly 8 inches (20.32 centimeters), the huge, scary-looking fruit bat, the goliath frog that can weigh as much as 33 pounds (14.98 kilograms), and the bizarre-looking anteater. These are but a few of the thousands of exotic life forms that crawl, slither, hop, fly, and teem about in the tropical rain forest.

CONSEQUENCES OF RAIN FOREST DESTRUCTION

Despite this great diversity and obvious abundance of life, tropical rain forests can be easily and severely damaged, and they take an extremely long time to recover. Their soil is usually ancient and poor in minerals that are mostly bound up in the incredible amounts of vegetation it has to support. Although rain forests are highly productive ecosystems, this productivity is based on the constant sunlight and steady rains, and not on rich, thick soil. When trees are cut down and burned in a typical practice called "slash and burn," the landscape suffers severely. This is usually done to clear the land for farming and roadbuilding. Logging also clears large areas. When this occurs, the thin soil is exposed and the steady rains wash it away, leaving behind "wet deserts" and causing devastating floods. An area twice the size of Maine is cleared this way every year, and with it often go the unique plants and animals it supported.

Rain forest destruction means not only plant and animal extinction because of habitat loss but possibly an increase in the "greenhouse effect" as fewer trees exist to absorb the increasing amounts of carbon dioxide people produce. This causes Earth's atmosphere to trap too much heat and could lead to global warming.

[*See also* **Biodivesity; Biome; Forest**]

Reproduction, Asexual

Asexual reproduction occurs when a new organism is produced from just one parent. It is a form of reproduction that does not involve the union of gametes (male and female sex cells), and therefore results in an offspring with the same genetic blueprint as the parent. As a result, this offspring is actually a clone of the parent.

BINARY FISSION

Reproduction is the process by which new organisms are produced from existing ones. Asexual reproduction means reproduction without sex, or without male and female sex cells uniting. The simplest form of asexual reproduction is when a single-celled organism like a bacterium splits into two. Called binary fission, this process occurs when a one-celled organism duplicates its DNA and divides into two to form two new identical organisms.

BUDDING

Other organisms like yeast, which is a microscopic, single-celled fungus, reproduce by budding or growing new cells that eventually separate from the parent. Some very simple animals, like hydras and corals, also reproduce this way. Like yeast, a new bud grows directly on the body of the parent. It eventually breaks off and establishes itself as a new, separate organism.

REGENERATION

Reproduction by fragmentation or regeneration is related to budding. It occurs when a part of the parent's body breaks off and grows into a complete, new organism. For example, if a starfish loses an arm, it can grow the arm back. Sometimes the severed arm itself can grow into an entire starfish. A flatworm can also be cut into two and each part can grow into a complete flatworm. Many plants also use a form of asexual reproduction called vegetative reproduction to duplicate themselves. This common method occurs when a plant splits in two, and each segment develops into a separate new plant.

RHIZOMES

Other plants like strawberries and certain types of grass form runners, or rhizomes, that spread out from the parent plant to form plantlets at their ends. The plantlets become independent plants when they develop roots, and the connecting runners disintegrate. Spider plants are excellent examples of plants that use vegetative reproduction.

A CLONE NAMED "DOLLY"

Whether it is a plant or an animal, or whether reproduction occurs by binary fission, budding, or vegetative reproduction, all reproduction that is asexual involves one parent passing on a duplicate of all of its genes to its offspring. This means that the offspring produced by asexual reproduction are genetically identical copies, or clones, of the parent. Until recently, only certain animal cells could be regularly cloned or reproduced asexually. However, in 1996 a sheep named "Dolly" was cloned from a cell taken from an adult sheep. The achievement of such a difficult and complex feat (that is, asexually reproducing a mammal from a single cell taken from an adult rather than an embryo) raises the possibilities of asexual human reproduction. However, such possibilities raise many legal, moral, and ethical questions.

THE ADVANTAGES AND DISADVANTAGES OF ASEXUAL REPRODUCTION

Humans aside, asexual reproduction is a fairly common occurrence in nature and it has its advantages and disadvantages. First of all, organisms that reproduce without sex do not have to expend any energy or resources toward the production of gametes (sex cells). Neither do they have to maintain an elaborate reproductive system or spend time and energy finding and fertilizing (or being fertilized by) a mate. Also, under certain conditions, a great number of individuals can be rapidly produced by asexual reproduction. For example, bacteria can divide every twenty seconds. Another great advantage is that even if there remains only a single individual, organisms capable of asexual reproduction can continue their species without a mate. Finally, when an organism is perfectly adapted to its habitat or particular environment, it will never change and always remain perfectly suited.

However, habitats or environments often change. If an organism does not have the capacity to change, what had been an advantage may become a disadvantage. With asexual reproduction, there is no opportunity for genetic variety. Since offspring are clones of the original parent, there is no way for any new (and sometimes advantageous) traits to be introduced into the population. When all the individuals are identical, that means if one cannot adapt then none can, and the entire species may be endangered.

[*See also* **Buds and Budding; Cell Division; Mitosis**]

Reproduction, Sexual

Sexual reproduction is the creation of new individuals by the joining of the separate sex cells of two parents. Each offspring produced by sexual reproduction has a unique collection of genes and are well-equipped to adapt to change. Most animals reproduce sexually.

Sexual reproduction describes the process in which the gametes (sex cells) of the two parents come together and form a fertilized egg cell called a zygote. The zygote then develops into a new individual. Since each parent contributes genetic information to the new and unique individual created, sexual reproduction is a far more complex phenomenon than asexual reproduction. (Asexual reproduction is when just one parent copies its genetic material creating a new, but identical, individual.) The gametes of each parent must have specific characteristics in order for sexual reproduction to work properly. Specifically, each set of gametes must have only half the total number of chromosomes that nonsex cells of that species contain. This ensures that when the nuclei (singular, nucleus; the cell's control center) of the male sperm and female egg join together, instead of having twice the normal number of chromosomes, the fertilized egg will have exactly the right number. In the case of humans, that number is forty-six chromosomes (with twenty-three obtained from each parent).

Sexual reproduction also applies to many plants—pollen is the equivalent of male sperm and it fertilizes the female sex cell of the flower, called an ovum. However, sexual reproduction in the animal world is the focus here. Organisms that reproduce sexually are usually fairly complex, and the individuals involved are usually either male or female, with the sex of each being separate. Males and females have different types of gonads or sex organs in which the gametes develop. The males produce sperm in gonads called testes, and the females produce egg, or ova, in gonads called the ovaries. Sperm are generally smaller than the egg and must swim through a liquid to get to the egg in order to fertilize it.

EXTERNAL AND INTERNAL FERTILIZATION

Although there are some instances where one individual produces both sperm and eggs, these are the exception. Fertilization or the union of a male sex cell and a female sex cell can occur inside the female (internal fertilization) or outside (external fertilization). Both methods have advantages and disadvantages. Aquatic organisms (those that live in water) more commonly use external fertilization. The sperm and eggs are released into the water where they meet, and fertilization occurs. (Actually, the sex cells are scattered into the environment and the rest is left to chance.) To increase the odds for fertilization, gametes are released in large numbers. For example, oysters release millions of sperm and eggs into the water. Although there may be great waste in this process, there is little cost to the parents who do not have to care for the offspring produced. Animals that use external fertilization, like fish and frogs, have generally short lives and do not reproduce many times.

Internal fertilization is practiced by most land animals, including humans. Since the sperm and egg are united inside the body of the female, both are protected, and there is a better chance the gametes will meet. Although there are still large numbers of sperm, fewer eggs are needed. The female's body also provides the proper environmental conditions for the survival of the gametes (unlike the harsh conditions of external fertilization in which many eggs are often devoured by predators).

For most animals, internal fertilization must take place within a certain time period. For example, in humans, there is only one twenty-four-hour period every twenty-eight days that the egg is able to be fertilized. Internal fertilization also requires special adaptations such as gamete delivery. This means that specialized sex organs (such as the male penis and female vagina) are used to place the sperm as close as possible to the egg inside the female's body. After internal fertilization occurs, the zygote (fertilized egg cell) is either released from the body within some sort of protective covering, like a shell, or it remains within the body where it develops fully. Development inside a shell or body means that the zygote goes through a series of cell divisions. These begin to specialize and form individual body parts.

ADVANTAGES OF SEXUAL REPRODUCTION

Probably the biggest advantage of sexual reproduction over asexual reproduction is that there is great genetic diversity since the new individual inherits genetic material from two different individuals. Because of this, populations (or the many individuals that make up a single species) are better able to survive any environmental changes that may occur. While those less-adapted might die, other better-adapted individuals would survive and therefore reproduce passing on their better-adapted genes.

[*See also* Egg; Embryo; Fertilization; Human Reproduction; Reproductive System; Sperm; Sex Chromosome; Sex Hormones; Sex-linked Traits; Zygote]

Reproductive System

The reproductive system is made up of the organs and processes that enable an organism to produce offspring. Although reproduction is one of the characteristics of living things, and each member of the five kingdoms of life (Monerans, Protists, Fungi, Plants, and Animals) is able to reproduce, only the more complex organisms have actual "systems" for reproducing.

Since every living thing has a limited life span, reproduction is the means by which organisms are able to continue their species. Among the simpler life forms, like bacteria, protozoa, and fungi, reproduction often takes place by processes like binary fission in which a cell simply divides in two. For plants and animals, which are more complicated forms of life, reproduction usually involves certain systems and processes. Whether they reproduce with a partner (sexually) or alone (asexually), plants and animals need a reproductive system that has certain essential parts and functions.

ASEXUAL REPRODUCTION

Asexual reproduction involves a single parent and is less complicated than sexual reproduction (which involves two organisms). Many plants reproduce asexually by a process known as vegetative reproduction. This involves a plant putting out stems or roots that develop into entirely new plants. Grass is an example of a plant that grows and spreads this way. Although each plant is a separate individual from the parent, each is an exact duplicate or clone of the parent plant. Some animals can also reproduce asexually. For example, a cnidarian such as a hydra can achieve reproduction by budding off small parts of itself. Compared to sexual reproduction, reproduction that involves only one organism is not very complex.

SEXUAL REPRODUCTION IN PLANTS

Sexual reproduction usually involves two parents. Even when it involves a single organism, it still requires two different types of gametes, or sex cells. In sexual reproduction the male and female gametes fuse or unite to produce a zygote (a fertilized egg cell), which develops into a separate, new individual.

Pollination. Many flowering plants that produce seeds are able to pollinate and fertilize themselves. Pollination is the process that transfers the flower's male sex cells to its female parts. Fertilization is the actual uniting of the male and female sex cells. A single flower contains both male (called a stamen) and female (called a pistil) reproductive organs. Not all flowers have both parts, and those that do are called perfect flowers.

Other flowering plants depend on animals, like bees and birds, to pollinate them. These animals often carry the male pollen to the female ovary of a plant. Animal-pollinated flowers are usually very showy or have a strong scent in order to attract these pollinators. Other flowers produce sweet nectar as a reward for animal pollinators. For plants, the end product of this process is the production of a seed, which is the beginning of another plant.

SEXUAL REPRODUCTION IN ANIMALS

Sexual reproduction among animals is a more complex process since animals are more complicated organisms. Unlike plants, animals must first find a mate. They must then deliver the spermatozoa, or sperm (the male sex cells), to the ovum, or egg (the female sex cells). Sperm delivery is accomplished by internal or external fertilization.

External Fertilization. Many animals that live in a watery environment, like fish and frogs, rely on external fertilization. This process takes place outside of the animals' bodies, as the female releases her eggs directly into the water while the male sprays them with his sperm. Animals that practice external fertilization usually have fairly short life spans and do not reproduce very often. They also produce large numbers of offspring who receive little or no care from the parents.

Internal Fertilization. Other animals practice internal fertilization. In this case, the male gametes unite with the female gametes inside the female's body. To accomplish this, both sexes need specialized sex organs as well as what are called accessory glands. The reproduction systems of mammals are probably the most complicated of animals that practice internal fertilization. Since the female carries the developing fetus inside her body, her reproductive system must accommodate itself to nourishing and eventually giving birth to a new individual. Animals that practice internal fertilization usually live a long time and reproduce more often, although they produce relatively few young. Their young usually need some degree of parental care after birth. The reproductive systems of mammals, as well as of all living things, are the products of evolution, meaning that they are best-suited and best-adapted to the reproductive needs of a certain species.

[*See also* **Egg; Embryo; Fertilization; Human Reproduction; Reproduction, Sexual; Sperm; Sex Chromosome; Sex Hormones; Sex-linked Traits; Zygote**]

Reptile

A reptile is a cold-blooded vertebrate (animal with a backbone) with dry, scaly skin that lays sealed eggs. Dinosaurs once dominated this class, which is now represented by turtles, snakes, lizards, crocodiles, and alligators. Reptiles have endoskeletons (internal skeletons) and are mainly carnivorous (meat-eaters). They do not move especially fast and their name "reptile" means "creeper."

All reptiles have a tough skin made of waterproof scales that resists drying out. In this and many other ways, they are entirely different from amphibians from whom they evolved and with whom they are often con-

Fox snakes, like this one, are good representatives of reptiles. (Reproduced by permission of Field Mark Publications. Photograph by Robert J. Huffman.)

fused. Reptiles do not go through any metamorphosis (a series of distinct changes in which an organism passes as it develops from an egg to an adult) and breathe air through lungs their entire lives. They do, however, lay eggs like amphibians—but even these eggs are substantially different. Reptiles always live on land, although they are ectothermic or cold-blooded like amphibians. This does not mean that they are cold, but rather that their body temperature reflects that of their environment. Unlike warm-blooded vertebrates that use food to keep their internal body temperature constant despite the outside temperature, reptiles have a body temperature that fluctuates with their environment. This can be an advantage since reptiles require less energy and therefore less food, and as a result are able to survive in a habitat where there is little food. As vertebrates, reptiles have an internal skeleton. Turtles are not an exception to this, but they may appear to be. Although they have hard, bony shells above and below their bodies and into which they can withdraw their head and legs for protection, they still have an endoskeleton.

All reptiles reproduce sexually through the joining of male sperm and female eggs. It was the ability of reptiles to produce a sealed egg, or one with a strong membrane, that allowed them to evolve beyond amphibians and remain on land, freeing them from needing water to reproduce or hatch in. The reptilian egg is fertilized internally or within the body of the female, and is called an amniotic egg because it contains the necessary water and food for the embryo to develop and grow before hatching. (This is different than amphibian eggs, which are fertilized than released by the female into the water where they will hatch.) These leathery eggs are usually buried in sand or soil where they hatch, releasing live, miniature versions of their parents.

Although reptiles range in size from a tiny lizard, like the gecko, to a 20-foot (6.1-meter) alligator, they all have skin that is dry to the touch. Reptile skin is made of scales created by a waterproof substance called keratin. The outer layers of this skin are regularly shed by most reptiles as they grow in size.

Reptiles can vary from the slow-moving turtle whose body is encased in a shell and has a jaw like a bird's beak, to the fiercely aggressive crocodile. The tiny gecko lizard can walk on ceilings, where as the basilisk lizard can run on two legs using its tail for balance and can even run across water. A chameleon can change its color to blend in perfectly with its surroundings and catch its prey with its tongue. Snakes can unhinge their jaws and swallow whole a prey that is larger than their own head. They also sniff the air with their tongue, which carries the chemical particles it catches in the air to a specialized detector in the roof of their mouth. Some snakes have hollow teeth to inject venom or poison into the prey they bite, while others coil around their prey and squeeze until it suffocates.

[*See also* **Dinosaur; Vertebrates**]

Respiration

Respiration, or cellular respiration, is a series of chemical reactions in which food is broken down to release energy. In order to live, all living things must be able to extract needed energy from the organic compounds they take in. The chemical process of respiration may be either aerobic or anaerobic.

The living cells of every organism need a constant supply of energy, or fuel, which they use to stay alive. Therefore, all living things obtain their energy from the food they make themselves (as plants are able to use light and chemicals to make their own food) or which they capture from their environment (by eating plants or other animals). In an animal, once this food is broken down into simpler forms by its digestive system, it is absorbed into the bloodstream. There the circulatory system (a network that carries blood throughout an animal's body) transports these small bundles of nutrients to each cell. It is at this level that the process known as cellular respiration takes place. During this process, cells convert the stored energy into usable energy. To do this, these bundles of food, or nutrients, must have their bonds broken so that the chemicals necessary to sustain life are released.

There are two types of cellular respiration. One involves oxygen and is called aerobic respiration, and the other does not need oxygen and is known as anaerobic respiration. Most cells use aerobic respiration. It is by far the most common and efficient method of obtaining energy. During aerobic respiration, nutrients reach the cells in the form of glucose (a form of sugar). The cell breaks down the glucose by combining it with oxygen, thereby releasing usable energy. This occurs in four separate stages and is called oxidation. The process of oxidation (the combining of glucose and oxygen) releases a large amount of energy to the cell. Oxidation also gives off carbon dioxide (a major atmospheric gases) and water as waste products.

Anaerobic respiration, which does not use oxygen to break down glucose, is less common and does not result in the release of as much energy as aerobic respiration. It is performed mainly by bacteria and some fungi, some of which use other inorganic compounds like nitrates or sulfates in place of oxygen. Fermentation is a type of anaerobic respiration since it breaks down glucose without using oxygen. The term respiration is also used to describe the process of breathing, in which oxygen is taken into an animal's body. This type of respiration is called external respiration.

[*See also* **Bacteria; Blood; Diffusion; Fermentation; Metabolism; Respiratory System**]

Respiratory System

The respiratory system is composed of those organs and processes that allow an animal to take oxygen into its body and expel carbon dioxide. All living things require oxygen to survive, and although respiratory systems may vary in size and the way they function, they share many basic features and operate on the same principles.

All animals need oxygen to survive, because oxygen is the fuel they use to convert their food into energy. As with any fuel that is consumed, there is always a byproduct given off, and in the case of animals, this waste product is carbon dioxide. Since all animals need to constantly take in oxygen and eliminate carbon dioxide, they need some system to perform this gas exchange, which is called respiration. Although a variety of systems and methods accomplish this, all operate on the same basic principle called diffusion.

DIFFUSION VITAL TO RESPIRATION

Diffusion can be described as the movement or spreading out of a substance from an area in which it is highly concentrated to an area of its lowest concentration. Diffusion takes place at the level of molecules, and since molecules are constantly in motion, they have a natural tendency to mix randomly with one another. Although it is not known exactly why molecules behave this way, they have a natural tendency to move from where they are all together to where there are the fewest of them, in an effort to spread themselves out more evenly. Although any given single molecule may not always behave this way, the net or overall movement of a group of molecules will always do so. This net movement is called diffusion. An everyday example of diffusion is the way in which tobacco smoke or strong perfume will spread throughout the still air of a closed room.

The respiratory system of an animal always carries out diffusion across a respiratory surface. There is always some sort of membrane across which the gases (oxygen and carbon dioxide) pass in and out of a body. When there is more oxygen in the environment outside a membrane than there is inside, oxygen will automatically drift through the membrane to equalize the pressure on both sides. Although this may sound like osmosis (which could be described as diffusion across a membrane), osmosis only involves the passage of a substance dissolved in a liquid solution. In respiration, however, gases are exchanged.

INTEGUMENTARY EXCHANGE

In the simplest animal respiratory system, gases are exchanged directly through the body tissues themselves. This is called integumentary exchange, since an animal's integument is its protective outer covering or skin. The one-celled organisms that practice this form of respiration are too simple to have any skin, and instead have a membrane that allows oxygen and carbon dioxide to diffuse right through it and reach every part of its "body." More complicated animals, like earthworms, also perform this type of "skin breathing," but they also use a simple type of circulatory system to move the gases from the inside of their body to their skin. Studying an earthworm also reveals a major characteristic of all respiratory systems—they must always be wet. The slimy, mucus-covered skin of an earthworm demonstrates that diffusion will only take place if the respiratory surface or membrane is always kept moist. If an earthworm dries out, it will suffocate.

TRACHEAL SYSTEM

Skin breathing may be fine for very small organisms, but when the outer area of an animal cannot provide a large enough surface area or is too thick or hardened to allow a good gas exchange, then the animal needs some type of specialized respiratory organs. One simple form of such specialized organs is the tracheal system found in insects. In this unique system, oxygen and carbon dioxide are exchanged through diffusion by means of a network of small, stiff tubes called tracheae that extend into the insect's body and are small enough to supply individual cells. Insects have no need of lungs or any connection to a circulatory system.

GILLS

The gills that fish use to breathe are the next most sophisticated system, and they are designed specifically to work in water. A gill is a collection of thin flaps (called lamellae) that are able to obtain oxygen dissolved in water. As water moves over the lamellae's thin membrane, dissolved oxygen diffuses into the fish's blood, while carbon dioxide diffuses out through the gills and into the water. Since water contains only five percent of the oxygen that air does, gills must be especially efficient.

Opposite: A labeled diagram of the human respiratory system. (Illustration by Hans & Cassidy. Courtesy of Gale Research.)

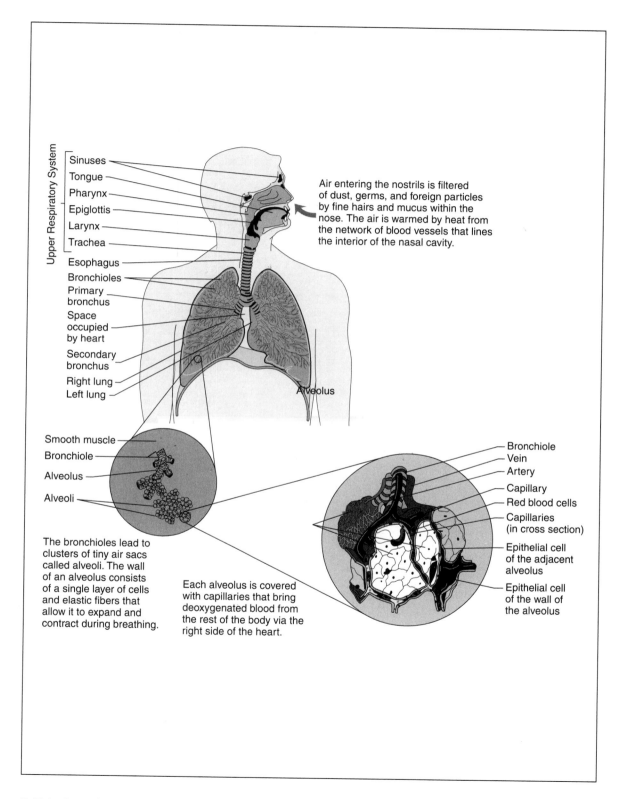

Upper Respiratory System

Sinuses
Tongue
Pharynx
Epiglottis
Larynx
Trachea
Esophagus
Bronchioles
Primary bronchus
Space occupied by heart
Secondary bronchus
Right lung
Left lung
Alveolus

Air entering the nostrils is filtered of dust, germs, and foreign particles by fine hairs and mucus within the nose. The air is warmed by heat from the network of blood vessels that lines the interior of the nasal cavity.

Smooth muscle
Bronchiole
Alveolus
Alveoli

The bronchioles lead to clusters of tiny air sacs called alveoli. The wall of an alveolus consists of a single layer of cells and elastic fibers that allow it to expand and contract during breathing.

Each alveolus is covered with capillaries that bring deoxygenated blood from the rest of the body via the right side of the heart.

Bronchiole
Vein
Artery
Capillary
Red blood cells
Capillaries (in cross section)
Epithelial cell of the adjacent alveolus
Epithelial cell of the wall of the alveolus

They only will work, however, if water keeps moving over their surface, and a fish needs to keep its mouth open as its swims to keep the water moving over the gills. When a fish is not moving, it closes its gills, takes a mouthful of water, and forces it out its gills. Fish cannot breathe out of water because the filaments that contain their lamellae collapse when they are not supported by water. The gills of most fish are located behind their head.

THE HUMAN RESPIRATORY SYSTEM

Lungs are the respiratory organs used by mammals, birds, and reptiles, as well as some amphibians. Lungs exchange gases, since it is the job of the circulatory system to collect and distribute gases throughout the organism. The human lungs are located in the chest cavity, although the human respiratory system actually begins at the nose and mouth where air is inhaled and exhaled. The mouth and nose are connected to a common tube at the back of the throat called a pharynx. Air then passes through the larynx, also called the voice box, into a branching system that resembles an upside-down tree. The larynx flows into the trachea (the tree trunk), which divides into two large limbs called the right and left bronchi. Each of these branch off into multiple smaller bronchi, which continue dwindling down into smaller and smaller tubes that finally end in terminal bronchioles. At the end of these bronchioles, like the leaves of tree, are clusters of moist air sacs called alveoli where the actual exchange of gases takes place. Tiny, thin-walled blood vessels called capillaries create vast networks surrounding the alveoli. It is across these thin walls that oxygen is passed into the blood and carbon dioxide out of the blood by diffusion. Humans have a total of 300,000,000 alveoli in both lungs. Air is actually forced into the lungs by a large muscle beneath the lungs called a diaphragm. When its muscles contract and pull down, the ribs above are lifted upward and outward, and air rushes into the elastic lungs. When air is automatically sucked into the lungs as they expand (inspiration), it is called negative pressure breathing. Expiration occurs when the diaphragm muscles relax, allowing the lungs to go back to their retracted state. Air containing carbon dioxide is then forced out of the lungs. Breathing is controlled by a brain command that sends a signal every few seconds. The average adult human takes between twelve and fifteen breaths a minute.

Because the human respiratory system brings in substances from the outside environment, there are safeguards to fight infectious agents that may enter with the oxygen. The normal human lung is sterile, meaning that there are no bacteria or viruses present. The first line of defense includes hair in the nostrils that filters large particles. The epiglottis between the pharynx and larynx acts as a trap door and prevents food and other swallowed substances from entering the larynx and then the trachea. If it does, we cough involuntarily and say that "something went down the wrong pipe." The acts of sneezing and coughing are usually both started by irritants in the respiratory system, and work to forcibly expel them. Finally, mucus exists throughout the system and serves to trap dust and infectious organisms. Cells called macrophages line the respiratory tract and engulf and kill anything they consider an invader.

Plants can be said to "breathe" since they exchange gases during photosynthesis (which is actually the reverse of respiration since it takes in carbon dioxide and gives off oxygen in the process of making food). However, they do not have any respiratory system approximating that of an animal, since plants exchange gases through simple openings or pores in their leaves called stomata.

[See also **Blood; Respiration**]

Rh Factor

Rh factor describes a certain blood-type marker that each human blood type either has (Rh-positive) or does not have (Rh-negative). As a further refinement of determining exactly what blood type a person is, the Rh factor is important not only for proper blood transfusions but also during pregnancy.

In 1909 the Austrian physician, Karl Landsteiner (1868–1943), explained why blood cells agglutinate, or clump, together when blood from different people were mixed. He showed that all human blood can be divided into four main groups, some of which are compatible and many which are not. He named these four groups blood type A, type B, type AB, and type O according to the particular type of antigen they had on their red blood cells. (An antigen is a protein that works as a type of chemical identification tag.) People from the same blood type could exchange their blood, but those with different blood types had to follow certain exact rules if they were to successfully receive a blood transfusion.

Overall, Landsteiner's discovery made blood transfusions fairly safe and saved many a life. However, despite his breakthrough in understanding blood types, there continued to be enough unexplained accidents during blood transfusions to send Landsteiner searching for the possibility that some other factor might exist that was yet unknown. By 1940, Landsteiner and his associates discovered a different factor in the blood of rhesus monkeys, and he later found that this factor also existed in human blood. As with the four major human blood types, each of which had (or did not have) a certain, specific type of antigen, certain human blood also was found to have an antigen that he named antigen D. If blood had this antigen, it was therefore Rh-positive. Those without the antigen were considered Rh-negative. The symbol Rh was used as an abbreviation for Rhesus. Studies have since shown that about 85 percent of the population are Rh-positive and 15 percent are Rh-negative.

Blood type, like a person's Rh factor, is inherited. The Rh factor only becomes important when a person receives a blood transfusion or when a woman is pregnant. If a person who is Rh-negative receives blood from an Rh-positive person, then the Rh-negative blood will produce antibodies against the Rh-positive factor. Antibodies are proteins in the plasma (the liquid part of the blood) that destroy foreign substances. Therefore, the next time that person's system encounters Rh-positive blood, it will cause what is called a hemolytic reaction and make the blood agglutinate together. This can cause serious injury or death to the patient.

The Rh factor is also critical during pregnancy. If an Rh-negative woman gives birth to an Rh-positive child whose father was RH-positive, there is a risk that her system will become sensitized to her baby's Rh factor and will begin to produce Rh-positive antibodies. While her first baby usually will not be affected, her next child may be in danger since the mother's system may send antibodies into the child's bloodstream while she is still carrying the fetus. This could threaten the child's life. This condition is known as erythroblastosis fetalis, or hemolytic disease of the newborn (HDN). It can cause severe anemia (lack of hemoglobin or red blood cells), brain damage, or even death.

Before the Rh factor became known, it was a major cause of stillbirth pregnancies (when the baby is born dead). Today, this situation can be prevented. At twenty-eight weeks into her pregnancy and immediately after birth, the mother can be given an injection that destroys any Rh-positive antibodies she has in her system. Also, the baby can be given a blood transfusion just before birth while it is still in the womb, or immediately after it is born. A check of blood type and Rh factor are now routine in all blood transfusions and pregnancies.

[*See also* **Antibody and Antigen; Blood; Blood Types**]

RNA (Ribonucleic Acid)

RNA, or ribonucleic acid, is an organic substance in living cells that plays an essential role in the construction of proteins and, therefore, in the transfer of genetic information. If deoxyribonucleic acid (DNA) is the storehouse of information for cells, RNA is the delivery system of that information. RNA copies the coded DNA instructions and carries them to the part of the cell that forms proteins.

Like DNA, RNA is a nucleic acid (so called because it is found in the cell nucleus). Because RNA is involved with making proteins, and because living tissue is made up of proteins, RNA is a critically important substance. Since proteins cannot reproduce themselves, DNA and RNA act together and tell the cells how and which protein to make. Each protein is responsible for a particular characteristic, and some proteins help nourish the cell itself while others determine how tall a person will be. All of this and much more information is encoded in genes in the DNA. However, since DNA is found in the nucleus of the cell and protein is made outside the nucleus in the cytoplasm (the jelly-like fluid that circulates inside the cell and surrounds its nucleus), information about a certain protein must be transferred from the nucleus where it is stored to

A computer-generated model of RNA. RNA is essential for the production of proteins and the transfer of genetic material. (Reproduced by the National Audubon Society Collection/Photo Researchers, Inc. Photograph by Ken Eward.)

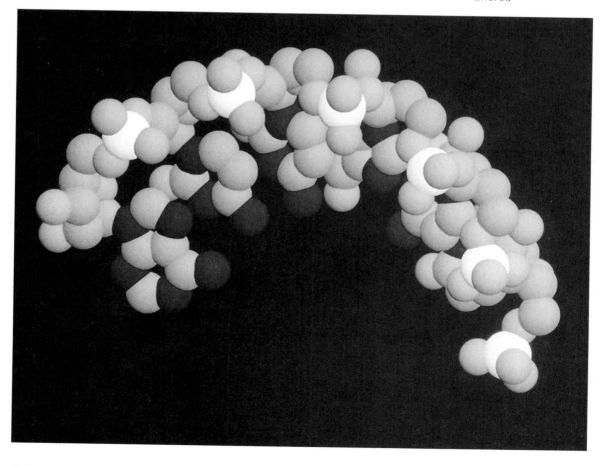

outside of the cell where it is manufactured. It is RNA that performs this important function.

There are actually two types of RNA that handle the information necessary to make proteins. The first is called messenger RNA (mRNA) because it copies the DNA code and carries it out of the nucleus to the ribosomes in the cell (the "factory" where proteins are actually made). This process has been compared to the photocopying of a cookbook. Just as we do not tear out the page of a booklet that contains a recipe, but instead photocopy it for use elsewhere, so the genetic information contained in the DNA is copied by the RNA. This occurs when the DNA double helix or "spiral staircase" splits down the middle, or unzips itself, allowing a single strand of it to act as a template or pattern for RNA to copy. When this has happened, in a process called "transcription," the single RNA strand leaves the nucleus and enters the cytoplasm. The two DNA strands then reunite.

After the mRNA has delivered the instructions to the cell's ribosomes (its protein factories), its code is read by another type of RNA called transfer RNA (tRNA). Transfer RNA also carries amino acids (the building blocks of protein molecules) to the ribosomes, which need them to make proteins. In this process, called "translation," the tRNA molecules read the instructions on the mRNA, and whenever the mRNA needs a particular amino acid, the corresponding tRNA molecule drags the correct amino acid into the protein factory. This process is going on constantly in our bodies, since every second of every minute, our cells are using what might be called gene recipes to make the specific proteins they need.

[*See also* **Amino Acid; DNA; Gene; Nucleic Acid; Protein**]

Root System

The root system of a plant is one of its three main organs. (The others are its stems and leaves.) Roots grow underground and perform several functions: they anchor the plant firmly in the soil, they absorb and transport water and nutrients throughout the plant, and they may also store food.

All seed-producing plants and most spore-producing plants have roots. The exceptions are bryophytes (a type of nonvascular plant, such as mosses, liverworts, and hornworts that grow only in moist environments), since they do not have true roots. Roots are essential to a plant for many reasons. Without a root system that penetrates the soil and spreads below ground, a plant would never be able to grow toward the life-giving Sun.

The beginnings of a plant root are already contained in the embryo found in a seed. When conditions are right and the seed begins to take in water and burst its seed coat (germination), a root or radicle breaks through the coat and begins to grow downward into the soil. Root tissue already has a specialized function, and since it is sensitive to the pull of gravity, it responds appropriately and grows downward. In this way it demonstrates positive geotropism (by growing toward the external stimulus of gravity). As the radicle becomes a mature primary root, it eventually develops secondary roots which, in turn, branch out even more in all directions. These are called fibrous roots. Grass is an example of a plant with a fibrous root system. Some plants also produce a taproot that is much larger than secondary roots and penetrates deeper into the soil. A taproot is a primary food storage root and may be fleshy like a carrot or woody like a tree root. If the taproot of certain plants is broken, they will die. Other roots that form slightly above ground level and go into the soil are called adventitious roots. Roots that emerge from the base of a corn stalk are adventitious roots or prop roots and serve to support the plant. Plants that have aerial roots, like certain orchids and mistletoe, are not in contact with the ground at all but absorb water from aboveground sources (like other plants). Other parts of a plant may grow underground, like tubers (potatoes), bulbs (onions), and corms (gladioli), but these are not really roots but rather only modified stems.

A root is made up of three types of tissue: the epidermis or surface layer; the cortex or root wall where water and food are stored; and the vascular core in its center, which carries food and water into the stem. The

A labeled diagram of a root. The root system is vital to a plant's health. (Illustration by Hans & Cassidy. Courtesy of Gale Research.)

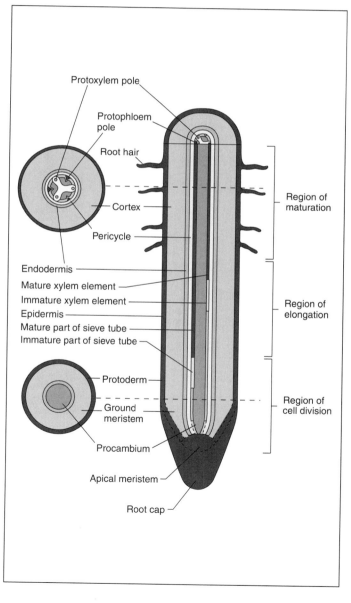

epidermis is a type of outer layer or protective skin. Roots also have hairs that are modified epidermis cells. These long, tubelike hairs give the root a larger surface area for absorbing substances from the soil. It is the root hairs that perform most of the absorption of water and minerals. The core (also called the stele) is made up of vessels and tubes that transport food and water up and down the roots and stem. The tip or apex of the root is its growing point, and it is protected by a thimble-shaped cap as it penetrates into the ground.

Roots help plants adapt to yearly cold seasons. In perennial plants (plants that live for many years), the entire plant survives the winter by using food stored in the roots and stems. In biennial plants, such as carrots, the leaves die off the first winter and a new plant develops from the root the following spring. After the second year, the plant flowers, forms seeds, and dies. In annual plants, the entire plant, including the root system, dies after flowering and producing seeds. The roots of many plants are edible. For example, important root crops include beets, carrots, cassava, parsnips, sweet potatoes, and turnips. Plant roots also benefit the environment by preventing soil erosion by wind and water.

[*See also* **Plant Anatomy; Plants; Seed; Tissue**]

Seed

A seed contains the embryo plant from which a new plant will develop. It also contains food storage tissue and a protective coat. The creation of a seed depends on pollination (the transfer of pollen containing male sex cells to the pistil containing female sex cells) and fertilization (the process in which an egg cell and a sperm cell unite to form one cell). Seeds are produced by more than 250,000 different types of plants. Seeds also vary greatly in size and the methods by which they are dispersed.

The first seeds are thought to have developed about 360,000,000 years ago, marking a major step in the evolution of land plants. These early seeds were gymnosperms or "naked seeds" since they were totally exposed. Over time, however, seeds came to develop a coating (called angiosperms) that protected the seed. This coating proved so successful that angiosperms are now the dominant type of plant. A seed is formed sexually when a grain of pollen containing male sperm fertilizes an ovule containing the female egg. This fused egg cell begins to divide rapidly and grows a structure called the embryo. This part of the seed will become the new plant. It contains, in miniature, the radicle or embryonic root that will grow into a primary root after germination (sprouting). It also has the beginnings of a shoot and early leaves, called cotyledon. After sprouting, the seed lives off its endosperm or stored food until it develops roots and leaves to make its own food.

Seed dispersal, or the methods plants have developed to scatter their seeds away from the parent plant, are extremely varied and interesting. In the simplest cases, seeds ripen on the plant, fall to the ground, germinate, and grow into a new plant. While this may seem like a good method, it soon creates an overcrowded situation where seedlings are competing for the same resources as the parent plant. Plants, therefore, have developed strategies and methods to disperse their seeds some distance from the parent plant. One method is the creation of fruit that is the ripened ovary of the plant and that surrounds the seed itself. Fruit can be hard and dry or fleshy and soft. Many plants enclose their seeds in tasty, attractive fruit to encourage an animal to eat it. Once eaten, the seeds pass through the animal's digestive tract and are deposited elsewhere in the animal's waste—often far away from the parent plant. The fruit of berry seeds, for example, are typically small, thin-skinned, and brightly colored with no smell. It is the fruit's bright color that attracts birds that then eat the fruit. Fruits that appeal to mammals are less colorful but often have a pleasant smell. Others have their nutritious seed enclosed in a hard shell (like a nut) that a rodent will chew through and eat. Sometimes rodents bury nuts to eat later. The ones that are not dug up will germinate and grow into a new plant. Some fruits are meant to be eaten, but contain toxins that make an animal regurgitate (vomit) them elsewhere allowing the fruit's seeds to be dispersed in a new location.

Animals also disperse seeds by carrying both fruit and seeds on their bodies. Certain plants produce seeds with sticky surfaces, while others have barbs or hooks that become attached to an animal's fur or feathers and are then taken away to fall elsewhere to the ground. Some plant species develop extremely light seeds that are easily blown great distances by the wind. The fluffy coverings of dandelion or cottonwood seeds are good examples of wind dispersal. Other plants use the wind more mechanically and have developed seeds with wings (like the sycamore tree) or appendages that act as parachutes. Tumbleweed is an example of an entire plant becoming loose and blowing away with the wind. Other plants develop seeds that can float on water and even have a waterproof coat, such as the coconut. Other mechanical means of dispersal are used by plants that produce capsules that explode when ripe, resulting in the scattering of seeds. Many such plants, like the popular impatiens, grow little curled capsules that build up tension as they develop. When they finally dry out in early fall, they split and abruptly uncurl, flinging their seeds as far as possible from the parent plant.

Many seeds require a period of dormancy or inactivity before they are able to germinate. The plant usually assures that such a seed will not sprout as soon as it ripens by giving it a hard coat or by including a growth-inhibiting hormone in the seed. Some seeds even require a period of freezing temperatures before they will germinate. Seeds are usually very dry and therefore need a great deal of water before they can sprout. By making sure that a seed stays dormant for a certain time, the plant ensures that it will only germinate under the best possible conditions, and not prematurely on a warm fall day. Some seeds can remain dormant for weeks, others months, and still others for years.

Seeds are a major source of food for both animals and human beings. Many species, such as cereal grains (corn, nuts, oats, rice), are a staple for people throughout the world. Many oils are obtained from seeds (sunflower, corn, peanut, and linseed), and are also used to make other products. Two of the most popular seeds consumed today—the cocoa bean and the coffee bean—give us chocolate and coffee.

[*See also* **Plant Anatomy; Plant Reproduction; Plants; Reproduction, Sexual**]

A close-up of grass seed on the tips of growing grass. (Reproduced by permission of The Stock Market. Photograph by Roy Morsch.)

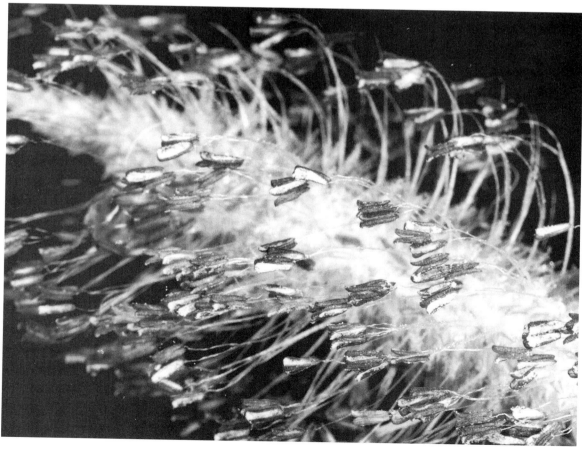

Sense Organ

A sense organ is any collection of cells in an organism that responds to information about certain changes in the organism's internal or external environment. Each sense organ reacts to a particular type of stimulus. The sense organ converts the stimulus into a nerve impulse that is sent to the organism's brain to be processed and identified. Human sense organs are the eyes, ears, nose, mouth, and skin—each having its own particular type of receptors.

Sense organs are essential if an animal is to obtain any information about its surroundings. Without them, the individual organism would probably not survive long. Therefore, sense organs are essential to survival since they are the key link to the external, or outside, world. The type of sense organs an animal has greatly determines how it will perceive its environment. Humans see a world rich in colors. Animals who hunt at night see things only as shades of gray. Dogs recognize others mainly by their smell. Insects see an ultraviolet world all their own.

SENSORY RECEPTORS

Although there is great variety in how different animals experience the world through their senses, they all have sensing systems that operate by using sensory receptors. Thus, all sense organs, no matter what they detect, have and need sensory receptors. A receptor is a group, or cluster, of nerve cells that react to a particular stimulus and receive information.

Sensory receptors make up the most familiar sense organs, such as the ears and eyes. These receptors can be classified according to the type of energy or stimulus to which they respond. Chemoreceptors (for taste and smell) respond to certain chemical compounds. Mechanoreceptors (for touch) respond to mechanical energy. Auditory receptors (for hearing) respond to sound wave vibrations, although some consider them to be a form of mechanoreceptor since the pressure waves of sound are a real, physical force. Photoreceptors (for sight) respond to light energy.

These four types of receptors correspond to the five human senses (taste and smell both use chemoreceptors) and, therefore, to our five major sense organs. However, there are other types of receptors that are used by organisms that are not necessarily linked to a particular sense organ. For example, certain insects such as ticks, and animals such as snakes, possess thermoreceptors with which they respond to temperature. A tick is aware of your presence and jumps on you by sensing your body heat.

Certain fish also have electroreceptors in their skin that allows them to detect electrical energy given off by other objects. Another important type of receptor is known as the proprioceptors. These are sensory receptors located inside an animal's muscles and joints. Proprioceptors allow the animal to be aware of its entire body position, as well as to keep its balance. It is because of this sense that a person is able to dress in complete darkness.

The human body has two senses that employ chemoreceptors—taste (gustation) and smell (olfaction). The first uses taste buds (mainly in the tongue) as the receptors for dissolved chemicals. The second uses olfactory epithelium ("smelling skin") in the nasal cavities to detect airborne chemicals. The sense of touch is located in the skin. Here, mechanoreceptors are activated when they change shape by being pushed or pulled. Auditory, or hearing, receptors are located in the cochlea, deep within the ear. They detect or respond to pressure waves (since sound is actually a vibration of the air). Finally, the rods and cones in the retina of the eyes are the photoreceptors that enable people to see.

Humans would have none of their five senses if they did not also have a vast, branching network of nerves. These nerves take all of the coded messages to the brain, which translates or interprets them. The brain tells a person exactly what he or she is sensing. As a result, people do not really see with the sense organs called the eyes, for it is the brain that interprets the signals the eyes are sending. The brain tells a person that he or she is seeing a beautiful rainbow and not a dangerous fire. The role of the sense organs then is only to gather the information. Understanding that information is left to the brain.

[*See also* **Brain; Hearing; Integumentary System; Organ; Sight; Smell; Taste**]

Sex Chromosomes

Sex chromosomes are the chromosomes within the nucleus of a cell that determine the sex of an organism. Chromosomes pass on genetic material from one generation to another, and different species have different numbers of chromosomes. Humans have forty-six chromosomes arranged in twenty-three pairs, but only a single pair decides what sex (male or female) an individual will be. These are the sex chromosomes.

In all animals and some plants, each cell contains sets of chromosomes that are arranged in matched pairs and are thus called "homolo-

A scanning electron micrograph of human sex chromosomes. The XY represents the male chromosome and the XX represent the female chromosome. (Reproduced by permission of Photo Researchers, Inc.)

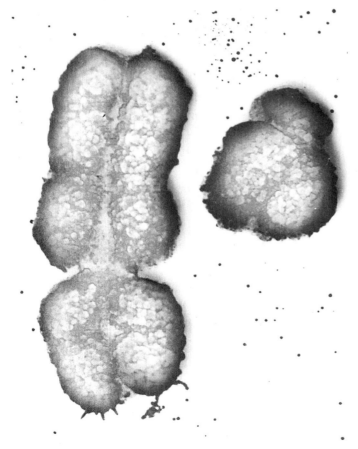

gous" chromosomes. Half of these chromosomes came from the organism's male parent and half came from the female parent. This explains why their offspring, or the unique organism produced by them, is similar to but not exactly like either parent. In humans, the sperm of the male contributes twenty-three chromosomes and the egg of the female also contributes twenty-three—totalling forty-six chromosomes for their offspring. When these two half-sets of chromosomes combine, every chromosome seeks and joins with its matching chromosome, each of which contains different versions (traits) of the same genes. For example, the gene for height that is contributed by the father will match up next to the mother's height gene, and so on. Of these twenty-three pairs of chromosomes that together form a unique individual (with a complete set of forty-six chromosomes), twenty-two pairs determine or affect every characteristic of that individual except its sex. These twenty-two pairs are called "autosomes." It is the remaining single pair of chromosomes that determines the sex of the individual, and these are called sex chromosomes. In females, the sex chromosomes are designated as XX, and in males the sex chromosomes are XY.

In human beings, the forty-six chromosomes in each body cell are arranged in pairs. When the chromosome pairs of a female are examined under a powerful microscope, they are seen to all have the same general appearance, resembling a slightly crooked X-shape. In males however, all but one pair of chromosomes have this same X shape, with only the twenty-third pair being noticeably different. In both men and women, this twenty-third pair is the sex chromosomes. However where for women, the twenty-third chromosome pair appears like all others as a crooked X, for a man, only one chromosome in the pair looks like an X. The other is considerably smaller and rather stumpy-looking and is called a Y chromosome. This is known as the XY chromosome pair and determines the sex of a child. At the moment when a single sperm fertilizes an egg, the sex of a child is determined. This is because each individual sperm carries only twenty-three chromosomes (since it is ready to link up with the egg's other twenty-three chromosomes), one of which is either an X or a Y (having split its forty-six in half). Since the sex chromosomes of the egg are always X (having two X chromosomes), if the egg is fertilized by an X-containing male sperm, the resulting egg will develop into a female (XX). If it is fertilized by a Y-containing sperm, then a male will be born (XY). Although the new child will inherit traits from both its parents, it is the father who determines its sex.

[*See also* **Chromosome; Nucleus; Human Reproduction; Reproduction, Sexual**]

Sex Hormones

Sex hormones are certain types of chemical substances that prepare an animal's body for reproduction. They are secreted by a gland or an organ. Sex hormones determine both male and female sexual characteristics and can also influence a person's behavior.

Hormones are chemical messengers in both animals and plants. In animals, they are produced by glands. Hormones travel through the blood to target tissues where the hormones act as chemical regulators. Hormones influence reproduction, growth, and overall bodily balance, among other things. Sex hormones are important to all animals, but are especially so to vertebrates (animals with a backbone). In humans, the sex hormones—androgens, estrogens, and progestins—are essential for those body processes that are related to reproduction.

Although scientists have only begun to understand sex hormones in the last fifty years, their effects have long been known and recognized. Farmers have known for millennia that castration (or removing a male animal's testes; the sperm-making organs) not only makes these animals more manageable but improves the quality of their meat. In Renaissance times (fourteenth to sixteenth century), boys in the church choir were sometimes castrated to keep their beautiful high voices from changing.

THE PITUITARY GLAND

In humans, the glands that produce hormones involved with sex and reproduction are the pituitary gland, the gonads, and the adrenal glands. The pituitary gland is a small organ below or at the base of the brain. It is about the size of a pea, yet it has a powerful effect on several other glands in the body. The pituitary gland releases eight different hormones. These stimulate other parts or organs in the body, including the gonads. For example, the pituitary gland's follicle-stimulating hormone (FSH) promotes the production of sex cells in males (sperm) and the maturing of sex cells in women (ovaries). The prolactin produced by the pituitary gland gets the female body ready to produce milk when needed.

THE GONADS

The gonads consist of the testes in males and the ovaries in females. These usually come in pairs. The ovaries produce egg cells or ova as well as the hormones known as the estrogens and the progestins. These hormones are usually produced in regular cycles and control female sexual development, thus triggering female secondary sexual characteristics like breasts. The hormones also prepare the body once pregnancy occurs and help ensure that it can sustain the developing fetus (the human embryo).

THE ADRENAL

The main estrogens are estradiol, estrone, and estriol. The main progestin is called progesterone. There are also several kinds of androgens (or male sex hormones) produced by the gonads, but the primary one is testosterone. This hormone stimulates hair growth and the lowering of the voices when a male goes through puberty. The adrenal glands also come in pairs in humans, and their name comes from being located so close to the kidneys. Only the outer part, called the cortex, secretes sex hormones, since it is made up of tissue that is similar to that found in the ovaries and testes.

THE IMPORTANCE OF SEX HORMONES

Sex hormones are important throughout life. They come into play at times other than sexual maturity. These hormones are working from the time of early development to influence the developing fetus. For example, testosterone begins to work before a baby is born by stimulating the growth of male genitals. Like all sex hormones, it also influences the development of other organs that are not directly related to reproduction. Later in life, the production of female and male sex hormones is gradually reduced with aging. Major changes can occur as a woman no longer produces eggs that can be fertilized.

Sex hormones also influence behavior. This is most noticeable in animals. Since sexual reproduction is mostly a joint, or cooperative, effort in which each partner supplies half of the needed ingredients (egg and sperm), many animals go through cycles during which they are receptive to mating. With the exception of humans and a few other mammals, most animals go through only one or two estrous cycles (called "heat") during which their hormones motivate them to reproduce.

Sex hormones also influence animals to do all the necessary things to care for their young. These include nest-building, nursing, and feeding. In males especially, sex hormones account for much of the aggressive behavior displayed during the mating season. Studies of rhesus monkeys have shown that those with the highest levels of testosterone in their blood are the ones doing all of the threatening, chasing, and fighting. These monkeys are dominant, or usually near the top of their social order. If the goal of all living things is to reproduce, then sex hormones are the key to all life. These hormones guide the reproductive process, and affect bodily changes as well as behavior.

[See also **Endocrine System; Hormone; Human Reproduction; Reproduction, Sexual; Reproductive System**]

Sex-linked Traits

Sex-linked traits are characteristics other than sex that are carried by the sex chromosomes (coiled structures in a cell's nucleus that carries the cell's genetic information). Sex chromosomes in humans do more than determine whether a person is male or female, and they can carry such traits as the condition color blindness and the disease muscular dystrophy. Most sex-linked traits occur only on the X chromosome since it is larger than the Y chromosome.

In humans and many other species, females have two X chromosomes (XX), while males have one X chromosome and one Y chromosome (XY). At fertilization (the union of sperm and egg), the new embryo that is created receives half (twenty-three) its chromosomes from the female parent and half (twenty-three) from the male parent. The twenty-three chromosomes in one cell join together as matched pairs with the twenty-three chromosomes in the other cell, so that genes for the same trait (such as height) are situated together on the same chromosome. Once this occurs, whichever gene is dominant (such as tallness) usually gets expressed in the offspring. However, since the male and female sex chromosomes are so different from the other twenty-two sets of chromosomes, which are called autosomes, different rules apply to them. This is because the X chromosome is much larger than the Y chromosome. Since it is larger, it naturally has room for more genes, which carry specific traits. Therefore, when the sex chromosomes pair off and an X chromosome matches up with a Y chromosome (to make a male), many of the genes on the X chromosome do not have matching partners on the Y chromosome. Since the X chromosome is larger and has space for genes that cannot fit on the smaller Y chromosome, males carry slightly less genetic information than females.

The fact that a male's sex chromosomes (XY) are different from a woman's (XX) and are able to carry fewer genes has certain implications that are sometimes very important. It definitely leads to different inheritance patterns between the sexes. Since females have two X chromosomes, if one of these contains a recessive mutation (some type of change in the genetic code), it is likely to be overridden or offset by a dominant, normal gene on the other X chromosome. However, when a male inherits an X chromosome with a recessive mutation, it will appear in him if his Y chromosome does not have a matching gene on it (which it usually does not). When a male has only one gene for a certain trait, it will always be expressed or appear in him.

A well-known sex-linked trait is color blindness. The typical form of this condition is an inability to tell the color green apart from the color red. This condition is caused by a recessive gene carried on the X chromosome, but the trait only shows up when there is no dominant gene to offset it. That is why color blindness shows up most often in males. If a female has an X chromosome with the defective gene carrying color blindness, chances are her other X chromosome has a gene with normal vision, and she will not be color blind. Males have no "other" X chromosome, and so whatever recessive gene they inherit on their one X chromosome is expressed. That is why females are considered "carriers" of certain conditions. One of the more serious conditions for which a female can act as a carrier is for the disease hemophilia, which prevents the blood from clotting. Another is muscular dystrophy, a disease in which the muscles waste away. For a woman to get either hemophilia or muscular dystrophy, both her X chromosomes would have to have the defective recessive gene.

[*See also* **Chromosome; Fertilization; Inherited Traits; Human Reproduction; Reproduction, Sexual; Sex Chromosome**]

Sight

Sight, or vision, is the sense that enables an organism to detect light. It serves mainly to allow an organism to see and move about its environment. As one of the five senses, the ability to see is critically important to the independence of the individual. Sight affects all aspects of an organism's survival.

Not all organisms that have receptors for light can actually see. Some of the simplest light-sensitive organisms (like certain cnidarians such as the jellyfish, or flatworms) have eyespots that detect light but cannot see objects. The best their light-sensitive cells can do is determine the direction and intensity of a light. Being able to form an effective image requires a much more complex organ. This organ is called an eye, usually with a lens.

Besides having a lens, which concentrates light for the photoreceptors, a complete system of sight needs a brain that can interpret the light images it receives. In the animal world, there are basically two types of eyes. These include the "camera" eye of vertebrates (animals with a backbone), and the compound eye of arthropods (a phylum that includes insects).

SIGHT IN HUMANS

As vertebrates, humans naturally have the "camera" eye common to higher animals. It is described as a camera because it has an adjustable lens. The human visual system consists of two eyes located in the front of the head, thus allowing both to be focused on the same object. Called "binocular vision," this creates an overlap of information that allows people to judge distance and depth accurately.

Sight begins when rays of light hit an object and bounce back, entering the eye through the cornea. This front part of the eye is a thin, transparent membrane. This membrane refracts, or bends, the incoming light through a watery fluid called "aqueous humor" and then through the lens. The elliptical, or egg-shaped, lens has muscles on either side of it that allow it to adjust its shape by expanding or contracting (according to whether the object is close or distant). The lens serves to focus this incoming light onto the retina at the back of the eye.

Once light reaches the retina, it is absorbed by its more than 100,000,000 photoreceptor cells. These are called cones and rods. Rods are very sensitive to light and enable people to see even in dim light. Cones need more light to work, but they allow people to see colors. These specialized light receptor cells generate electrical impulses that stimulate the optic nerve. The optic nerve carries the impulses to the visual cortex at the back of the brain. At this point, the brain decodes and integrates all this information and produces an image, or a picture.

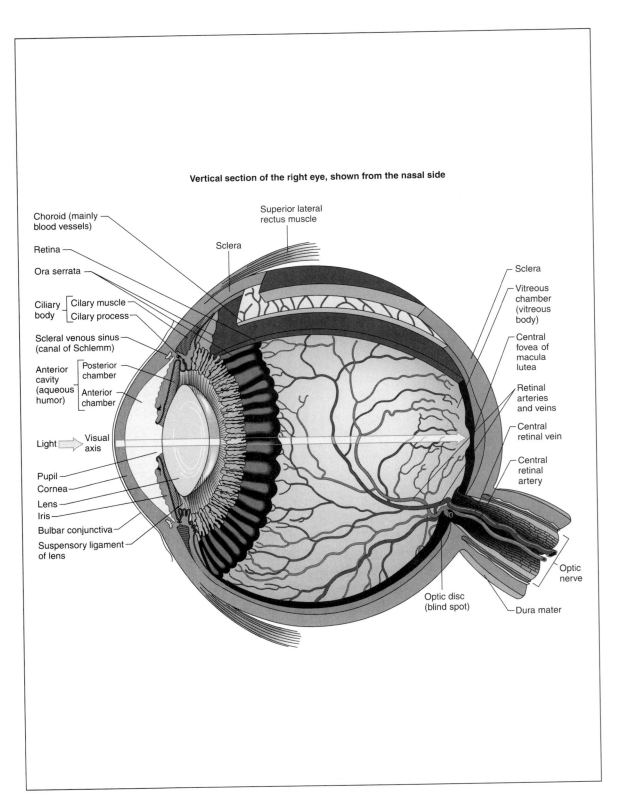

Vertical section of the right eye, shown from the nasal side

Choroid (mainly blood vessels)

Superior lateral rectus muscle

Sclera

Retina

Ora serrata

Ciliary body — Cilary muscle
              Cilary process

Scleral venous sinus (canal of Schlemm)

Anterior cavity (aqueous humor) — Posterior chamber
                                  Anterior chamber

Light → Visual axis

Pupil

Cornea

Lens

Iris

Bulbar conjunctiva

Suspensory ligament of lens

Sclera

Vitreous chamber (vitreous body)

Central fovea of macula lutea

Retinal arteries and veins

Central retinal vein

Central retinal artery

Optic nerve

Optic disc (blind spot)

Dura mater

SIGHT IN ANIMALS

The vertebrate eye is made so it will form sharp images. However, not all vertebrates see the same thing when they look at an object. Each animal species sees in a way that best helps it to survive. For example, animals that hunt at night, like cats or owls, have many more rods than cones, making them capable of night vision. They cannot, however, distinguish color. Such night hunters also have a type of pigment in their eyes that reflects any available light into their photoreceptor cells, explaining why a cat's eyes shine in the dark. Birds and primates who hunt by day need sharp vision. Birds that soar high above their prey have phenomenally sharp sight.

Unlike vertebrates whose eye has a single lens, the compound eye of arthropods (crustaceans and insects) is made up of thousands of separate, little lenses. Each lens is covered by its own cornea. A dragonfly has about 28,000. Each one of these receives light from a narrow field of view. The animal's brain puts these all together to form a single image. This type of vision is not geared to giving a clear, sharp image. Instead, it detects the slightest movement in a very wide field of view. Some insects can see an area as wide as 180 degrees without moving their eyes or their head.

THE BRAIN IS ESSENTIAL TO SIGHT

Like the other four senses that necessarily involve the brain, vision would not work if the brain was unable to tell a person what his or her eyes are seeing. If the part of the brain that processes visual information is damaged, a person may not be able to recognize a visual object despite having a pair of healthy eyes. Real blindness can result from an injury or disease of the eyeball, the optic nerve, or the nerve connections to the brain.

EYE DISORDERS

A common eye condition that is correctable is nearsightedness, or myopia. In this case, the lens bends the light too much so that it focuses before it reaches the retina. Another condition is farsightedness, which is also correctable, and happens when the lens does not bend the light enough. As a result, the light reaches the retina before it is focused. Astigmatism results in blurred vision caused by a misshapen cornea. Glasses, contact lenses, and laser surgery can help these problems.

Cataracts, or a clouding of the lens, common among elderly people, and can be corrected by surgery. Glaucoma, which is a type of high blood

Opposite: A cutaway anatomy of the human eye. (Illustration by Hans & Cassidy. Courtesy of Gale Research.)

pressure in the eye, can cause blindness, although it is controllable. It is not true that one's vision can be damaged by reading in poor light or by sitting too close to a television, but these habits can tire the eyes and make them sore.

[*See also* **Organ; Sense Organ**]

Skeletal System

The skeletal system is the structural framework that supports an animal's body. It also provides protection for an animal's soft tissues and internal organs and serves as an attachment for the body's muscles that push against it and apply force, resulting in movement. The skeletal system of invertebrate animals (animals without a backbone) is on the outside and is called an exoskeleton. Most vertebrates (animals with a backbone) have a skeleton on the inside of the body, called an endoskeleton.

Without some type of strong, rigid frame for support, an animal's body would be a soft mass of tissue without any real shape. Only animals have skeletons, and because of them, their muscles have an anchor or something to push against. Muscles and bones are really inseparable, since they were designed to always work together to allow an animal to move. The skeletal system of vertebrates has been described mechanically as bones that act as levers that, in turn, apply a force that muscles have generated.

HYDROSKELETON

The simplest and most primitive of all skeletal systems, the hydrostatic skeleton, does not resemble any type of rigid framework. Rather, it is what a soft-bodied animal, like an earthworm or a jellyfish, uses to keep its shape. Since these and other animals, like the hydra, have no rigid parts and are composed of fluid and soft tissue, they maintain their shape and get their support from the internal pressure of fluid pushing against the outer walls of their body cavity. Like air inside a balloon, the fluid that fills the animal's body cavity pushes against its sides and keeps it "inflated." These animals often live in water and move about by contracting their bodies and squeezing water out. Thus, when a jellyfish propels water from one opening, it darts quickly in the opposite direction. Earthworms make their internal fluid move inside their many segments in a particular, coordinated way and are able to lengthen and shorten their bodies and, as a result, crawl.

EXOSKELETON

Evolution transformed the primitive hydrostatic skeleton into an exoskeleton by simply hardening its outer wall. An exoskeleton covers all or part of an animal's body like a suit of armor, and gives it support from the outside. All arthropods (such as crabs, lobsters, spiders, and insects) have exoskeletons, and their muscles are attached to its inside and pull against it to create movement. The typical arthropod body is divided into several jointed regions all composed of a hard shell of dead tissue called chitin. This shell covers every part of the arthropod, and is especially thick and hard around its vital organs. However, it is thin and flexible at the joints so that the animal can move. Although a hard outer shell provides excellent protection, it also limits the size that an animal can reach since the larger it gets, the heavier its shell becomes. It also makes growing difficult and complicated, since the exoskeleton is made up of dead tissue and itself cannot grow. Arthropods achieve growth by periodic molts or splitting and shedding of an outer case. Molting is always a time of danger for arthropods, since they are vulnerable to attack and cannot move well. Mollusks (like clams and snails) have solved this problem since the space inside their extremely hard, outer shell gets bigger as the animal grows.

ENDOSKELETON

Unlike an exoskeleton, an endoskeleton cannot be seen since it is found inside the soft flesh of an animal. It is also very different from most exoskeletons because it grows in step with the rest of the body. Since endoskeletons are lighter than those carried on the outside, they can grow much larger in size. It is no surprise therefore that the largest animals on Earth have endoskeletons. An interior skeleton may be light, but it also provides little protection. While some vital organs may be surrounded by bones (like the ribs around the heart and lungs), other organs (like those below the ribs) are totally vulnerable to injury by force.

Surprisingly, there are some animals that, despite being invertebrates, nonetheless have an endoskeleton. Sponges do not have backbones, but they do have a form of endoskeleton. Other invertebrates, such as echinoderms like sea urchins and starfish, seem to have an exoskeleton, but their spines are really only extensions of their endoskeleton that lies just below their skin. Both squid and octopi are also invertebrates with an endoskeleton. There are also animals that are considered to be vertebrates but who do not have a single, real bone in their body. This is because their supporting framework is usually made up of cartilage. Cartilage is a tough, slippery substance that is both strong and flexible. The shark, ray, and lamprey are examples of vertebrates with an endoskeleton of cartilage, and they swim in a noticeably different way than true fish do.

PARTS OF AN ENDOSKELETON

All other vertebrates have an endoskeleton made of bone. As a living substance, bone is made up of cells surrounded by layers of hard mineral salts, such as calcium phosphate. Most bones have three structural parts: the periosteum or compact bone that is its dense outer layer and gives it strength; spongy bone, which is the light, softer inside layer; and marrow that fills its inside core and makes red and white blood cells. Before vertebrates are born, their skeleton exists in a cartilage form, which "ossifies" or hardens and turns into real bone at birth. After birth, some of the bones fuse together. For example, a human baby has 270 bones at birth. However, by the time the baby reaches adulthood many of the bones will have fused together, leaving only 206 separate bones in the human skeletal system.

For a skeleton to really work, however, it cannot be all bone. Bones must be connected to one another to make it all work together, and ligaments are the connective material that links bone to bone at the joints. A ligament is made up of many bands of tissue that, if torn, can heal; but if severed, must be surgically sewn back together. Muscles are connected to bones by connective tissue called tendons. Although tendons act like a very tough cord, they cannot be stretched. If severed, they must be surgically repaired or the muscle will not work the bone (since the connection is broken). Cartilage is also a form of connective tissue and serves to fill the spaces between bones and prevents them from scraping painfully against one another. Cartilage is slippery (called "gristle" in animals) and it allows bones to slide over each other at the joints.

Because vertebrate skeletons are jointed, they allow movement. There are six types of moving joints in vertebrate skeletons: ball-and-socket joints (like the hip and shoulder joint); gliding joints (wrist and ankle); pivotal joints (allow two kinds of movement—side-to-side and up-and-down); saddle joints (thumb joint); hinge joint (elbows, fingers, and knees); ellipsoid joints or condyloid joints (movement in two axes such as the tiny bones in people's fingers, toes, and jaw). Joints move easily because of their slippery cartilage but also because they are lubricated by a special fluid called synovial fluid. There are also some body joints that do not move, such as the bones of the skull and hip. In these joints, bones come together in joints that are really more like seams.

The basic form of all vertebrate skeletons is essentially the same for many different types of animals and is made up of an axial skeleton and

Opposite: A diagram showing some of the major bones that make-up the human skeletal system. (Illustration by Kopp Illustration, Inc.)

Skeletal System

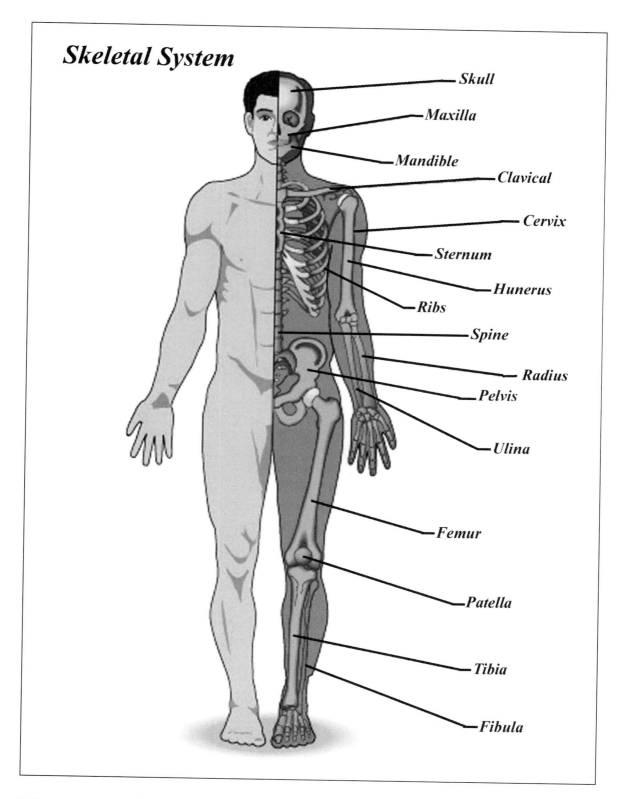

- Skull
- Maxilla
- Mandible
- Clavical
- Cervix
- Sternum
- Hunerus
- Ribs
- Spine
- Radius
- Pelvis
- Ulina
- Femur
- Patella
- Tibia
- Fibula

an appendicular skeleton. The standard axial model (for a typical mammal) has a vertebral column made up of individual small bones (vertebrae) that provide up-and-down or lengthwise support while also being flexible. The vertebrae (singular, vertebra) also connect the skull to the rest of the body. Ribs, also part of the axial skeleton, provide support and protection for the chest area.

The appendicular skeleton is made up of the forelimbs (arms and hands), the shoulders, and the pelvic bones to which the hindlimbs are attached. Finally, ligaments keep the bones securely attached at the joints. There are naturally many variations to this model. For instance, a snake is a vertebrate but it has no limbs at all. A manatee and a whale have only forelimbs (flippers). Humans have arms and birds have wings. The long, flexible human thumb allows us to perform many precise movements, whereas the chimpanzee, our close relative, has a shorter, much less useful thumb. While the number, size, and shape of skeletal elements may vary greatly within species during their development, and sometimes even between sexes, the basic vertebrate model is always the same.

Smell

Smell is the sense that enables an organism to detect airborne chemicals. It serves as a way of identifying, sorting out, and warning an organism about its environment. As one of the five senses, the sense of smell plays a key role in human development and is also linked to human emotions and memory.

Smell is technically called "olfaction," and it is one of the senses an animal uses to orient itself to its surroundings. Olfaction is sometimes described as a "sensitivity to substances in a gaseous phase." This means that smell allows an odor (which is an airborne chemical or a gas) to be detected. Being able to smell is one sense that the earliest life forms probably used to find food and avoid being eaten themselves.

Smell can be very important to the survival of both humans and other animals. It affects people's quality of life, or how much they enjoy life. Like the sense of taste, smell involves a complex process called chemoreception. Described simply, things can be smelled if they give off molecules (small particles) into the air. Organisms that have the sense of smell have specialized receptors, or cells, that receive these molecules. Substances that give off molecules are called "volatiles."

THE SENSE OF SMELL IN HUMANS

For humans, smell begins with the nose. The nose breathes in air carrying these molecules. This air enters through the nasal cavities, or nostrils (and sometimes the mouth). It passes over the body's "smelling skin," called its olfactory epithelium. This is a small patch of moist, specialized cells located in the upper part of the very rear of the nasal cavities just above the bridge of the nose. Here the body's chemoreceptors are stimulated by the gas molecules. The chemoreceptors are covered with extremely tiny hairs, called cilia, and a fluid. When the gas molecules dissolve in the fluid and touch the cilia, the cell reacts. Scientists still do not know if there is a special receptor for every different type of possible scent, or if there are certain receptors that are triggered in a different sequence by a particular odor. Most think that the latter is probably true.

When a chemoreceptor cell reacts, a nerve impulse is produced. The impulse travels to the brain's olfactory cortex (a layer of gray matter that

A diagram showing the process by which olfactory information is transmitted to the brain. (Illustration by Hans & Cassidy. Courtesy of Gale Research.)

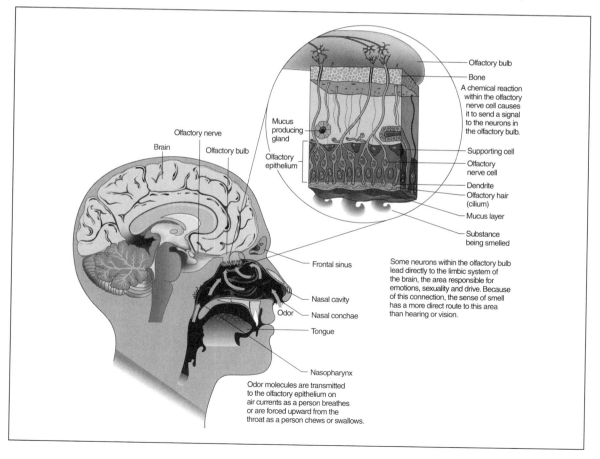

Olfactory bulb

Bone

A chemical reaction within the olfactory nerve cell causes it to send a signal to the neurons in the olfactory bulb.

Mucus producing gland

Olfactory nerve

Brain

Olfactory bulb

Olfactory epithelium

Supporting cell

Olfactory nerve cell

Dendrite

Olfactory hair (cilium)

Mucus layer

Substance being smelled

Frontal sinus

Some neurons within the olfactory bulb lead directly to the limbic system of the brain, the area responsible for emotions, sexuality and drive. Because of this connection, the sense of smell has a more direct route to this area than hearing or vision.

Nasal cavity

Odor

Nasal conchae

Tongue

Nasopharynx

Odor molecules are transmitted to the olfactory epithelium on air currents as a person breathes or are forced upward from the throat as a person chews or swallows.

covers most of the brain's surface) where the smell is identified. If the smell is recognized from a previous experience it is easily identified. If it is new, it is stored and remembered for the next time. In humans, the olfactory cortex is located deep within the brain's limbic system. This is the part of the brain that is the source of people's emotions. Smell is also linked to the brain's hippocampus and amygdala in the limbic system, which controls memories. It is thought that this link to the parts of the brain that control emotion and memory is the reason why smells can cause people to feel certain emotions or have strong memories. All people have experienced a particular smell bringing back a flood of childhood feelings or making them remember an event. In this way, smell plays a large role in forming life experiences and influencing moods. Odors associated with a pleasant experience instantly bring back fond memories, while those associated with an unpleasant experience trigger negative emotions.

In humans, smell is closely related to taste since they both operate by chemoreception. If food has a foul smell, it becomes unappetizing and someone knows not to eat it. Without a sense of smell, humans' ability to taste would be severely impaired. People experience this when they are badly stuffed up from a head cold and cannot smell. Newborn babies recognize their mother within three days of birth by her smell. People with no sense of smell can hardly taste cheese and pepper. The sense of smell can be damaged or lost as a result of a head injury, infection, a brain tumor, or exposure to toxic chemicals.

THE SENSE OF SMELL IN ANIMALS

While the sense of smell does not play an obvious role in the lives of humans, it is a critically important sense for many animals. Those animals who depend a great deal on their sense of smell usually possess an acute hunting ability, and smelling plays many different roles in their lives. It is known that a dog's area of "smelling skin" in its nose is roughly fifty times larger than a human's olfactory epithelium. Such extreme sensitivity to odor by animals is exemplified by a shark, which can smell a few drops of blood mixed with sea water from great distances.

While many mammals smell with their noses, some animals and insects smell with their tongues, feet, or antennas. For example, a snake picks up chemical odor molecules from the air by flicking its tongue, while a butterfly senses sweetness with its feet and detects the smell of the opposite sex with its antennas. Ants and bees also smell with their antennas, and salmon are guided upstream by their sense of smell. Other animals, like fish and amphibians, have scent-detecting organs all over their bodies.

In the natural world, animals use smell to identify their own kind, find food, and avoid predators. They also use this sense to communicate using pheromones, or "messenger substances." These chemicals indicate when an individual is receptive, or ready, to mate. They also can guide a predator to its prey or warn the prey that a predator is close by. Many mammals use their urine to mark their territory and signal others to keep out. Animals of the same species can smell a number of things about the "marker" of the territory, such as its sex, readiness to mate, and even its general age.

Mammals have the best sense of smell among all vertebrates (animals with a backbone). Within the group of mammals, carnivores (animals that eat other animals) and rodents have the best sense of smell. Primates, like humans and apes, have the poorest sense of smell.

[*See also* **Organ; Sense Organ**]

Species

A species is a group of organisms of the same type. The term species is one of the seven major classification groups that biologists use to identify and categorize living things. These seven groups are hierarchical or range in order of size. Species is the last and smallest complete group. The classification scheme for all living things is: kingdom, phylum, class, order, family, genus, and species.

Species can be considered the basic unit of scientific classification. It is used to describe a group of closely related, physically similar organisms that can breed with one another. Members of the same species often are so close in features that it is difficult to tell them apart. For example, although a wolf and a dog look similar, they do not belong to the same species. The wolf belongs to the species *lupus* (*Canis lupus*), while the dog to the species *familiaris* (*Canis familiaris*). Some organisms, however, are more difficult to differentiate. This is the case with sunflowers of different species. Some species of organisms may differ very little in their conspicuous features, shape, behavior, and habitat. However, only members of the same species will share a common gene pool.

The only correct way to identify one species from another is by the binomial (two-word) scientific name. For example, the correct way to distinguish between two species of seabirds would be to use their binomial names: *Sula sula* and *Sula nebouxii*. In these examples, *Sula* is the genus name, while *sula* and *nebouxii* are the species names. (The species name is always the lowercase Latin word that follows the uppercase Latin genus word.) Very often, however, it is the common name for the species that is most used to refer to one particular type. So, for the example above, most people would refer to the two species of seabirds as the red-footed booby and the blue-footed booby instead of using the binomial scientific name.

[*See also* **Class; Classification; Family; Genus; Kingdom; Order; Phylum**]

Sperm

A sperm cell, or spermatozoon, is a sex cell produced by male organisms. In humans and other vertebrates (animals with a backbone), sperm are produced in great numbers by the male gonads or testes (sex organs). The job of a sperm is to swim to the female egg, penetrate its surface, and deliver its package of genetic material. This is called fertilization and usually results in the production of an offspring.

Sexual reproduction involves the fusion, or uniting, of male and female gametes (sex cells) to produce a new individual. It also usually involves a male parent that produces sperm and a female that produces an egg, or ovum. The egg is large and does not move, while sperm are usually small and highly mobile. When a sperm contacts and penetrates an egg, fertilization occurs. This fertilization produces a zygote that will develop into a genetically unique offspring. All animals that engage in sexual reproduction manage to unite a sperm with an egg.

For some species, the sperm fertilizes the egg externally (as do frogs or fish in water). The method of external fertilization used by aquatic animals would barely work if only a few sperm and eggs were released each season because the eggs and sperm are unprotected and left to unite by chance. That is why each aquatic parent produces very large quantities of sperm or eggs. Land animals, like mammals, are more complex, and their reproductive systems are more specialized. They engage in internal fertilization where the sperm it directly deposited in the female's body. While the male produces sperm in great numbers, the female makes only a very small number of eggs available for fertilization at any one time.

Sperm moving over the surface of a uterus. Sexual reproduction involves the union of an egg and sperm to produce a cell that is genetically different than the parent cells. (Reproduced by permission of the National Audubon Society Collection/Photo Researchers, Inc. Photograph by Fawcett/Phillips.)

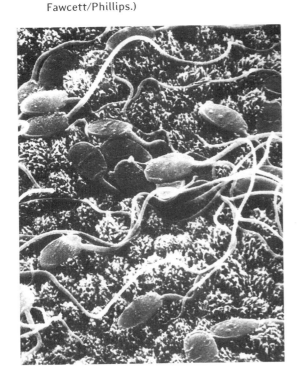

Nearly all male animals produce sperm as their reproductive cell. With the exception of certain worms, decapods (like crayfish), diplopods (like millipedes), and mites, all sperm have two main parts. These include a head and some form of a whiplike tail. The tail, or flagellum, whips side-to-side and gives the sperm cell its movement. The head of a sperm is different for each species and is made up mainly of a nucleus (the cell's control center). It is there that the sperm carries chromosomes, the important genetic material responsible for transmitting certain characteristics to the new individual it helps create.

It is the sperm (and not the egg) that also carries the chromosome that determines the sex of the offspring. The head of the sperm is covered with a cap called the acrosome. This cap contains chemicals that eat through the egg's protective covering and help the sperm burrow into the egg and fertilizes it. When the sperm nucleus and egg nucleus meet, their membranes fuse together and form a new nucleus. This new nucleus receives twenty-three chromosomes from the sperm and twenty-three from the egg to make a complete set of forty-six. Once an egg is fertilized by one sperm, it prevents any others from penetrating its outer layer. Sperm that do not fertilize an egg keep swimming either in water or in the female's reproductive tract until they die.

Most animals release sperm in large numbers, and a healthy human male can release 250,000,000 sperm in a single ejaculation (the ejection of sperm and fluids from the penis). Human males do not start producing sperm until puberty begins (between the ages of twelve and fourteen when they evolve from children into adolescents). The male gonads or testes where sperm are produced are housed outside the body in a bag of skin called the scrotum. Since sperm are unable to survive at normal body temperature, they are housed outside the body where it is at least 5°F (-15°C) cooler.

[*See also* **Fertilization; Human Reproduction; Reproduction, Sexual; Reproductive System**]

Sponge

A sponge is an invertebrate (an animal without a backbone) that lives underwater and survives by taking in water through a system of pores. A sponge has no organs or nervous system and lacks most features that are common to animals. It is the simplest and one of the oldest of all multicellular organisms.

There are about 5,000 species of sponges. All of these belong to the phylum Porifera, which means "to have pores." Most inhabit a saltwater environment and live in one place on the seabed. They always attach themselves to something hard and unmoving. Although biologists consider the sponge to be an evolutionary dead end, it is nonetheless a very successful organism in terms of its ability to survive.

CHARACTERISTICS OF SPONGES

All sponges have certain things in common. First, all are filter feeders, meaning that they get their food by trapping whatever their watery environment provides them. They allow water to enter and leave their body cavity through a system of tiny holes or pores. In this way, sponges obtain the water, oxygen, and nutrients they need. They rid themselves of waste like carbon dioxide by using the same system. Sponges expel their waste out of their largest opening called the osculum. As water travels through the sponge, any small food particles in the water are captured and absorbed by its cells.

A vase sponge with fishes swimming inside of it. Sponges are one of the simplest and one of the oldest of all multicellular organisms. (Reproduced by Photo Researchers, Inc.)

This points out a unique thing about sponges: each of their cells is in a sense on its own. For example, although each cell responds to stimuli, the sponge as an organism cannot react as a whole. Similarly, digestion and waste disposal is the job of each cell. This is necessary since a sponge has no specialized tissues or organs to perform these functions. A sponge might therefore be described as a loose association of cells.

While a sponge may be as small as a fingernail or as large as a chair, all have some sort of skeleton or framework that supports them. In fact, sponges are classified according to the type of skeleton that they form by secretion. One class of sponges has a chalky skeleton made of calcium carbonate spikes. Another class has needle-like glass spikes, while a third class has a supporting skeleton made of a fibrous protein called spongin. The "natural" sponge we associate with taking a bath is actually a dried spongin skeleton minus the sponge's living cells. Most of today's household sponges are synthetic (man-made) plastic versions of a sponge.

As an invertebrate, most sponges are hermaphroditic, meaning that the same individual can produce both sperm and eggs. They can reproduce sexually, although they must obtain the sex cells of another individual. After fertilization (the union of a male sex cell and a female sex cell), a free-swimming larva is released that eventually attaches itself to the bottom of the ocean where it remains anchored for its entire life. Sponges can also reproduce asexually (without another individual's sex cells). This happens when a small fragment is broken off and settles on an appropriate spot on the ocean floor where it buds or develops into a new sponge. It is estimated that this extremely simple organism, from which few multicellular organisms have evolved, has successfully lived on Earth for more than 5,000,000,000 years.

Spore

A spore is an extremely tiny, specialized package of cells used by some organisms during reproduction. Plants use spores as they do seeds, for reproduction; while certain algae, fungi, bacteria, and protozoans use spores to help disperse themselves widely and to protect themselves from unfavorable conditions. Spores vary in size but all are microscopic and usually contain a single cell.

In botany (the study of plants), spores are regarded as reproductive cells that are capable of developing into a new individual plant, either directly or after fusion with another spore. Plants that do not flower, like mosses and ferns, do not grow from a seed that was created sexually by male pollen combining with a female ovule. Instead, they reproduce by means of spores. The plant that develops from a spore does not resemble the parent plant, since this plant is in the first phase of a life cycle called the "alternation of generations." This means that in the life cycle of a plant, two generations exist alternately, one after the other. For example, for centuries no one knew how ferns actually reproduced. Most thought that since a fern was a green plant, it had to produce seeds (and therefore reproduce sexually with male and female sex cells). Yet it was impossible to find a fern's seeds until botanists studied the entire life cycle of a fern. Finally, they discovered that ferns reproduce with spores. They also discovered that a fern has a sexual stage (producing sperm and egg) that alternates with an asexual stage (producing spores). In the life cycle of a fern, a mature fern plant develops little brown spore cases called sporangia that are attached to the underside of their leaves, or fronds. When the spores are ripe, the cases split open in the dry air and the dustlike spores are carried away by the wind. When the spore lands where there are damp conditions, it germinates (begins to sprout) and grows into a very small, heart-shaped plant. This tiny plant begins to mature and develops sex organs which, after fertilization (the process in which an egg cell and a sperm cell unite to form one cell) occurs, grows into a plant we recognize as a fern.

A fern leaf with spore clusters. Spores, not seeds, are the reproductive cells of ferns. (©National Audubon Society Collection/Photo Researchers, Inc. Photograph by Hugh Spencer.)

Organisms besides plants use spores for other purposes. Certain kinds of algae, bacteria, fungi, and protozoans all form what are described as survival spores. Besides the ability of spores to be easily and widely dispersed, they also have the ability to survive under harsh conditions. For fungi that are not able to move, spores are an ideal way to spread themselves around, and when conditions are right, fungi produce dispersal spores that function like seeds and germinate quickly under proper conditions. They grow, mature, and produce more spores out of which more fungi will grow. But when the environment becomes unfavorable—too hot or cold or too dry—fungi produce survival spores that may live for years before germinating. Certain types of bacteria form spores for protective reasons. Bacterial spores, which are bacterial cells that have gone dormant (resting) and developed a thick, hard wall, can usually survive even in hot, boiling water. Protozoans—most of which are parasites that live in or on other animals—also form protective spores by a type of cell division. The protozoan that causes malaria is injected into a healthy person by a mosquito carrying its spores. Although the spores cannot move, they multiply by cell division in the person's liver and then enter the blood cells. Soon the blood cells burst and release the spores into the liquid part of the blood. When a mosquito stings this infected person and takes its blood, it also takes the spores and eventually deposits them into yet another healthy person. For plants and other organisms, spores have proven to be a successful means of establishing themselves in new environments as well as a way of surviving unfavorable conditions.

[*See also* **Algae; Botany; Bacteria; Fungi; Plant Reproduction; Plants; Protozoans**]

Stimulus

A stimulus (plural, stimuli) is any event that triggers a response in an organism. When an organism reacts, or changes, its behavior because of some environmental change, it is responding to a stimulus. An ability to respond to what is going on around them is one of the characteristics of living things.

In order to survive in a world full of constant change, activity, and motion, organisms have developed a wide range of receptors that react to particular types of stimuli. If organisms are not immediately aware of changes in their environment, they may not be able to adapt. Therefore, an organism must be able to detect change and to adjust itself. The organism must respond to change in an appropriate way, or it will not live long. Vertebrates (animals with a backbone) have developed elaborate and sensitive nervous systems that enable them to know what is going on about them. This system enables them to react quickly to each new situation.

Vertebrates have five main senses. Each have specialized receptors that respond to certain types of stimuli. A person's eyes have receptors that detect light, while ears detect sound; the skin detects pressure and temperature; the tongue detects dissolved chemicals; and the nose detects airborne chemicals. Although each type of receptor reacts to only one particular type of stimulus, they all work on the same principle. A sense receptor is activated by a certain type of energy change. Therefore, when a certain energy change, or stimulus, occurs in the external environment, the appropriate cell, or nerve ending, reacts and converts this into a nerve impulse. The nerve impulse is carried to the brain by sensory neurons. The brain decodes the signal and tells a person what he or she is sensing.

It also transmits any necessary signals to the muscles or glands (organs in the body that produce a special substance like hormones or enzymes) to carry out a particular action.

Organisms also have rapid or immediate responses to certain stimuli that are built into their nervous systems. These are called reflex actions and are usually geared to matters of well-being and survival. As a result, a person will instantly pull his or her hand away from a hot stove without thinking. The heat sensed by the person's skin is the stimulus and the hand jerking back is the response. Such an instantaneous reaction is called an unconditioned response because it occurs with no learning or experience involved. The idea of stimulus is closely associated with that of life or living, since all organisms, from the simplest to the most complex, are geared to receive and react to stimuli.

[See also **Brain; Hearing; Integumentary System; Sight; Smell; Taste**]

Stress

Stress is a physical, psychological, or environmental disturbance of the well-being of an organism. The body's nervous and endocrine systems usually respond automatically to stress. Some stress is unavoidable and even natural, but prolonged stress can be harmful.

All organisms seek to maintain homeostasis, which can be described as a balanced, constant, or stable internal environment. Some of the major mechanisms that organisms use to maintain homeostasis include the control of temperature, fluid balance, blood pressure, and the production of energy. The body's many mechanisms and processes are constantly adjusting themselves in order to cope with these highly dynamic internal and external situations. Stress, however, is something that is slightly out of the ordinary.

Stress can be considered something that strains or interferes with the functioning of an organism. Stress is a real challenge to homeostasis. Stress can come in many shapes and forms. It can be temporary or long-lasting, and it can be mild or severe. Stress can be purely physical, such as a lack of food, an injury to a muscle or bone, or an infection. It can be the result of certain undesirable environmental conditions, such as extreme altitude, humidity, heat, or cold. It can also be psychological, such as a person's fear of public speaking, or an animal's fear of being hunted by a predator.

All organisms experience stress at one time or another. While each organism may react differently to stress, all of them experience the same general physiological, or bodily, reactions. Many of these reactions happen without the organism knowing it. Most of these responses are difficult, if not impossible, to consciously control. In humans, most responses are controlled by the body's autonomic nervous system. As it sounds, this is the part of the nervous system that controls involuntary muscles and glands. When a stressful situation is perceived by the nervous system, the brain sends a stimulating message to the adrenal gland. This gland sits above each of the kidneys and secretes adrenalin and other hormones (chemical messengers) when stimulated. These hormones enable a person to be instantly ready for "fight or flight." This means that the major systems take measures to prepare for the worst and get the body ready to fight harder, run faster, and think quicker than normal. The body's heart rate skyrockets and the blood moves from the internal organs to the muscles. The body interrupts all nonessential processes and causes the rate of breathing to speed up, taking in as much oxygen as the body needs. As a result, the body becomes ready to either fight if necessary or use its strength to get away as quickly as possible. Besides adrenaline, the adrenal gland also produces cortisol when stimulated. This powerful hormone provides the body with a ready supply of energy and enables it to function at peak efficiency.

All of these reactions to stress are normal and sometimes necessary for survival. However, prolonged and repeated stress (with no resolution) is damaging to the body. This situation is called chronic stress, and it can be very common given the way people live today. People may encounter situations in everyday life that are not threatening but cause the body to have the same "fight or flight" response, sometimes over and over again. When the body is preparing for a physical extreme, and the situation does not require or permit it, people "stew" in their hormones that are urging them to take action.

Chronic stress can be damaging to the body, since it has been found that regularly high levels of cortisol can damage the body's immune system. Also, steady adrenaline can cause high blood pressure and high cholesterol. Animals often show signs of abnormal behavior when stressed. They may rock or pace when caged too closely together. Plants suffer physical stress when they do not receive enough water or light. Each living thing has developed some ability to cope with stressful situations. For people, it helps to be aware of what makes them feel stressed. If they cannot remove the stressor from their lives, they can attempt to minimize its effects. Relief can come through exercise, meditation, psychotherapy, and biofeedback (in which a person tries to control the body's hormone level). Overall, stress can be a major factor in people's health.

[*See also* **Endocrine System; Homeostasis; Nervous System**]

Survival of the Fittest

Survival of the fittest is a simple way of describing how evolution (the process by which gradual genetic change occurs over time to a group of living things) works. It describes the mechanism of natural selection by explaining how the best-adapted individuals are better suited to their environment. As a result, these individuals are more likely to survive and pass on their genes.

The theory of natural selection was first offered by English naturalist, Charles R. Darwin (1809–1882), during the 1850s to explain how evolution worked. Darwin suggested that all living things were connected to one another because they had evolved from a few common ancestors. He used the mechanism of natural selection to explain how this could be possible. Natural selection is based on the idea that although the individuals that make up a given species all seem alike, there are in fact many important characteristics that make each slightly different from the other. These differences were inherited from the individual's parents. Organisms would pass these differences on to their own offspring if they lived long enough to reproduce.

Darwin's idea proposed that since each individual was different from any other, certain ones possessed particular traits, or characteristics, that favored individual over another. For example, a single pair of rabbits can produce up to six litters a year. Darwin realized that if each of these offspring of every species of rabbits survived to reproduce, the entire world be overrun with rabbits, to the point where there would not be enough resources to keep them all alive. Since there was a limited amount of resources, Darwin argued that each individual had to compete with others for what it needed to stay alive, grow, and reproduce.

Darwin explained that it is the environment or nature itself that "selects" which individuals are best adapted to it or are best "fit." For the six litters of rabbits, those whose particular traits give them an advantage in their particular environment are the ones who most likely will survive. These offspring also will grow strong, and pass on these "fit" traits to their offspring. Depending on the environment, it may not always be the fastest rabbit that survives. Instead, it could be the one with a certain coat color that allows it to be easily camouflaged that has the "fit" advantage. This point was recognized by scientists who adopted the term "fitness" to refer to the members of a group whose traits made them the best-adapted. For this reason, natural selection is often called "survival of the fittest." Darwin did not use these words. Instead, they were first used by the nineteenth-century English philosopher, Herbert Spencer (1820–1903), to help explain Darwin's theory of evolution.

[*See also* **Evolution; Evolutionary Theory; Natural Selection**]

Symbiosis

Symbiosis describes the relationship, close association, or interaction between two organisms of different species. Although the term is often used to describe a relationship that benefits both species, there are different types of symbiosis. Symbiotic relationships that have occurred over very long periods of time can sometimes result in evolutionary changes in the organisms involved in the relationship.

Symbiosis literally means "living together," and there are many examples in nature of organisms of entirely different species that are in-

A cape buffalo with an oxpecker on its back in Kenya, Africa. The relationship between the oxpecker and the buffalo is a type of symbiosis called mutualism since the oxpecker feeds from the supply of ticks on the buffalo, which in turn benefits from the tick removal. (Reproduced by permission of JLM Visuals.)

LYNN MARGULIS

American biologist Lynn Margulis (1938-) has suggested some of the more revolutionary ideas in the history of modern biology. Her symbiotic theory of evolution has offered a new approach to both evolution and the origin of cells within the nucleus. She also subscribes to the "Gaia" hypothesis, which states that the Earth acts a superorganism, or single living system, that can regulate itself.

Lynn Margulis was born in Chicago, Illinois. Her parents, Morris and Leone Alexander, had three other daughters. An exceptional student, Margulis was fifteen when she completed her second year at Hyde Park High School and was accepted into an early entrant program at the University of Chicago. There she was immediately inspired by her science courses and took to reading the original works of the world's great scientists. She also became interested in the deeper aspects of heredity and genetics. While at Chicago, she met Carl Sagan (1934-1996), who would become an astronomer (a person who studies the universe beyond Earth) and one of the best-known scientists in the world. Sagan was a graduate student and Margulis was nineteen in the year she both received her bachelor's degree and married Sagan. She then entered the University of Wisconsin to pursue a joint master's degree in zoology and genetics, and in 1960 she and Sagan moved to the University of California at Berkeley where she conducted genetic research for her doctoral dissertation. The marriage to Sagan produced two sons but ended before she received her Ph.D. in 1965. After teaching at Brandeis University, she joined Boston University and married crystallographer (a person who studies crystal structure) Thomas N. Margulis, with whom she had two children before they divorced in 1980. Since 1988, Margulis has been a distinguished university professor at the University of Massachusetts at Amherst.

Margulis has regularly questioned the commonly accepted theories of genetics yet she has been called the most gifted theoretical biologist of her generation by numerous colleagues. As a graduate student she became in-

volved in some form of close, beneficial relationship or association. In fact, there are some symbiotic relationships that are necessary for the survival of the participating organisms. There are three types of symbiosis—mutualism, commensalism, and parasitism—depending on the nature of the relationship. As with any classification system, there are always exceptions, and sometimes it is difficult to categorize a certain situation. It is also a mistake to make a judgment of one type of symbiosis being better than another, since each is simply an organism's adaptation to survive.

terested in what is called non-Mendelian inheritance, which is when the genetic makeup of a cell's descendants cannot be traced solely to the genes in the cell's nucleus (the cell's control center). This puzzling phenomenon led her to search for genes in the cytoplasm of cells, that is, inside the cell but not inside its nucleus. In the early 1960s, Margulis actually found deoxyribonucleic acid (DNA, which is the carrier of genetic information) in the cytoplasm (jelly-like substance) of plant cells, suggesting that heredity in higher organisms might not be totally determined by genetic information carried only in the cell nucleus. This led her to eventually formulate her most startling idea, called the serial endosymbiotic theory (SET). Margulis stated that prokaryotes (cells that do not have a nucleus, such as very simple life forms like bacteria), which simply carry their genetic information inside the cell's cytoplasm, were the evolutionary forerunners of the more complex eukaryotes (which are cells that have a separate nucleus). All plants and animals have eukaryotic cells. She argued that eukaryotes evolved from prokaryotes when different types of prokaryotes formed symbiotic systems to increase their chances of survival. Symbiosis means that they had some sort of relationship, usually a type of partnership in which both members benefitted. An example of this, she says, is a cell's mitochondria (specialized structures inside a cell that break down food and release energy) that process oxygen.

Most scientists now agree that these cell structures evolved from oxygen-using bacteria, which joined with fermenting bacteria. Margulis is unique in her argument that traditional evolutionary theory cannot explain what she calls the "creative novelty" of life. Margulis also extends her concept of symbiosis to the entire biosphere (that part of Earth that contains life) and therefore accepts the Gaia hypothesis put forth by English chemist James E. Lovelock. This theory states that all life, and Earth itself, including its oceans and the atmosphere, are parts of a single, all-encompassing symbiosis that in turn form a single "organism," or a single living system. For Margulis, the concept of symbiosis is a powerful explanatory tool.

Mutualism is a type of symbiotic relationship that results in a mutual benefit. Both species realize some type of gain by living together and cooperating within the same habitat. An example of mutualism would be the close relationship between a certain bacteria (*Rhizobia*) that lives under the soil and is attached to the roots of certain plants like peas, beans, clover, and alfalfa. These bacteria are nitrogen-fixing, meaning they are able to take in nitrogen gas that exists in the atmosphere and change it into nitrates that plants can use. This plant/bacteria relationship is mutualistic because both organisms benefit: the plant gains the necessary nitrogen in a usable form, and the bacteria gains access to a source of energy (using the plant's ready-made glucose). This is also an example of what is called "obligatory mutualism," since both partners are completely dependent on each other. Another example of this type of mutualism is the lichen, which is really made up of a fungus (plural, fungi), and an alga (plural, algae) living together. An alga can make its own food but can only live in wet places. A fungus cannot make its own food but can store a great deal of water. Together, they can live anywhere since the alga makes food (and lives inside the fungus), while the fungus provides it with its necessary water.

The other form of mutualism is called "facultative" and describes a relationship in which both partners benefit, but which each could still survive if the relationship did not exist. The relationship between the ox-pecker (also called the tickbird) of Africa and the black rhinoceros is a good example, since these birds spend most of their time clinging to the bodies of large animals like the rhinoceros and eating ticks and maggots that infest the rhinoceros' hides. The birds also make a hissing sound that alerts the rhinos to possible danger. The rhinoceros benefits by having blood-sucking insects removed from its body, as well as having an early warning system. However, although both animals benefit from their relationship, the bird could obtain insects elsewhere if the rhino were to vanish, and the rhino could survive being infested with ticks.

Commensalism is the second type of symbiosis and describes a relationship in which one species benefits while the other experiences basically no effect (it neither benefits nor suffers). A bromeliad (an air plant) growing on the high branch of a rainforest tree is an example of such a relationship since it benefits by being closer to the sunlight while the tree is not harmed in any way (it also does not receive anything beneficial from the bromeliad). Another example is the tiny mollusks or crustaceans called barnacles that attach themselves to the body of a humpback whale enjoy the benefit of being moved through the water so they can filter microscopic food. The whale is neither bothered nor benefitted by the mollusks. Commensalism is usually practiced by one species on another to obtain something it cannot provide for itself such as transportation, protection, or nutrition.

Finally, a symbiotic relationship is described as parasitism if it results in the host organism being somehow harmed. In this type of relationship, the organism that benefits is called the parasite, while the organism that the parasite lives in or on is called the host. Disease-producing organisms are probably the best examples of parasitism. Such is the case with a tapeworm that lives inside the digestive organs of mammals. Because the tapeworm takes nutrition from the host, the host is left weakened and may also suffer tissue damage. An example of a strange and interesting form of parasitism is that conducted by a brood parasite. In this phenomenon, one species of animal uses the adult or parent of another species to raise its young. The common cuckoo bird does this regularly by laying its eggs in the nest of a species with similar-looking eggs. As soon as the cuckoo hatches, it pushes all the other eggs from the nest and eats all the food provided by its foster parents (which have been tricked into raising the cuckoo as their own).

[*See also* **Parasite**]

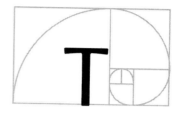

Taiga

The taiga is a geographical region characterized by dense, coniferous (evergreen) forests broken up by bodies of water. With its long, cold winters and low light, the taiga does not support a wide variety of species. However, the taiga covers a larger area than any other type of forest in the world.

The name taiga comes from a Russian word used to describe the evergreen forest of Siberia. It is also called a boreal forest and is taken from the word *boreas* meaning north wind. The taiga is always subject to the north wind because it is located only in the northern latitudes of the Northern Hemisphere, from Alaska, through Canada, across Eurasia, to Siberia where the largest tracts of taiga are located. At a similar latitude in the Southern Hemisphere, the land is too narrow, and therefore influenced by the ocean, to support a taiga-like environment.

PLANT LIFE IN THE TAIGA

A typical taiga forest is cold and dark, and broken up by lakes, rivers, and swamps. The dominant tree is the conifer, an evergreen that reproduces by making cones. The conifer is well-adapted to the taiga. It has branches that slope downward to prevent snow from building up, as well as a pointed shape and flexible trunk to cope with high winds. Growing conditions are harsh, since winters are extremely long. The taiga soil is poor because decomposition (breaking down of waste) takes so long. The soil is also highly acidic and low in minerals. Ground-level vegetation consists mostly of ferns, mosses, and shrubs that have adapted to the short growing season. Because of the slow rate at which things decompose, there are usually dense layers of peat (rotted vegetable matter) in the ever-present bog (wet, spongy ground consisting of decaying plant matter).

ANIMAL LIFE IN THE TAIGA

Animal life in the taiga includes woodland caribou, moose, brown bears, beaver, lynx, and wolves. Most animal life is medium to small-sized, including rodents, rabbits, sable, and mink. Most birds migrate (seasonally move) to warmer climates for the winter. Swarms of biting insects during the summer make the taiga a miserable place for humans and other warm-blooded animals (their internal temperature remains constant despite their environment). Most of the taiga is not well-suited for farming, although it does yield great quantities of lumber and support a fur trade in mink, sable, and ermine, among others.

[*See also* **Biome**]

Autumn colors of a taiga in Alaska. *Taiga* is a Russian word that means "land of little sticks." (©Photographer, The National Audubon Society Collection/Photo Researchers, Inc.)

Taste

Taste is the sense that enables an organism to detect dissolved chemicals. It serves primarily to tell an animal the difference between something that is good to eat and something that is dangerous. As one of the five senses, the sense of taste is closely associated with the sense of smell. Taste is influenced by habit, learning, and other cultural and psychological factors.

HOW THE SENSE OF TASTE WORKS

Humans are born with the ability to taste. The sense of taste begins with the tongue. The skin over this muscular organ located inside the mouth is covered with about 10,000 receptor cells, or chemical-sensing bodies. These are called taste buds. Each of these funnel-shaped clusters has an opening called a taste pore. Molecules (small particles) of dissolved substances, containing chemicals, flow into these holes and trigger, or activate, a receptor cell.

The taste buds also respond to other stimuli. When people smell or think of a food they like, their mouth starts to water. This means that people start to produce saliva. In order for humans to actually taste something, it has to be dissolved in saliva. Like smell (called olfaction), taste (also called gustation) operates on the principle of chemoreception. Certain receptors are triggered when chemicals contact them. It was once thought that certain parts of the tongue responded only to one of the four basic categories or sensations of taste (sweet, sour, bitter, salty). Now it is thought that individual receptors are not specifically sensitive to only one sensation.

Unless the brain is involved in this process, a person will not be able to actually identify anything he or she has dissolved on the tongue. Science still does not know exactly how this occurs. Somehow, when a dissolved molecule triggers a taste bud, or cell, certain nerves at the root of the cell are also stimulated. These carry impulses to the brain stem, then to the thalamus or the front of the brain stem. The impulses finally end up in the cerebral cortex of the brain, the brain's taste control center. The brain interprets this signal, or impulse, and tells people what they are tasting. As with each of the senses, all of this happens instantaneously.

THE SENSE OF TASTE IN ANIMALS

Some invertebrates (organisms without a backbone) do not have a separate sense of taste or smell. Both are linked in a sense called chemoreception, which means the ability to detect chemicals. Single-celled protozoans as well as most insects and crustaceans (like crabs, shrimp, and lobster) all use chemoreception.

Among vertebrates (animals with a backbone), the organs of taste can be very different. Although birds have their taste receptors on their tongues, adult amphibians, like frogs and toads, and certain fish have chemical receptors in their mouths and over parts of their skin. Most mammals have their taste receptors on their tongue.

THE SENSE OF TASTE IN HUMANS

The sense of taste plays an important evolutionary role for all animals. It allows them to know what is good to eat and what is to be avoided. A fruit that has not yet ripened usually tastes very sour. Humans will probably not eat much of it since they cannot tolerate something that is strongly sour. On the other hand, ripe fruit tastes sweet—a taste people prefer. Interestingly, many plants that are toxic to people also have a sour

The taste regions of the tongue (left) and taste bud anatomy (right). (Illustration by Hans & Cassidy. Courtesy of Gale Research.)

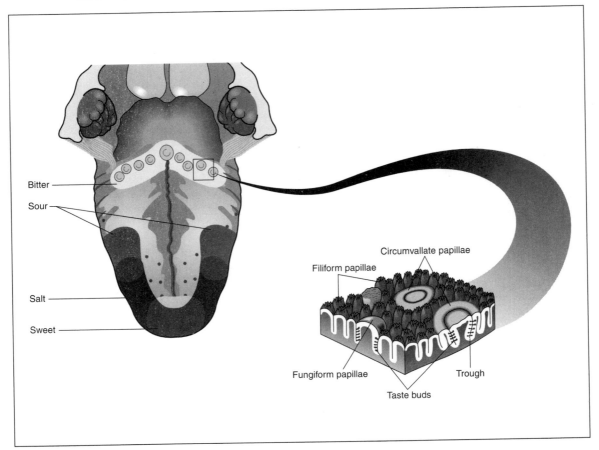

Bitter

Sour

Salt

Sweet

Circumvallate papillae

Filiform papillae

Fungiform papillae

Trough

Taste buds

or bitter taste. When the body is salt-depleted from overwork, it usually craves something salty to eat. Babies who are Vitamin D deficient seem to prefer the strong fishy taste of cod-liver oil, whereas it seems to revolt almost everyone else.

In humans, taste is also affected by other sensations such as temperature, texture or feel, and even looks. Certain foods have a particular feel in people's mouths that affect whether or not they like them. Some cold drinks are not good at room temperature. Finally, human culture, habit, and learning play a major role in what people find appetizing and enjoyable to eat. For many people, these psychological factors are even more important than their basic biological needs.

[*See also* **Organ; Sense Organ**]

Taxonomy

Taxonomy is the science of classifying living things. It follows rules and procedures for classifying organisms according to their differences and similarities. Classifying living things enables scientists to see how an organism is related to others and to trace its evolution (the process by which gradual genetic change occurs over time to a group of living things).

Until modern taxonomy was invented by the Swedish naturalist, Carolus Linnaeus (1707–1778), a name for any given organism was usually a long, detailed description rather than an actual name. Since there were no rules, or standards, to follow when naming a newly discovered form of life, most people went about it in an unscientific and rather individual way. Linnaeus realized that some system of order had to be imposed on the great diversity of life if people were to understand one another. As a result, Linnaeus not only devised a system that identified and named each living thing, but was able to place each living thing in one of several related categories.

HIERARCHICAL CLASSIFICATION

Most people do this type of organizing in their daily lives without thinking about it. For example, a music store groups all CDs together and keeps them separate from music on tape. Within the CD section, the store makes more detailed categories of music, like rock, jazz, hip-hop, and others. Within one of these categories, it may further break it down into groups or solo artists, and alphabetize within one of those categories. This type of systematic arranging that goes from general groups to more specific groups is called hierarchical classification.

It was hierarchical thinking that Linnaeus used when he first built his classification system. He divided all forms of life into the first and largest group called kingdoms. In the mid-eighteenth century, science recognized only two kingdoms, plant and animal. With more knowledge, scientists have added three more: fungi, protists, and bacteria.

Taxonomy is an always-growing and adaptable science that allows room for additions, changes, and even corrections. As a result, each kingdom was divided into smaller and smaller categories, with each level more general than the one below it. These seven categories are kingdom, phylum, class, order, family, genus, and species. A useful trick to remember this order is the sentence, *"King Philip Came Over From Great Spain."* These categories, or taxonomic groupings, are also called taxa (singular, taxon). For example, the taxon Carnivora is an order that includes many different families. Amazingly, the seven taxa, or hierarchical levels, that were finalized by Linnaeus in 1758 are still the ones used today.

BINOMIAL SYSTEM OF NOMENCLATURE

Linnaeus made another major contribution to organizing the natural world. He gave a two-part scientific name to every living thing. Since this method was based on certain standards, or rules, and was made up from Greek or Latin words, it gave everyone an agreed-upon name to use for a particular organism. This system avoided the confusion that could arise when different languages or countries used different names for the same animal. It also allowed all scientists to speak the same language. As a result, a Russian researcher knows exactly what organism is discussed in a paper published by a French biologist.

The Linnean system came to be called the "binomial system of nomenclature," and there are several strictly followed rules that govern its use. The system uses two Latin names—the genus and species to which an organism belongs—for its scientific name. Binomial names are always underlined or italicized. The first letter of the genus is always capitalized, while the species is always written in lowercase letters. For instance, *Homo sapiens* is the scientific name for humans. The genus name may be used alone, but the particular species name is never used without the genus name. There are now taxonomic rules that govern the worldwide classification of organisms. No changes can be made without the approval of the appropriate international body.

NEW METHODS OF CLASSIFICATION

Since taxonomy is an evolving science, it is not surprising that it includes more sophisticated ways of grouping and classifying organisms.

One new method is to take into account new molecular and biochemical information. Another looks only at the chromosomes (coiled structures in the nucleus of a cell that carries the cell's genetic information) of an organism to see how it the organism is related to others. In many ways, the aim of modern taxonomy is to arrive at an evolutionary-based classification system that will let scientists see more clearly the real relationships between all living organisms.

[*See also* **Class; Classification; Family; Genus; Kingdom; Order; Phylum; Species**]

Territory

A territory is an area that an animal claims as its own and that it will defend against rivals. Competition for territory often comes from within an animal's own species. Territorial animals usually have a better chance at survival and reproduction than animals with no territory of their own.

Many animals that reproduce sexually exhibit a type of behavior that is called territorial. These animals will defend a certain territory or portion of their habitat against other individuals of their own species. Territoriality is often described as adaptive behavior. This means that being territorial somehow works to the advantage of the organism that engages in this behavior. Being territorial means being willing to defend a certain area by using threats or by engaging in actual fighting. Studies have shown that when an animal is successfully territorial (meaning that it is able to exert control over a certain area and keep all rivals out) it obtains many benefits, all of which have survival value. One of these benefits could be protection from other species that want to eat it. Other benefits might be plentiful food and safe breeding areas. A male animal that controls a certain area also demonstrates its dominance to females. These females may then want to mate with the territorial male.

An animal may choose a particular area as its place to defend for many reasons. Whatever the reasons, they all are based on the idea that the place contains resources vital to the animal's survival. Territories are usually smaller segments of a larger habitat, but some predators, like wolves, actually claim and defend several square miles of territory. On the other hand, a sea bird may be territorial only around its actual nesting site.

Territoriality can be permanent, as when an eagle returns to and will defend the same general area every nesting season. Prairie dogs remain

IVAN PETROVICH PAVLOV

Russian physiologist (a person who studies how an organism and its body parts work or function normally) Ivan Pavlov (1849–1936) is best known for his systematic studies of the conditioning of dogs. His work on animal behavior and inborn reflexes revealed a great deal about animals' true nature. His work has also been applied to understanding human learning behavior.

Ivan Pavlov was born in Ryazan, in western Russia. Since his father was a priest, it was expected that he would become one too, and he was sent to study at a theological seminary. There, however, the young man somehow happened to read English naturalist Charles Darwin's *On the Origin of Species,* and he turned immediately toward the study of science. By the time he was twenty-one, he had transferred from the seminary and the study of religion to St. Petersburg University and the study of science. There he had the good fortune to study with two of Russia's best chemists, and in 1879 he received his medical degree from the St. Petersburg Military Medical Academy. Four years later he earned his Ph.D. For the next few years he studied and did more research in Germany, and by 1890 he had returned to St. Petersburg and become a professor of physiology there.

By then, Pavlov had already begun his surgical experiments on the physiology of digestion (how digestion actually works). He demonstrated this skill by actually disconnecting a dog's esophagus (the tube leading to its stomach) so that when the dog ate, the food would drop out and not enter the stomach. Since he found that the stomach produced gastric juice as if there were food being put in it, he suggested correctly that a message must have been sent from the brain by way of nerves to the digestive glands, which then secreted the gastric juices. This helped establish the importance of the autonomic nervous system, which is that part of the nervous

in the same burrows all their lives and will drive away any others of its species. Territoriality can also be temporary, as when a bird abandons a certain shrub on which it has been feeding after the bush stops producing the food it needs. Possessing control means benefits to the territorial animal, but it also means that the animal must expend some resources to enforce that control.

The most important of these enforcing actions is called marking. Many animals use their own urine or feces to mark the perimeter (boundary) of their territory. Dogs and cats do this, although they will also "mark" another's territory temporarily as they are passing through it. Other marking systems includes howls and shrieks by monkeys and sea lions, calls and whistles by birds, and aggressive displays and warnings by certain system that controls an animal's involuntary actions. It was for this work on the physiology of digestion that Pavlov won the 1904 Nobel Prize in physiology and medicine. He then went on to develop the idea of the conditioned reflex, the discovery for which he is most famous. Pavlov began this work studying an animal's natural reflexes, which could be described as the simplest form of instinct. Instinct is a behavior pattern that is inherited, or which is built into its nervous system. Instinct is thus handed down from one generation to another. It was Pavlov's goal to see if he could somehow change, or alter, in some way an animal's instincts. Noticing that a dog would naturally salivate, or drool, when it thought it was about to be fed, he rang a bell before giving it food. Soon the dog would salivate whenever Pavlov rang the bell, whether food was produced or not. With this, Pavlov had actually changed its natural reflex and developed in the dog what he called a learned, or a conditioned, reflex. This led to his theory that a good part of an animal's behavior patterns are actually the result of conditioned reflexes.

The notion of an animal's territory is a good example of instinctive behavior. In territorial species, or those that will defend a certain part of a habitat against intruders, this behavior is simply part of their genetic makeup. When a male bird selects a territory at the beginning of the breeding season, he does this because of the high concentration of sex hormones in his blood. Despite the fact that territoriality is an inborn trait for many species, Pavlov's work demonstrated that it, like most other instinctual behavior patterns, can be conditioned or modified. Pavlov's contribution of the notion of the conditioned reflex showed life scientists that an animal's reaction is not always purely instinctive but may also have been somehow learned through a sequence of associations.

animals if a rival gets too close. Bears are known to scratch deep gouges on certain trees as markers.

Although territoriality may sometime involve conflict or actual fighting, studies have shown that in the long run, it tends to reduce conflict within a species. Once territories are established and understood, most respect the boundaries of others and fighting actually diminishes. This might have something to do with another interesting fact. In most species, the "owner" of a certain territory almost always wins a fight with an intruder, often despite a difference in size. It has been shown that the same animal that acts timid and surrenders in a conflict located on neutral ground becomes an unbeatable fighter when it is defending its "home field." Scientists also say that individual humans are often territorial when they display a need for privacy or for personal space in crowded situations.

Tissue

Tissue is the name for a group of similar cells that have a common structure and function and which work together. Tissues fit together to form organs in higher animals These animals have four basic types of tissue.

The animal body is made up of many different kinds of cells. These specialize to perform certain functions, or specific tasks. A group of closely associated or similar cells that work together to do one thing is called a tissue. All the cells in a tissue look very similar and all do the same work.

A microscopic view of human fetal tissue. (Reproduced by Custom Medical Stock Photo, Inc.)

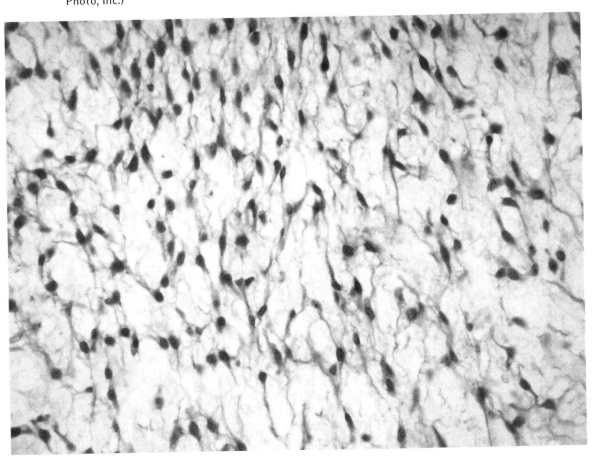

TYPES OF TISSUE

There are four types of animal tissue: epithelial, connective, muscle, and nervous tissue. Every cell in each of these tissues is an independent unit, yet all of the cells in a given tissue interact with one another. They must do this in order to perform a certain necessary function for the animal's body. For example, an animal's brain is made of nerve tissue that is composed of millions of connected nerve cells. In animals, when two or more tissues are associated and work together, they form an organ such as the stomach or the heart.

The same is true for plants, except they have only three types of tissue. Plant tissue, like animal tissue, is also organized into organs, so that epidermal plant tissue makes up the organ known as a leaf. For both plants and animals, a tissue is the "stuff," or specific type of cellular material, out of which specialized organs are made.

HUMAN TISSUE

As animals, humans have four different types of tissues: epithelial, connective, muscle, and nervous tissue.

Epithelial Tissue. The epithelial tissue, whose closely packed cells make it ideal for forming a lining or a covering, is what makes up the skin. This tissue also makes up the lining for the organs and the many passageways. Because its cells are so tightly packed together, it allows the skin to be an excellent barrier and protects the body against injury and invading microorganisms (any form of life that is too small to be seen without a microscope). It also regulates fluid loss.

Nervous Tissue. The nervous tissue is made up of cells called neurons. These are designed to carry impulses. This highly specialized tissue carries electrical signals from one part of the body to another and allows it to function as an organized unit.

Muscle Tissue. Muscle tissue is responsible for producing movement. Its cells are designed to work by contracting and relaxing. They also are built to respond to stimuli transmitted by neurons. There are three types of muscle tissue. Smooth muscle makes up organs that people do not control, such as the intestines. Striated, or skeletal muscle, is under people's control and makes up the muscles that allow people to move. Cardiac muscle is also called heart muscle and is responsible for the regular and powerful contraction of the heart. Unlike skeletal muscle, it never needs to rest.

Connective Tissue. Finally, connective tissue is the most common tissue in the body, and it is what holds the entire body together. Bone, cartilage, and blood are made of connective tissue. Bone is a type of mineralized connective tissue, cartilage is found between joints, and blood is considered to be a connective tissue in liquid form since it circulates throughout the body.

PLANT TISSUE

Plants have three types of tissue. Their epidermal tissue serves a purpose similar to humans, in that it covers the surfaces of leaves, stems, and roots and protects its inner parts. The tissue through which a plant transports materials is called its vascular tissue. Its cells are elongated and form tubelike organs. The rest of a plant is made up of what is called fundamental plant tissue. In plants and animals then, tissues are the intermediary stage between an organism's individual cells and its specialized organs. Therefore, cells are arranged into groups, called tissues, and tissues are eventually grouped into organs.

[*See also* **Cell; Organ**]

Touch

Touch is the sense that enables an organism to get information about things that are in direct contact with its body. As one of the five senses, touch allows a person to feel heat, cold, pain, and pressure. Touch is a very important sense, since it tells an organism a great deal about its immediate environment.

Touch is one of the least-thought about senses, perhaps because it does not involve a complex and highly specialized organ or specific organs that are identified with that sense. The eyes, ears, nose, and mouth are linked immediately and automatically with vision, hearing, smell, and taste. Yet the sense of touch is identified with the largest organ in the human body—the skin.

HOW THE SENSE OF TOUCH WORKS

Touch is detected by sensory nerves in the skin called "mechanoreceptors." These receptors are designed to respond to specific stimuli, because touch actually involves a variety of very different sensations. On the human body, there are well more than 500,000 sensory cells unevenly distributed over the skin's surface, and not all of them are alike. There are at least a half dozen different types of known touch receptor cells in humans. Some respond to light pressure, others to vibrations, and others to pain or temperature changes.

Each of these different types of receptors has a different structure. For example, capsule-like receptors called "Merkel's discs" are located in parts of the body that are extremely sensitive, such as the fingertips. As one would expect, there are far fewer of these type of cells where there is less need for them, such as on a person's leg or shoulders. Certain other parts of the body have uncovered nerve endings called "free endings." The skin around the hair roots has the largest amount of these free nerve endings.

In order for a person to feel sensation, one of these points on the skin must be stimulated in some way. When this happens, the receptor cells respond by generating a nerve impulse. The impulse is transmitted along pathways via the spinal cord to the brain. The nerves that carry impulses or information from the skin to the spinal cord are called spinal nerves. Each pair of these nerves transmits signals from a particular skin area. The first stop in the brain is the thalamus. The thalamus directs the signals to the appropriate part of the brain's cerebral cortex (the outer layer of gray matter covering the cerebrum) responsible for processing touch information. The brain then decides whether to pay attention to the signal and if so, how to respond to it. These steps all must happen instantaneously, since any sort of delay could mean serious injury or worse.

Little is known about the exact way that the brain interprets what is basically a coded impulse, which it then converts into the actual sensation that we experience or feel. The normal brain correctly lets people feel pain when they burn their finger, and pleasure when a sore muscle is massaged. It also allows people to gently squeeze a fruit and tell if it is ripe, sense an ant crawling up their leg, check a child's temperature with their hand, or "read" the raised dots of a Braille book. Touch also acts as an early warning system, informing people of serious or dangerous conditions before they encounter them fully.

THE SENSE OF TOUCH IN ANIMALS

The sense of touch is no less important for all other organisms. The variety found in the sense organs of animals is based on evolution according to the particular needs of the species. In other words, nature keeps what works best, even if it is a little different. Examples from nature make this point very well. The overly large ears of most rabbits best serve an animal whose first and only defense is a quick getaway. Rabbits' acute hearing sometimes gives then a slight edge over predators. As for the sense of touch, certain animals rely more on this sense than others. An earthworm that spends its life crawling about and has a minimal amount of specialized organs has special hairs that generate a nerve impulse when they contact something. Some insects have similar hairs on their legs and antennas that "touch" the air and sense changes in currents. This is why it is so difficult to swat a housefly, which knows what is coming by the moving air it senses.

Fish also have a sense of touch founded in their lateral line. These are nerves running lengthwise on their bodies that allow them to detect the presence of nearby organisms or objects. The tongues and beaks of many birds have a well-developed sense of touch. The whiskers of a cat or a rat enable them to "feel" things with their long bristles almost in the way humans do with their fingertips.

For all organisms, including humans, touch allows us to coordinate bodily movements. Because of touch, people unconsciously sense where their legs, arms, head, eyes, muscles, and internal organs are. Touch disorders can range from the minor but troublesome itching caused by allergies, diseases, infections, or bites. Numbness or pins-and-needles can signal a more serious nerve injury or can result from a blood clot, tumor, heart attack, or stroke. Chronic pain, which has no explanation, is another type of touch disorder.

THE BENEFITS OF TOUCH

Science has only recently realized that touching and being touched has important psychological and physical advantages, especially to mammals. It is now known that the stimulation of the skin an infant receives by being held while feeding is as important as the food. Studies have shown that in cases where mammals, like a cow or horse, lick their newborn, licking the skin actually stimulates the nervous system and gets it working. Newborn animals that are not licked usually die, because their intestinal or urinary systems never begin working. Human babies that were never held often display signs of "failure to thrive." Finally, humans have a psychological need to touch and be touched. For example, studies have shown that seniors who live alone but have an animal to care for and "pet," are in better health and spirits than those who do not.

[*See also* **Organ; Sense Organ**]

Toxins and Poisons

Toxins and poisons are chemical substances that destroy life or impair the function of living tissue and organs. Although used interchangeably, a toxin is usually considered to be any poison produced by an organism.

A poison, however, is more generally any type of substance that harms an organism by its chemical action.

As a chemical harmful to living things, a poison can be almost anything. Nearly every prescribed drug can have negative effects if taken in the wrong dosage. In certain situations, whether or not something is harmful depends entirely on the dosage or amount taken. Other substances can be beneficial to one living form (penicillin cures a sick person) but deadly to another (it kills bacteria). Although in common usage, the words toxic and poisonous are often used interchangeably, as are the words toxin and poison, it is safe to say that poison is the broader term.

Poisons are so diverse in their origin, chemistry, and toxic action that it is nearly impossible to classify them simply. Many have natural origins, such as those that are produced by living things. Some of the most potent toxins known are produced by simple bacteria. For example, bacteria are responsible for the diseases botulism, diphtheria, and tetanus.

All of these common household products are toxic and poisonous when absorbed into the systems of humans and animals. (Reproduced by permission of Field Mark Publications. Photograph by Robert J. Huffman.)

Certain mushrooms are highly toxic, while a fungus is responsible for the usually deadly disease called ergotism. More complex plants contain a large variety of poisonous substances that are part of the alkaloid group. Many of the better-known drugs, such as quinine, curare, morphine, and nicotine, come from this family of plants. These drugs can be poisonous depending on the dosage. Many animals also produce toxins, including certain snakes, frogs, and insects. A mammal, like the shrew, can produce a poison in its salivary glands.

Poisons are also found in the nonliving part of the natural world. Some organic elements like mercury, arsenic, and lead, all called heavy metals, are poisonous when absorbed into the systems of living things. Many strong acids and bases are damaging to soft tissues. A number of gases, like chlorine and ammonia, are toxic even at low doses. Many alcohols and solvents (a liquid that dissolves other substances) can do extreme damage to people's organs, while many plastics made from petroleum can be toxic. As a result, today's industrial society has come to present people with a major source of human-made poisons.

The action of these and other poisons is generally described in terms of what part of the body they affect or what biochemical changes they produce. While the actual chemical mechanism may be different for each poison, they can be grouped generally according to their effects. Many poisons block, or inhibit, something that should be happening in the body. Thus, the toxic gas carbon monoxide makes the body's cells unable to transport necessary oxygen. Other poisons prevent a certain critical enzyme (a protein that acts as a catalyst and speeds up chemical reactions in living things) from being released, while others block a crucial step in a person's metabolism (which are all of the chemical reactions and sequences that happen in living things).

The effects of toxins are classified according to time-based categories. That is, an acute effect happens immediately, as would the distress caused by a venomous snake bite. Acute effects often involve damage to organs. If the effects appear over days, weeks, or months, they are called subacute. For example, a tetanus infection takes some time to develop and show its worst symptoms. Effects that appear very gradually and last for an extended period of time are called chronic effects. A cancer caused by exposure to toxic waste is described as chronic. Often, an individual's susceptibility to toxins and poisons varies depending on his or her genetic background, age, weight, gender, overall health, and previous exposure to the toxin or poison.

[*See also* **Pollution**]

Tree

A tree is a tall, woody plant with one main trunk and many branches. It is perennial (grows for many years) and distinguished from a shrub by its size (usually 15 feet [4.6 meters] or taller) as well as by its single woody stem or trunk. A shrub is a short, woody plant that usually divides at its base. Trees are the most visible and dominate part of a forest. They also play an important role in the world's environment and economy.

Trees vary greatly in size, with the tallest being the redwood trees of coastal California that reach well over 350 feet (106.7 meters). Trees began their evolution more than 400,000,000 years ago. The oldest known living trees are the bristlecone pine (*Pinus aristata*) growing in the Rocky Mountains which are believed to be more than 4,500 years old. The widest tree is a giant sequoia (*Sequoia gigantea*) growing in central California. Nicknamed the "General Sherman," it has a circumference (measured completely around) of 115 feet (35.1 meters). Trees also make up the largest living organism in the world, with some stands or groups of trembling aspen trees covering as many as 100 acres (404,700 square meters). These trees reproduce by sending out roots that send up new sprouts that in turn become trees. Since the trees are all genetically identical and actually con-

A pine forest. Pine trees are classified as conifers because they reproduce using cones. Pine trees also are classified as softwoods. (Reproduced by permission of JLM Visuals.)

nected, they can be said to represent a single organism. Trees are found in every region of the world except deserts, the Arctic, and Antarctica.

Woody plants, like trees, have tough stems covered by bark that do not die when the growing season has ended. It is their tough, woody stems that allow them to grow as tall as they do. Trees can be divided by the type of wood they form. Conifers (produced in cones) like pine and spruce are called softwoods, while most others are considered hardwood. A tree is like any other green plant in that it draws in water from its roots and makes food in its leaves through photosynthesis (the process by which plants use light energy to make food from simple chemicals). Deciduous trees, like maples and oaks, lose their leaves for a season and grow new, flat broadleaves each spring. Evergreen trees, like pines, are always covered with leaves (which have evolved into sharp needles), although they are constantly losing them and replacing them in small numbers. As with all plants, trees are either angiosperms (producing flowers and seeds with coverings), or gymnosperms (producing naked seeds). Conifers are gymnosperms since they produce seeds on modified leaf structures called scales that are on their cones. Most other trees produce flowers and are angiosperms. While spring flowers on a fruit tree are obvious and beautiful, the flowers on some trees do not resemble anything like a flower. The age of a tree can be determined by counting its rings after it has been cut down. Each year new wood is formed in a layer that is outside that of the previous year's wood growth. Very dry years result in thin rings, and years of good rainfall result in thicker rings.

Forests of trees have been called the "lungs of the world," since they provide an enormous amount of oxygen to the environment as a by-product of photosynthesis. Besides providing oxygen, trees and the forests they make up form the habitat for many animals, and virtually every part of a tree has been put to some use by humans—even a tree's sap and bark. Trees supply wood for fuel as well as for lumber, paper, and plastic products. Humans dependence on trees for products has begun to have a negative impact on forests. Today, deforestation is a growing problem, especially in less developed countries where trees are being cut down faster than they are able to grow.

[See also **Forest; Plants; Rain Forests**]

Tundra

The tundra is a geographical region that is a cold, treeless, boggy (wet, spongy ground) plain with a permanently frozen layer of subsoil. Its harsh conditions will not support a wide variety of species. Tundra occupies approximately one-fifth of Earth's land surface.

The tundra can be found only in the extreme northern latitudes where snow melts only in the summertime. It has extremely long, cold winters and short, cool summers, along with regularly low precipitation. Despite receiving barely more rain than a desert does, it is among the wettest landscapes on Earth. This is because it is usually overcast, which minimizes evaporation. All tundra have permafrost, which is a layer of permanently frozen earth that lies just below the surface. This permafrost (permanently frozen subsoil) also prevents water from draining downward. For about fifty days in the summer, the tundra has temperatures warm enough to partially thaw the permafrost. The name tundra comes from the Finnish word *tunturi* meaning "completely treeless heights." All tundra are treeless, mainly because tree roots could only spread horizontally along the surface of the ground since they cannot penetrate the permafrost. These roots would therefore not be able to anchor themselves and grow tall.

A view of the alpine tundra in Kizlar Sivrisi, Turkey. (Reproduced by permission of JLM Visuals.)

PLANT LIFE IN THE TUNDRA

As with every demanding climate, the plants and animals that live in the tundra have adapted to it in order to live. The soil that lies above the permafrost is a thin layer of cold, moist earth that contains little nutrients for plants. The cold kills off most of the bacteria, so decomposition (breaking down of waste) barely occurs. The common plants found in all parts of the tundra are blankets of fast-growing moss and lichen. Both are able to grow or go dormant at any time and can quickly respond to any sudden weather change. Wildflowers do bloom, however, sometimes through the melting snow so as to take full advantage of the short summer growing season.

ANIMAL LIFE IN THE TUNDRA

The animals that survive in the tundra are also well-adapted to its demands. The larger animals, like the musk ox and polar bear, are well insulated by thick fur. Other predators like the Arctic wolf, wolverine, peregrine falcon, snowy owl, and white fox, prey on lemmings and Arctic ground squirrels. Caribou also migrate (seasonally move) from the taiga (coniferous forest) to the tundra in the summertime in search of food. Many birds migrate north to the tundra in summer to nest and feed on heavy swarms of insects. There are no reptiles or amphibians in the tundra.

Because of its scarce resources and delicate balances, the tundra is one of nature's more delicate biomes (particular types of large geographic regions). It has been shown that the tundra is most susceptible to environmental damage, mainly because it takes so long to regenerate after being disturbed. Ecologists know that even small disturbances can have immediate and devastating chain reactions throughout the entire system.

[*See also* **Biome**]

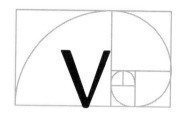

Vacuole

A vacuole is a large, fluid-filled storage sac inside a cell. Many types of cells contain vacuoles, but they are most prominent in plant cells. A vacuole can store materials that a cell needs. It also provides the necessary internal pressure for a plant to remain erect and not wilt.

A vacuole is an organelle or a specialized structure inside a cell that has a particular function. Its main purpose involves storage and transport of materials inside a cell. Vacuoles in animal cells can store a variety of substances, including lipids (a kind of fat) and carbohydrates. In plants, vacuoles are very prominent, and when seen under a microscope they appear as large, round, clear structures. Vacuoles are filled with a watery fluid called cell sap (made up of water, salts, and sugar). In some plant cells, a vacuole may occupy as much as 90 percent of a cell's total volume. When a vacuole takes up this much space in a cell, it presses the cytoplasm (jelly-like fluid in a cell) against the cell wall, which eventually remains stretched out under this force. As long as the vacuole remains full, the plant maintains its turgor pressure (like the air pressing against the inside wall of a balloon). When the vacuole loses this fluid and decreases the pressure, it collapses temporarily and the plant wilts. Maintaining this cellular pressure is the prime responsibility of the vacuole in a mature plant. When pressure is maintained, the entire plant is able to keep its crisp shape. When it does not, the whole plant wilts.

[*See also* **Cell; Organelle; Plant Anatomy**]

Vascular Plants

Vascular plants are plants with specialized tissue that act as a pipeline for carrying the food and water they need. All plants, except bryophytes like mosses, liverworts, and hornworts, have developed special, internal systems to transport their requirements from one part to another. Vascular plants have systems that move nutrients and water from the soil to the stems and leaves and transport food to where it is needed.

A green plant is about 90 percent water, but it loses much of its water through evaporation from its leaves. Because of this, plants need a steady supply of water to grow and reproduce. Much of this need for water is satisfied by the plant's root system that develops in a network spreading down and out from the stem. Once the roots reach water, however, they must be able to get the water back up to the branches and leaves. Plants are able to achieve this by having tissues, or cells that are specialized, to perform a particular function. Tissue moves water is called vascular tissue. Vascular comes from the Latin for "little vessel." There are two types of vascular tissue in a plant: xylem tissue and phloem tissue. The xylem is a ring or a series of hollow tubes that extend from the roots, up through the stem, and out to every branch and leaf. The xylem is located near the surface of the stem and in a tree, it forms a band just below the bark. The xylem is made up of dead, hollow cells arranged end-to-end so that they look like a tube or a straw. The xylem carries water and minerals, like sap, from the roots on a one-way trip to the stem and leaves.

The second part of a plant's circulatory system is the vascular tissue called phloem. Unlike xylem, the cells that make up phloem are living. The phloem carries food (in the form of organic molecules) that the leaves and stems have made by photosynthesis (the process by which plants use light energy to make food from simple chemicals) to parts of the plant that are unable to make their own food (such as the roots and stem tip). In a vascular plant, xylem and phloem are always found together in groups that are called vascular bundles. These bundles may be distributed evenly through the body of a stem, grouped in rings near the outside, or found in a ring in the outer part of the stem according to the type of plant.

Water and minerals are moved from the belowground roots to the aboveground stem and leaves by a phenomenon known as water potential. Although plants do not have a pump (as animals have a heart) to push water up from their roots, they nonetheless are able to move water upwards by water potential without expending any energy. Water potential works according to the laws of physics. When a wet and dry place are joined by a tube of water, the water always flows toward the dry area. This is similar to the law of physics that says when hot and cold objects come together, the heat always travels toward the cold. In a plant, there is usually a large moisture difference between roots (which are surrounded by water) and leaves (which are constantly losing water through their surface pores). This steady water loss is called transpiration. As the roots absorb water, the pressure builds up in them, causing the water to move up the xylem to the drier parts of the plant (stem and leaves). As a result of water potential and transpiration, water always moves on its own from the roots to the leaves.

Plants also rely on the water supplied by their vascular systems to keep their shape. Water that is drawn into its cells create what is called "turgor pressure" and, like an inflated balloon, the cell becomes full or rigid. If a plant loses more water through its leaves than it is able to take in from its roots, it will lose some of this turgor and begin to go limp or wilt. If such a situation continues for any length of time, the plant will eventually die.

[*See also* **Plant Anatomy**]

Vertebrates

A vertebrate is an animal with a backbone. They also have internal skeletons and a system of muscles and bones that allows them to move about easily. All vertebrates have bilateral symmetry, well-developed body systems, and a brain that controls many functions. Vertebrates are divided into five groups, all of which vary in structure, life cycle, and behavior. These five groups are further divided according to whether or not they are cold-blooded or warm-blooded.

CHARCTERISTICS OF VERTEBRATES

All five major classes of vertebrates—fish, amphibians, reptiles, birds, and mammals—belong to the phylum Chordata. The animals in these five classes all have a true backbone, meaning that it is made of bone and not cartilage. A backbone, or spinal column, is made up of individual vertebra (plural, vertebrae) that first form as cartilage in the embryonic stage and then ossify, or harden, into bone. The vertebrae all lock together and give the entire column rigidity and support as well as flexibility. The vertebrae are separated and cushioned from each other by soft, flexible structures known as discs. Inside the hollow center of each vertebra runs a col-

ALFRED SHERWOOD ROMER

American paleontologist (a person who studies animals, plants, and other organisms that lived in prehistoric times) Alfred Romer (1894–1973) was one of the most influential evolutionary biologists of the twentieth century. Romer's detailed studies of the evolution of extinct fishes, amphibians, and reptiles enabled him to be able to trace the basic changes in their structure and function that came about as they evolved into more complex land animals. As the ultimate authority on the evolution of vertebrates, Romer can be said to have demonstrated Darwin's ideas.

Alfred Romer was born in White Plains, New York, the son of a newspaper man. Since his family moved many times, he was eventually sent back to White Plains at the age of fifteen to live with his grandmother. At age eighteen, he spent a year doing odd jobs to earn money for college, and entered Amherst College entirely on his own initiative. He was able to pay for his schooling through scholarships, jobs, and loans, and finally graduated in 1917 knowing that he wanted to become a paleontologist (one who studies the life of the past by examining its fossil remains). During World War I (1914–18), the army sent Romer to France, and on his return home in 1919, he entered graduate school at Columbia University and earned his Ph.D. in

umn of soft nervous tissue called the spinal cord that is connected to the brain and is an essential part of the animal's nervous system. The hard, bony, yet flexible vertebrae protect the delicate cord.

Vertebrates also have several other things in common. All have what might be called a "head end" containing a control center and sensory organs. As vertebrates are forward-moving animals, it is important that their sense organs be located in the front-most part of their bodies. Vertebrates also have bilateral symmetry, which means that a line drawn lengthwise (top-to-bottom) through the center of the body divides it into halves that are mirror images of each other. This could only be the case for an animal that has a head end, a tail end, and a right and left side.

All vertebrates have an endoskeleton, which is a hard bone and cartilage framework located inside their bodies and which supports and maintains their body shape. An endoskeleton linked to a system of muscles enables vertebrates to move. Vertebrates also have a brain and highly developed nervous systems. Finally, vertebrates have a closed circulatory system and a well-developed heart that pumps blood to all parts of the body. Although there are some 40,000 species of vertebrates in the world just two years. His dissertation on myology (the scientific study of muscles) became a classic in that field. In 1923 Romer joined the University of Chicago, and in 1934 moved to Harvard University where he remained until his retirement.

Romer spent nearly all of his career investigating vertebrate evolution (the process by which all living things change over generations). His comprehensive books, *Vertebrate Paleontology* and *The Vertebrate Body* among others shaped much of the thinking of his subject for decades. Romer was able to focus attention on the importance of form and function as it related to an animal's environment as being the key to how it evolved. His painstaking studies of fossils enabled him to document the slow changes that occurred over long periods of time. Romer's work would bring English naturalist Charles Darwin's theory of evolution to life as Romer used evidence taken from comparative anatomy and even embryology (the study of the early development of organisms). His work also contained scores of examples of specific anatomical adaptations that had taken place in organisms as a result of or in response to environmental changes. Romer not only shaped and defined his field, but was able to give tangible evidence of Darwin's ideas of adaptation through natural selection.

today, vertebrates actually make up only a very small percentage of the total number of animals.

FISH

Fish are the most successful group of vertebrates and belong to the class, Osteichthyes which means "bony fishes." As the name implies, these fish have skeletons made of real bone and cartilage, like eels, sharks, and rays, which are not true fish. A fish is a vertebrate animal that lives in the water and breathes through gills. The bones of a fish are usually thin and light since they can use the natural buoyancy of water to support their bodies. Fish are also ectotherms ("cold-blooded") which means that their body temperature changes with that of their surroundings. Fish spend their entire lives in water and, therefore, have a respiratory system with gills that uses the oxygen that is dissolved in water. They cannot take oxygen directly from the air. Fish are streamlined in body design and made to move forward efficiently. Fish also have fins that are winglike structures used for balance and control. Most fish have overlapping scales that are covered with mucus to help them glide through the water. They have a heart, but their circulatory system is the simplest of the vertebrates. Fish reproduce sexually through the union of male sperm and female eggs, and they lay these eggs.

AMPHIBIANS

Amphibians are the second group of vertebrates and they, like fish, are also cold-blooded. Amphibians are considered to be the first vertebrates to develop legs and move from water to the land. Their name is taken from Greek words meaning "to have two lives." This is so because the natural life cycle of an amphibian requires that it live partly on land and partly in the water. An amphibian, like a frog, spends part of its life underwater as a tadpole having the characteristics of a fish. The tadpole then undergoes a metamorphosis, or total change in body shape and function, and develops into a land animal. Amphibians, therefore, have "two lives." Most amphibians, like a salamander, frog, toad, and newt, lack a waterproof layer to the skin and, therefore, must keep their skin moist. They usually have two pairs of limbs as adults. Amphibians reproduce sexually and the female lays her eggs in the water. When the eggs hatch they look like little fish and even breathe with gills. Soon, however, with the release of a certain hormone (chemical messenger), they will begin to grow legs as their tails shrink and the body enlarges, and they will develop air-breathing lungs and lose their gills.

REPTILES

The third group of cold-blooded amphibians is made up of reptiles. Although people immediately think of giant dinosaurs that dominated Earth when they think of reptiles, the name now includes snakes, lizards, turtles, and alligators and crocodiles. A reptile is a vertebrate with dry, scaly skin and sealed eggs. Reptiles are not to be confused with amphibians because reptiles have fully adapted to life on land. Although many live in and around water, they always breathe air through lungs. The complete transition to land was made possible when reptiles began laying eggs with a thick, leathery shell that contained water and food. This allowed the egg to be laid on dry land where it would remain safe until it eventually hatched. With the exception of snakes, reptiles usually have four limbs. Snakes have long, thin bodies, no legs, and a jaw that can unhinge and open wide to swallow large prey. Lizards are much like snakes but have two pairs of legs. Turtles have hard protective shells above and below their bodies, but they also have an endoskeleton. Alligators and crocodiles are similar and have very tough armored skin and a powerful tail for swimming. Reptiles reproduce sexually and most lay eggs.

BIRDS AND MAMMALS

Birds and mammals make up the warm-blooded vertebrates. A warm-blooded animal is able to maintain a constant body temperature no matter how hot or cold its surroundings are. Unlike cold-blooded animals, which slow down in the cold, warm-blooded animals can remain active because they convert their food into body heat. They also have a covering of feathers or hair that keeps them warm.

Birds are the only animals with feathers, and along with bats, are the only vertebrates able to fly. A bird is a warm-blooded animal with wings and feathers. All birds have a beak, two legs, and reproduce by laying eggs. They are found in nearly every environment. The act of flying consumes a high amount of energy, and birds have very efficient respiratory and circulatory systems. They also have powerful breast muscles to push their wings back against the air, and hollow bones that are extremely light. Birds' beaks and feet are especially adapted to their habitat and diet, and the shape of a bird's beak and the type of feet it has can usually give clues to what the bird eats. Birds reproduce sexually and lay eggs that have a hard shell. Being able to fly gives a bird a definite competitive advantage since it allows them to escape quickly and easily from danger, as well as leave, or migrate, to another place where food is more plentiful.

A mammal is a warm-blooded vertebrate with hair that feeds milk to its young. Mammals are named after the mammary glands of females that secrete milk and provide food for their young. There are about 4,500 species of mammals, which include humans. Rats and elephants are mammals as are bats and horses. All mammals have some hair or fur on at least part of their body that helps to keep them warm. The mammal brain is also larger than other vertebrates and allows for greater learning. Mammals breathe air through lungs and have specialized teeth and a four-chambered heart. Mammals also exhibit complex behavior that is often directed by instinct, or an inborn pattern, of doing things a certain way. In most mammal species, the unborn young remain inside the mother's body until they are fully developed. Female mammals that mate and are fertilized develop a special organ called a placenta that carries food and oxygen to the embryo and also takes waste away. Most mammals live on land, although whales, dolphins, seals, and manatees live in water. The current geological era is called the Age of Mammals because mammals have successfully spread throughout the world. Mammals are considered by humans (who themselves are mammals) to be among the "higher" vertebrate animals. Although mammals may earn this distinction because they demonstrate evidence of obvious learning and exhibit complex behavior, mammals may also be classed as "higher" vertebrate animals since humans are the ones making up the rules of classification.

[*See also* **Amphibians; Birds; Fish; Invertebrates; Mammals; Reptiles**]

Virus

A virus is a package of chemicals that infects living cells. Composed only of some genetic material inside a protein coat, it is not considered a living thing since it does not reproduce on its own nor does it carry on respiration (the process by which living things obtain energy). A virus is only able to do these things while inside a host cell, which it usually kills in the process of duplicating itself, often causing a disease.

Ever since the existence of viruses was first demonstrated just before the twentieth century, viruses have regularly puzzled biologists who sought to classify them. Examining their characteristics seems to place viruses on the borderline between living and nonliving things. Viruses are smaller than the smallest bacteria, and were not able to actually be seen until the postwar invention of the electron microscope. Being able to see them and watch how they behaved did not make it any easier to classify them, however. Viruses at first appear to be a living organism since they are made of some of the same compounds and chemicals that are found in living cells. However, they are not themselves cells nor are they made up of cells (as all living things are). Furthermore, viruses do not have a nucleus or any other cell parts, and they cannot reproduce unless they are inside another living cell. In fact, they do not carry out any of the typical life processes, or metabolic activity, that living cells do. Despite all of this, when they find an appropriate cell, they quickly reproduce themselves, usually to the disadvantage of the host cell and sometimes the entire organism.

Anyone who has ever had a case of the chicken pox, measles, or the flu has been infected by a virus. Some viral diseases like polio, AIDS, yellow fever, meningitis, encephalitis, and rabies can be fatal. Others, like herpes or the common cold, only make us sick temporarily. Overall, viruses are responsible for at least 60 percent of the infectious diseases around the world. A virus can also infect bacteria and fungi as well as plant and animal cells. Viruses are incredibly tiny and come in different shapes according to what type of cells they invade. Animal viruses are usually round and look like little puffballs. Plant viruses resemble rods, while bacterial viruses look like tadpoles with little tails. Despite their appearance, they do not have a true cell structure with a nucleus or other parts of a cell. Instead, viruses consist of a core of nucleic acid covered by a protective coat of protein called the capsid. The nucleic acid (either DNA or RNA) contains directions for making more viruses.

Unlike a living cell, a virus has one job only—to reproduce or replicate itself. Once inside, it acts like a computer program for making new viruses. When it enters or infects a cell, a virus takes over the cell's metabolism or its chemical reactions, since it does not have the machinery, the energy, or the raw materials to do anything on its own. Like an invader, it takes charge of the cell and instructs it to produce everything that the virus needs to reproduce itself. In a sense, it "reprograms" the cell it invades so that the infected cell's systems and energy are available to and controlled by the virus.

Biologists have been able to study viruses in action by observing how they infect bacteria. First, viruses do not attack just any type of cell. Viruses do not cross kingdoms, so a virus that attacks a plant cannot infect an animal. Other viruses only attack certain species within a kingdom, while others will only attack certain types of cells in a species. Once a virus finds its proper cell type, it first attaches itself at a certain place on the surface of the cell. It next penetrates the cell by drilling into it, which immediately stops the cell from making its own genetic material.

Three labeled diagrams showing differently shaped viruses. (Illustration by Hans & Cassidy. Courtesy of Gale Research.)

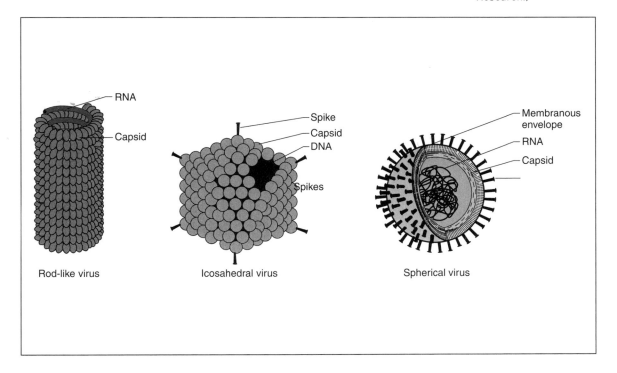

U·X·L Complete Life Science Resource

With the virus DNA or RNA now inside the cell, the cell begins to go to work copying and making virus DNA. After a half-hour or so when the cell has made many copies (one polio virus can produce 100,000 copies of itself inside a single cell), it makes a certain enzyme called a lysozyme. This enzyme attacks its cell walls, which soon burst open, killing the cell but releasing the many virus copies. These go on to invade and take over more cells, all the while reproducing more and more of the virus. Some viruses do not destroy the cell but simply join their DNA to that of the cell which, when it divides, also reproduces the virus. The organism whose cells are infected by the virus becomes diseased either because the virus is destroying its cells or damaging those that it takes over.

Fighting a virus is very difficult. Drugs that work against bacteria cannot work on viruses since viruses have no metabolic activities (the internal processes that make a cell work) of their own to attack. Since viruses use all of the infected cell's systems, anything that would stop a virus from reproducing would also attack the cell itself. By destroying the virus, the cell is also destroyed. An organism's natural defenses are the best antivirus weapon, so virus-caused diseases can be prevented by the use of certain vaccines. A vaccine is a substance that contains a weakened version of a virus that, although it can no longer cause a disease, encourages the body to create substances called antibodies that will later specifically attack and kill the virus when it invades. Vaccines have proven successful for many virus-caused diseases like polio, measles, and the many different types of influenza.

Viruses have ways of fighting back, including mutating or changing their makeup. Viruses like the flu or HIV (the Human Immunodeficiency Virus that causes AIDS) are able to change frequently enough so that a certain type of vaccine that may have been successful will no longer work on the new version. Other viruses can stay hidden for a long time. This type of virus is called a latent virus, and it does not take control of the cell as soon as its penetrates it. It still duplicates itself but does not harm the cell until at some later time when it becomes active and begins its destruction.

Although modern medicine has made great strides in fighting or preventing viral infections, it has proven especially difficult to create new drugs that will limit or stop the growth of a virus inside a cell without doing the same to the cell itself. Ever since their discovery, viruses have proven to be not only a baffling phenomenon but also an ultimate type of parasite that has proven to be a potent and highly resourceful enemy.

[*See also* **AIDS; Immune System; Immunization; Nucleic Acid**]

Vitamins

Vitamins are organic compounds (substances that contain carbon) found in food that all animals need in small amounts. Although they usually cannot be made by the body, they are essential to its proper functioning. Vitamins are not a source of energy, but instead serve to help enzymes (proteins that act as catalysts and speed up chemical reactions in living things) make important chemical reactions occur.

Vitamins are essential to life. Although all animals need them for proper metabolism (the chemical processes that take place in a living thing), different animals need different types or varying amounts. All animals need some vitamins in their systems, since most vitamins are necessary coenzymes. A coenzyme is something that helps an enzyme speed up a chemical reaction in the body. Specifically, it helps regulate the chemical reactions that take place inside an organism when an organism converts food into energy. Some enzymes cannot work at all by themselves and require a vitamin to do their job.

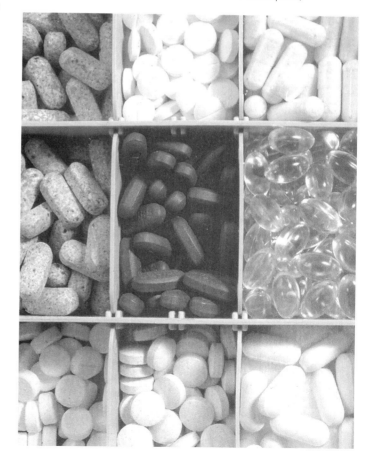

Some of the different types of vitamin supplements. An overdose of some vitamins can accumulate to harmful levels in the human body. (Reproduced by permission of Archive Photos, Inc.)

Vitamins are named by letters, and there are thirteen vitamins that have been identified as being necessary for human health. They are vitamins A, C, D, E, K and eight B vitamins. Since the B vitamins were originally thought to be one vitamin, they were first given different numbers, like B_1, B_2, etc. Later, all but B_6 and B_{12} were given actual names. The deficiency, or lack, of one certain vitamin usually shows itself in a very specific condition that is described as a deficiency-related disease.

TYPES OF VITAMINS

There are two types of vitamins: water-soluble vitamins and fat-soluble vitamins. Something is soluble if it is capable of being dissolved. Fat-soluble vitamins are stored in the body in the fats and oils that are taken

FREDERICK GOWLAND HOPKINS

English biochemist Frederick Hopkins (1861–1947) discovered the existence of "accessory food factors"—now known as vitamins—which are needed in animal diets to maintain health and life. He also laid the foundation for the concept of essential amino acids (those that cannot be made by the body and must be supplied in the diet).

Frederick Hopkins was born in Sussex, England, and had an especially lonely and unhappy childhood being raised by a widowed mother and an unmarried uncle who ignored him. When he was seventeen, his uncle found him a job in the insurance business. Despite doing this for several years, he managed to take part-time courses at the University of London and eventually earned a degree in chemistry when he was twenty-seven. By then he had received a small inheritance and was able to attend medical school at Guy's Hospital in London. After receiving his medical degree at the age of thirty-three, he finally began his real career at Cambridge University when he was thirty-seven years old. Although a very late starter, Hopkins made up for lost time, and in 1900 made his first discovery in his area of dietary research. He found that rats fed only gelatin would not live and grow, despite the fact that gelatin was a protein. He then found that the important amino acid called tryptophan was missing in gelatin. Additional research revealed that tryptophan (as well as several other amino acids) could not be manufactured in the body. He discovered that this amino acid had to be supplied in the diet. In doing this, Hopkins thus laid the foundation for the

in. Water-soluble vitamins are not able to be stored, and any excess passes out of the body. Vitamins A, D, E, and K are fat-soluble vitamins. Vitamin A is essential for the sense of sight, and a lack of Vitamin A is a common cause of blindness in developing countries. Vitamin D is important for healthy bones and teeth (a lack causes the disease rickets), and is found mainly in fish and eggs. It is also formed in the skin when it is exposed to sunlight. Vitamin E plays a major role in the reproductive system, and Vitamin K helps the blood to clot.

The other nine vitamins are water-soluble vitamins. Vitamin B_1 is called thiamin and is found in the outer layer of cereal grains. It helps break down carbohydrates (group of naturally occurring compounds that are essential sources of energy for all living things). B_2 is known as riboflavin and is necessary for cellular respiration (the breaking down of food into energy). B_3 is called niacin and also works in cellular respiration. B_5 is pantothenic acid which helps convert carbohydrates, fats, and proteins into energy. B_6 does not have a commonly used name, although

concept of the essential amino acid, which was detailed by others a generation later.

Hopkins then went on to study diet and its effect on metabolism (all of
the chemical processes that take place in a living thing). At this point in
time, nutritional science was not very advanced, and most scientists believed that such diet-related diseases as scurvy, beriberi, or rickets were
caused by some sort of toxic substances in food. Hopkins' research soon
led him to have serious doubts about this thinking, and his experiments
only confirmed this. He had already noticed that his laboratory rats failed
to grow when fed a diet of artificial nutrients. However, those whose artificial nutrients contained a tiny amount of cow's milk grew rapidly. This
led him to suspect that normal food must contain substances missing from
the artificial nutrients that contained only pure fats, proteins, and carbohydrates. Hopkins never was able to isolate them or find out what these
trace substances were, but in 1906 he wrote a paper in which he described
them as "accessory food factors." He pointed out that whatever they were,
they were obviously essential for growth. This paper is considered to be
the first explanation of the concept of vitamins. In 1925, the young man
who started life as an insurance man and whose determination got him his
first teaching job at thirty-seven, was knighted and thereafter was called
"Sir." Four years later he was awarded the Nobel Prize in physiology and
medicine for being the first to suggest what became known as the "vitamin concept."

it is technically called pyridoxine, and it helps break down fatty acids and
amino acids (the building blocks of proteins). B_{12} can be called cobal-
amin and helps make proteins. Biotin also is a B vitamin and is necessary for the formation of some fatty acids. Folic acid is needed to help
make nucleic acids (genetic material). Finally, Vitamin C, also called
ascorbic acid, is needed for healthy teeth, gums, and bones as well as for
healing. While each of these thirteen vitamins plays a very specific role
in the body, each also fills a more general need in promoting overall well-
being or good health.

HOW TO OBTAIN VITAMINS

Most physicians say that the best way to get the right amounts of vitamins into our systems is to eat a regular balanced diet. This means that
a variety of foods from each of the basic food groups (fats, carbohydrates,
proteins, and minerals) should give people the relatively small amounts
of the thirteen vitamins they need. Today, however, many people take vi-

tamin supplements just to be sure they are getting enough. Recent trends in taking what are called megadoses of certain vitamins are more controversial, and some physicians warn that large doses can be dangerous. While some of the water-soluble vitamins people take are simply excreted in their urine, if they take too many fat-soluble vitamins they will not pass the body and can accumulate to harmful levels.

Humans' knowledge about vitamin deficiency diseases is fairly certain. For example, it is known that Vitamin C cures scurvy and Vitamin D can cure rickets. However, we do not yet fully understand all of the biochemical roles played by vitamins, nor are all of the interactions among vitamins and other nutrients known.

[*See also* **Malnutrition; Nutrition**]

Water

Water is a liquid that is essential to life and plays many important roles. Water molecules (small particles) are the most common molecules in the body of every organism. Water is the ideal medium for transporting essential nutrients into the body and for transporting waste products out of the body.

Water is a chemical compound made up of one oxygen atom bonded to two hydrogen atoms (H_2O). Without water, it is safe to say that there would probably be no life on Earth. Virtually all of the chemical reactions that occur in every organism take place in some sort of a watery environment. Because it is an excellent solvent (meaning that it has the ability to dissolve many different substances), water plays a key role in life. Water is the best way to move substances into and out of cells because of its ability to be a "universal solvent." Since many substances dissolve in water, they are able to cross cell membranes and enter cells. Water also is the major constituent of all living things. If all the molecules in an organism were sorted and counted, the majority would be water molecules. In some living things, this percentage is as low as 60 percent water, but in some ocean animals like the jellyfish, the percentage is closer to 90 percent. The human body is about 65 percent water.

Humans know that they cannot live without drinking water. Although some people can go as long as six weeks without any food, without water they would die in a matter of days. Water is the primary component of blood, lymph (a colorless liquid that bathes the tissues of the body), and the fluids in all of the body's tissues. The body regulates its temperature with water by perspiring, and eliminate wastes with water.

Water is just as essential to plants as it is to all animals. Water is a key raw material that plants use during photosynthesis (when they make their own food). During photosynthesis, plants use the hydrogen atoms from water molecules (H_2O) and add them to carbon atoms to make carbohydrates (a group of naturally occurring compounds that are essential sources of energy for all living things) and other forms of food. The oxygen molecules (O_2) given off during photosynthesis come from water molecules.

Water is a unique substance with special properties. Water is able to absorb a great deal of heat, and on a global scale (that is, on something the size of Earth), it can act as an enormous moderating influence. When Earth's surface temperatures begin to rise too high, the oceans act like thermal sponges and soak up much of the excessive heat. Water also has a high surface tension, which means that its molecules closely stick together. This explains why it is able to support a broad, flat object, like a boat, and why certain insects can glide across its surface.

Water molecules are the most common molecules in the body of every organism. Without water there would probably be no life on Earth. (Reproduced by permission of the National Park Service.)

Water is also the only common, natural substance that is able to be found in three different physical states. Ice is its solid state, and water assumes a rigid crystalline structure at or below 32°F (0°C). It is found as snow, hail, frost, glaciers, and ice caps. Its liquid state has no particular shape and exists up to a temperature of 148°F (64.4°C). Water in this form covers three-fourths of the Earth's surface in the form of oceans, lakes, rivers, swamps, as well as rain clouds, dew, and ground water. The gaseous state of water occurs above 148°F and does not have a definite volume. This means it takes on the exact shape and volume of its container. It occurs naturally as fog, steam, and clouds.

Because of water's unique hydrogen bonding, ice is less dense than water. If this were not so and ice did not float, then all bodies of water would freeze from the bottom up, becoming solid masses of ice and destroying all life in them. Water also is a major force for changing the Earth's surface, as erosion regularly carves away softer parts and can cause major alterations and changes in the Earth's natural features. The major use of water by humans is for crop irrigation, although a great deal is used industrially, as well as to keep individuals, homes, and communities clean. Since much of the water used to irrigate crops either evaporates or is given off by plants, humans are a major factor in the hydrologic or water cycle. The water cycle describes the process in which water circulates between the sea, the atmosphere, living things, and the land in a continuous cycle

[*See also* **Ocean; Pollution; Wetlands**]

Wetlands

Wetlands are a diverse group of areas in which land is saturated with water for prolonged periods. They are among the most productive environments on earth and support a wide range of plant and animal life. Wetlands can be freshwater, saltwater, or brackish (part fresh and part salt) and are one of the most delicate and complex ecosystems (areas in which living things interact with each other and the environment).

Wetlands are nether totally aquatic (watery) nor terrestrial (dry land), but rather are in the zone between permanently wet and normally dry conditions. Wetlands can be found on every continent, and are often called marshes, swamps, or bogs. Despite their fragility, wetlands perform a variety of important, natural functions. Where the sea meets the land, tidal estuaries or salt marshes form a buffer zone, protecting the mainland from the onrushing sea. Wetlands improve water quality by filtering the water that passes through them. They also remove much of the excess carbon and nitrogen that humans pump into the air. Wetlands contain a great deal of food for sea life and other animals, while providing a safe haven for spawning (egg laying and hatching).

CHARACTERISTICS OF WETLANDS

No matter what wetlands are called, they all have three characteristics. First, they all have waterlogged soil. In such soil, water is at or above the soil surface for a long enough time during a year to influence and determine what grows there. Second, a certain type of plant called a "hydrophyte" grows in wetlands. Although there are as many as 5,000 species of such specialized plants, from mangroves and cattails to bald cypress and rushes, all are hydrophytes because they have in some manner developed their own way of getting a steady supply of air to their submerged roots. Third, the soil found in a typical wetland is mostly poor in oxygen and very acidic. This also determines what can grow there.

Wetlands, such as the one pictured here, are a diverse group of areas in which land is saturated with water for prolonged periods. (Reproduced by permission of Field Mark Publications. Photograph by Robert J. Huffman.)

Wetlands are usually either freshwater wetlands or saltwater wetlands, although there are some in which the two meet and mingle. Saltwater wetlands naturally occur at the coasts where the sea meets the land. Tidal salt marshes with salt-tolerant plant species can be found along the Arctic and Atlantic seaboards of North America, the Gulf of Mexico, and the European coastline. Mangrove forests whose thick trees are concentrated in the Indian Ocean and West Pacific region, are the subtropical equal of tidal salt marshes. Most of the wetlands in the temperate parts of the world are freshwater marshes. In the continental United States, 90 percent of the wetlands are freshwater marshes. Worldwide, wetlands account for about 6.5 percent of the Earth's total land surface, and the bulk of them are found in the world's tropical zones.

A river like the Mississippi River, which cuts down across the United States from Minnesota to the Gulf of Mexico, is a good example of how such a large moving body of water with seasonal flooding can build wetlands and keep them alive. Each spring, as the gorged river would search for the shortest route to the Gulf of Mexico, it would overflow its banks, depositing rich sediment. The river also pushed most of the saltwater at the Gulf back into the sea. The combination of sediment buildup and freshwater infiltration allowed wetlands to develop. Many plants that were sensitive to salt were able to take hold and grow, keeping the land in place.

Until the eighteenth century, wetlands were considered worthless and places to be avoided, and this annual flooding process was left undisturbed. But with the development of the levee system (a bank of earth along a river to prevent flooding), begun in New Orleans in the early 1700s, the flooding was stopped and the now-dry land became "useable" by people. With the continued development of levees and permanent flood control, the Mississippi River now has no choice but to deposit its wealth of sediment into the Gulf of Mexico. Since then, the wetlands of New Orleans have been disappearing.

PLANT AND ANIMAL LIFE IN WETLANDS

The variety of plant and animal life found in and around wetlands is huge and amazing. They are home to all types of birds, snakes, fishes, turtles, raccoons, beavers, alligators, and shellfish. All these and many more animals depend on wetlands for food and shelter. Wetlands also provide a welcome resting and feeding place for migrating (seasonally moving) birds. Many animals need to be in wetlands in order to reproduce. A great deal of today's commercial fishing industry depends in some way on the fertility of wetlands. Because they are so rich in nutrients and in all manner of interdependent life forms, wetlands are very delicate, intricate, and vulnerable ecosystems. Major changes in wetlands can produce a ripple effect.

HUMAN EFFECTS ON WETLANDS

Despite national laws and international agreements protecting critical wetlands, the impact of human development has had a profoundly negative effect on wetlands. Wetlands are, therefore, among the most threatened of habitats, and hundreds of thousands of acres are disappearing every year in the United States alone. Without the enforcement of laws put in place to protect wetlands, they may be one of the first ecosystems to vanish completely.

[*See also* **Biome; Water**]

Worms

A worm is a common name given to a diverse group of invertebrate animals that have a long, soft body and no legs. All worms used to be classified together in one phylum called Vermes, but biologists now divide them into three phyla. The bodies of worms mark a higher level of complexity on the invertebrate evolutionary ladder, and they are by no means the simplest of animals.

The least complex of the worms is the flatworm, a member of the phylum Platyhelminthes. As their name implies, they are flat like a ribbon and are either free-living or parasitic (organisms that live in or on another organism and benefit from the relationship). Flatworms include planarians, flukes, and tapeworms—the last two are parasitic. Planarian are found living in bodies of water. They are very small and have a simple digestive system and one opening that both receives its food and excretes its waste. Planaria can crawl and swim with hairlike cilia and reproduce sexually and asexually. Flukes are flatworms that live as parasites in the liver or blood of an animal host, and tapeworms are found in the intestines of vertebrates.

Members of the phyla Nemotoda (roundworms) and Annelida (true, or segmented worms), have bodies with three cell layers—a trait common to all "higher" animals. This advance means that they have a fluid-filled cavity in which internal, specialized organs can be suspended. Roundworms, or nematodes, are an abundant species and are more complex than flatworms. They have a mouth at one end and an anus at the other through which waste is excreted. They are not really round but have long, tapered bodies than come to a point at each end. They move about by contracting a single, long muscle that pulls their head and tail end closer together. They are covered by a hard, outer layer called a cuticle. Many roundworm are parasites, and some are very harmful to humans. One example is the hookworm that enters the human body by boring through the soles of the feet, entering the bloodstream, and traveling to the lungs. There they bore through the bronchi and the windpipe and enter the throat to be swallowed, passing eventually into the intestines where they finally attach themselves. Hookworms drain a host's blood and cause severe anemia (lack of blood). Another dangerous worm is the trichina roundworm. Humans can contract trichinosis by eating meat infected by the trichina roundworm. This worm reproduces in the intestines and its larva pass into other body parts and form cysts in muscle tissue, causing pain, fever, weakness, and even death.

Few segmented or true worms are parasitic, although the leech is one of them. The leech is a segmented worm with a sucker at each end of its body. It lives by feeding off the blood of other animals. Called annelids, segmented worms have bodies composed of identical ringlike sections or segments. The word annelid means "little ring" in Latin. Annelids have three tissue layers and therefore can support specialized organ systems. They also have a hydrostatic skeleton, which means that they keep their

Worms are beneficial because their digging action improves the soil. (Reproduced by permission of Field Mark Publications. Photograph by Robert J. Huffman.)

JEAN-BAPTISTE LAMARCK

French naturalist Jean-Baptiste Lamarck (1744-1829) founded modern invertebrate zoology. He was the first to use the words "vertebrate" and "invertebrate" and also popularized the word "biology." He was a pioneer of evolutionary theory and was the first scientist to describe the adaptability of organisms.

Born in Picardy in northern France, Jean-Baptiste Lamarck's full name was Jean-Baptiste Pierre Antoine de Monet Lamarck and he had the title of "Chevalier." This was, in fact, the lowest rank of the French nobility, and although his family was part of the aristocratic class, it was still very poor. As one of eleven children, he was supposed to become a priest, but entered the army instead when his father died. Six years of fighting for France left him with medals for bravery but also bad health, so he resigned and tried several different occupations. Having taken an interest in plant life when he was stationed on the Mediterranean coast, he wrote a book about the plants of France, which caused him to be noticed by the well-known French naturalist, Georges Louis Leclerc Buffon (1707-1788). It was through Buffon that Lamarck eventually was appointed botanist (a person who studies plants) to King Louis XVI. After the French Revolution (1789-99), Lamarck became professor of zoology at the Museum of Natural History in Paris. Nearly fifty years old, Lamarck finally started to focus his energies on one thing.

The object of his attention was a large group of organisms that, until Lamarck, had been hardly considered at all. In fact, the great Swedish botanist Carolus Linnaeus (1707-1778) himself had grouped these creatures

body shape by the pressure of their internal fluid pushing against the walls of their body. This is similar to the air inside a full balloon. Annelids can move about on the ground by contracting different sets of muscles that move their segments.

Earthworms are a type of roundworm that have a complex digestive system. This system includes a mouth and a tubelike esophagus that leads to the storage crop, which connects to a gizzard where food is broken down. From there, food passes into an intestine and eventually waste is expelled through the anus. Earthworms also have a closed circulatory system and several "hearts" that pump blood. They lack a respiratory system since they exchange gases or breathe through their skin (which must always be coated with mucus). Their nervous system consists of a simple brain and a main nerve cord. Earthworms are not only an important food source for many animals, but they improve the soil by their digging into only two general categories: insects and worms. Although Linnaeus had basically not even attempted to classify these organisms, Lamarck set out to give this huge group some order. The first thing he did was to name the entire group "invertebrates" since they did not have a backbone and were therefore different from "vertebrates," or animals with a backbone. He then set out to classify invertebrates according to their anatomic similarities. So he said that eight-legged arachnids (spiders) were different from six-legged insects, and that echinoderms, like starfish and sea urchins, were different from crustaceans, like crabs and shrimp. He continued this work on invertebrates even as a very old man and finally produced a huge, seven-volume *Natural History of Invertebrates* that essentially founded modern invertebrate zoology and became his most important contribution to the life sciences.

While he was creating his classification of invertebrates, Lamarck began to develop an evolutionary theory to explain the differences between living animals and fossils. He soon proposed the idea that species gradually change over time and argued that all living things could be arranged in such a way as to show how some species gradually changed into another. However, it was in his specific explanations as to how this actually came about that he created the incorrect theory now known as "Lamarckism." This theory wrongly states that characteristics, or traits, acquired by an individual during its lifetime are passed on to its offspring. Despite his errors, Lamarck's concern with evolutionary theory gave it much-needed attention, and he should be credited as a true pioneer of evolutionary theory as well as the founder of invertebrate zoology.

action (which allows air and water to filter in) and by their waste, which fertilizes it. Most segmented worms have both male and female organs, although they cannot fertilize their own eggs. Fertilization is accomplished when worms exchange sperm with one another. They can also regenerate or grow back a part that has been cut off.

[*See also* **Invertebrates**]

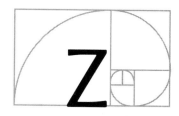

Zoology

Zoology is the scientific study of animals. Its subjects are highly diverse, and it includes a wide range of other disciplines. Some of these study the whole animal in a very broad way, such as animal ecology, while others examine animals on a smaller scale, such as their anatomy (structure) or physiology (function).

Zoology is one of the two main branches of biology. The other branch of biology is botany or the study of plants. Zoology includes the study of every type of animal, from the 180-ton blue whale to the one-celled bacteria. Animals make up the largest of the five kingdoms that were created by biologists to organize and describe the living world. Besides animals, the other kingdoms are monerans, protists, fungi, and plants. Described in the simplest way possible, animals are multicelled organisms that move about and live by taking in food. They are classified into two main groups: vertebrates have bony internal skeletons and invertebrates do not. There are eight different groups, or phyla, of invertebrates, all of which differ greatly in body structure, where they live, and how they reproduce. Vertebrates all belong to the same phylum and are classified as cold-blooded (the internal body temperature changes with the environment) or warm-blooded (internal body temperature remains the same despite the environment). Finally, animals react to what goes on in their environment. Much of this behavior involves communicating with other animals, and searching for food, mates, and a place to live.

As a science, zoology began with the Greek philosopher Aristotle (384–322 B.C.), who developed his own system to classify animals. His accomplishments and reputation were so great that much of what he wrote about animals remained unquestioned for nearly 2000 years. It was not until the middle of the eighteenth century that a modern system of classifying animals was created by the Swedish botanist, Carolus Linnaeus (1707–1778). Another century would also pass before biology, and therefore zoology, would be given a theory of evolution (the process by which living things can change over time) to explain the origins and development of animal life. That great theory, published in 1859 by the English naturalist Charles Robert Darwin (1809–1892), laid a new foundation for zoology.

Since the nineteenth century, the field encompassed by zoology has grown so large that it eventually became divided up into many other fields or branches. Some of these are broad subject areas, like embryology, which studies the development of individual animals, and anatomy that studies the structure of an animal's body. Other branches focus on only one type of animal, such as ichthyology, which studies fish, or entomology, which studies insects. There are also other fields in zoology that focus only on animal behavior.

Technical advances have always played a major role in the advancement of science, and they have allowed zoology to progress rapidly as well. Beginning with the seventeenth-century invention of the microscope, zoology benefitted by the new ability to see not only tiny life forms but also smaller details of other animals that had not been known. Further improvements allowed zoologists to examine animals at their cellular level. Recent breakthroughs in gene technology have given zoologists the ability to manipulate an animal's genetic makeup for a number of scientific and commercial purposes. Zoological research benefits humans in many ways, one example of which is the use of bacterial studies to learn how to protect people from being infected by disease. Since cattle and chicken are key to humans' food supply, zoologists regularly search for ways to produce healthier animals. Finally, zoologists also work to preserve those animal species that are endangered and could possibly go extinct.

Zygote

A zygote in animals is a fertilized egg or ovum. It is the first cell produced when a male gamete (sperm) unites with a female gamete (egg). Since it contains one set of chromosomes from each parent, the zygote will develop into a unique individual.

The act of fertilization brings together the sex cells of two different members of the same animal species. It eventually produces a fully developed offspring, which begins as a one-celled fertilized egg called a zygote. Whether fertilization is external (as when a frog sprays his sperm over the female's eggs in the water) or internal (when a male mammal deposits them inside the body of the female), the moment an individual sperm makes physical contact with the egg, fertilization begins. The egg is surrounded by a jelly-like film called the "zona pellucida" that the sperm must break through. It does this by actually contacting the film, which causes the tip of the sperm head to rupture. This releases a chemical that opens a hole through the outer layers of the egg.

As the sperm head descends through the layers, tiny projections called "microvilli" emerge from both the sperm and the egg, and it is these that first fuse together. Following this, the actual membranes of both sperm and egg fuse and the cytoplasm (jelly-like fluid) of the egg engulfs the sperm. The sperm releases its genetic material into the egg as the nucleus (the cell's control center) of both merge into one new nucleus. At this point, the sperm and egg have fully merged. The sex of the new offspring

An electron micrograph of a fertilized human zygote. This zygote is seen one day after fertilization and is preparing for its first cell division. (©Photographer, Science Source/Photo Researchers, Inc.)

and all the instructions needed to produce this new organism are already in place and are beginning to work. Because each parent has donated one set of chromosomes, the genetic information (or genome) of the offspring will represent a unique combination of deoxyribonucleic acid (DNA). The DNA contains the genetic instructions for each cell.

The zygote, therefore, is the first cell of this future offspring. As soon as the zygote is formed, a series of rapid cell divisions called cleavage begins. The zygote divides into two cells, then four cells, then eight, and so on. Each new cell has the same genetic makeup as the original zygote. As the cleavage process continues and the developing cell mass grows, it forms a berry-like, compact ball called a "morula." This ball soon develops different layers, which eventually begin to form their own specialized cells. Some layers become muscle and bone while others become part of the different organs and systems. In humans, five days after fertilization and the creation of a zygote, the zygote has been transformed into the multicelled beginnings of an embryo, which will eventually become a fully developed offspring.

[*See also* **Egg; Embryo; Fertilization; Human Reproduction; Reproduction, Sexual; Sperm**]

For Further Information

Books

Abbot, David, ed. *Biologists*. New York: Peter Bedrick Books, 1983.

Agosta, William. *Bombardier Beetles and Fever Trees*. Reading, Mass.: Addison-Wesley Publishing Co., 1996.

Alexander, Peter and others. *Silver, Burdett & Ginn Life Science*. Morristown, N.J.: Silver, Burdett & Ginn, 1987.

Alexander, R. McNeill, ed. *The Encyclopedia of Animal Biology*. New York: Facts on File, 1987.

Allen, Garland E. *Life Science in the Twentieth Century*. New York: Cambridge University Press, 1979.

Attenborough, David. *The Life of Birds*. Princeton, N.J.: Princeton University Press, 1998.

Attenborough, David. *The Private Life of Plants*. Princeton, N.J.: Princeton University Press, 1995.

Bailey, Jill. *Animal Life: Form and Function in the Animal Kingdom*. New York: Oxford University Press, 1994.

Bockus, H. William. *Life Science Careers*. Altadena, Calf.: Print Place, 1991.

Borell, Merriley. *The Biological Sciences in the Twentieth Century*. New York: Scribner, 1989.

Braun, Ernest. *Living Water*. Palo Alto, Calf.: American West Publishing Co., 1971.

Burnie, David. *Dictionary of Nature*. New York: Dorling Kindersley Inc., 1994.

Burton, Maurice, and Robert Burton, eds. *Marshall Cavendish International Wildlife Encyclopedia*. New York: Marshall Cavendish, 1989.

Coleman, William. *Biology in the Nineteenth Century*. New York: Cambridge University Press, 1977.

Conniff, Richard. *Spineless Wonders*. New York: Henry Holt & Co., 1996.

Corrick, James A. *Recent Revolutions in Biology*. New York: Franklin Watts, 1987.

Curry-Lindahl, Kai. *Wildlife of the Prairies and Plains*. New York: H. N. Abrams, 1981.

Darwin, Charles. *The Origin of Species*. New York: W.W. Norton & Company, Inc., 1975.

Davis, Joel. *Mapping the Code*. New York: John Wiley & Sons, 1990.

Diagram Group Staff. *Life Sciences on File*. New York: Facts on File, 1999.

Dodson, Bert, and Mahlon Hoagland. *The Way Life Works*. New York: Times Books, 1995.

Drlica, Karl. *Understanding DNA and Gene Cloning*. New York: John Wiley & Sons, 1997.

Edwards, Gabrielle I. *Biology the Easy Way.* New York: Barron's, 1990.

Evans, Howard Ensign. *Pioneer Naturalists.* New York: Henry Holt & Sons, 1993.

Farrington, Benjamin. *What Darwin Really Said.* New York: Schocken Books, 1982.

Finlayson, Max, and Michael Moser, eds. *Wetlands.* New York: Facts on File, 1991.

Goodwin, Brian C. *How the Leopard Changed Its Spots: The Evolution of Complexity.* New York: Simon & Schuster, 1996.

Gould, Stephen Jay, ed. *The Book of Life.* New York: W.W. Norton & Company, Inc., 1993.

Greulach, Victor A., and Vincent J. Chiapetta. *Biology: The Science of Life.* Morristown, N.J.: General Learning Press, 1977.

Grolier World Encyclopedia of Endangered Species. 10 vols. Danbury, Conn.: Grolier Educational Corp., 1993.

Gutnik, Martin J. *The Science of Classification: Finding Order Among Living and Nonliving Objects.* New York: Franklin Watts, 1980.

Hall, David O., and K.K. Rao. *Photosynthesis.* New York: Cambridge University Press, 1999.

Hare, Tony. *Animal Fact-File: Head-to-Tail Profiles of More than 100 Mammals.* New York: Facts on File, 1999.

Hare, Tony, ed. *Habitats.* Upper Saddle River, N.J.: Prentice Hall, 1994.

Hawley, R. Scott, and Catherine A. Mori. *The Human Genome: A User's Guide.* San Diego, Calf.: Academic Press, 1999.

Huxley, Anthony Julian. *Green Inheritance.* New York: Four Walls Eight Windows, 1992.

Jacob, François. *Of Flies, Mice, and Men.* Cambridge, Mass.: Harvard University Press, 1998.

Jacobs, Marius. *The Tropical Rain Forest.* New York: Springer-Verlag, 1990.

Johanson, Donald, and Blake Edgar. *From Lucy to Language.* New York: Simon & Schuster, 1996.

Jones, Steve. *The Language of Genes.* New York: Doubleday, 1994.

Kapp, Ronald O. *How to Know Pollen and Spores.* Dubuque, Iowa: W. C. Brown, 1969.

Kordon, Claude. *The Language of the Cell.* New York: McGraw-Hill, 1993.

Lambert, David. *Dinosaur Data Book.* New York: Random House Value Publishing, Inc., 1998.

Leakey, Richard. *The Origin of Humankind.* New York: Basic Books, 1994.

Leakey, Richard, and Roger Lewin. *Origins Reconsidered.* New York: Doubleday, 1992.

Leonard, William H. *Biology: A Community Context.* Cincinnati, Ohio: South-Western Educational Pub., 1998.

Levine, Joseph S., and David Suzuki. *The Secret of Life: Redesigning the Living World.* Boston, Mass.: WGBH Boston, 1993.

Little, Charles E. *The Dying of the Trees.* New York: Viking, 1995.

Lovelock, James. *Healing Gaia.* New York: Harmony Books, 1991.

McGavin, George. *Bugs of the World.* New York: Facts on File, 1993.

McGowan, Chris. *Diatoms to Dinosaurs.* Washington, D.C.: Island Press/Shearwater Books, 1994.

McGowan, Chris. *The Raptor and the Lamb.* New York: Henry Holt & Co., 1997.

McGrath, Kimberley A. *World of Biology.* Detroit, Mich.: The Gale Group, 1999.

Magner, Lois N. *A History of the Life Sciences.* New York: Marcel Dekker, Inc., 1979.

Manning, Richard. *Grassland.* New York: Viking, 1995.

Margulis, Lynn. *Early Life.* Boston, Mass.: Science Books International, 1982.

Margulis, Lynn, and Karlene V. Schwartz. *Five Kingdoms.* New York: W.H. Freeman, 1998.

Margulis, Lynn, and Dorian Sagan. *The Garden of Microbial Delights.* Dubuque, Iowa: Kendall Hunt Publishing Co., 1993.

Marshall, Elizabeth L. *The Human Genome Project.* New York: Franklin Watts, 1996.

Mauseth, James D. *Plant Anatomy.* Menlo Park, Calf.: Benjamin/Cummings Publishing Co., 1988.

Mearns, Barbara. *Audubon to X'antus.* San Diego, Calf.: Academic Press, 1992.

Moore, David M. *Green Planet: The Story of Plant Life on Earth.* New York: Cambridge University Press, 1982.

Morris, Desmond. *Animal Days.* New York: Morrow, 1979.

Morton, Alan G. *History of the Biological Sciences: An Account of the Development of Botany from Ancient Times to the Present Day.* New York: Academic Press, 1981.

Nebel, Bernard J., and Richard T. Wright. *Environmental Science: The Way the World Works.* Upper Saddle River, N.J.: Prentice Hall, 1998.

Nies, Kevin A. *From Priestess to Physician: Biographies of Women Life Scientists.* Los Angeles, Calf.: California Video Institute, 1996.

Norell, Mark, A., Eugene S. Gaffney, and Lowell Dingus. *Discovering Dinosaurs in the American Museum of Natural History.* New York: Knopf, 1995.

O'Daly, Anne, ed. *Encyclopedia of Life Sciences.* 11 vols. Tarrytown, N.Y.: Marshall Cavendish Corp., 1996.

Postgate, John R. *Microbes and Man.* New York: Cambridge University Press, 2000.

Reader's Digest Editors. *Secrets of the Natural World.* Pleasantville, N.Y.: Reader's Digest Association, 1993.

Reaka-Kudla, Marjorie L., Don E. Wilson, and Edward O. Wilson. *Biodiversity II: Understanding and Protecting Our Biological Resources.* Washington, D.C.: Joseph Henry Press, 1997.

Rensberger, Boyce. *Life Itself.* New York: Oxford University Press, 1996.

Rosenthal, Dorothy Botkin. *Environmental Science Activities.* New York: John Wiley & Sons, 1995.

Ross-McDonald, Malcom, and Robert Prescott-Allen. *Man and Nature: Every Living Thing.* Garden City, N.Y.: Doubleday, 1976.

Sayre, Anne. *Rosalind Franklin and DNA.* New York: W.W. Norton & Co., 1975.

Shearer, Benjamin F., and Barbara Smith Shearer. *Notable Women in the Life Sciences: A Biographical Dictionary.* Westport, Conn.: Greenwood Press, 1996.

Shreeve, Tim. *Discovering Ecology.* New York: American Museum of Natural History, 1982.

Singer, Charles Joseph. *A History of Biology to about the Year 1900.* Ames, Iowa: Iowa State University Press, 1989.

Singleton, Paul. *Bacteria in Biology, Biotechnology and Medicine.* New York: John Wiley & Sons, 1999.

Snedden, Robert. *The History of Genetics.* New York: Thomson Learning, 1995.

Stefoff, Rebecca. *Extinction.* New York: Chelsea House, 1992.

Stephenson, Robert, and Roger Browne. *Exploring Variety of Life.* Austin, Tex.: Raintree Steck-Vaughn, 1993.

Sturtevant, Alfred H. *History of Genetics.* New York: Harper & Row, 1965.

Tesar, Jenny E. *Patterns in Nature: An Overview of the Living World.* Woodbridge, Conn.: Blackbirch Press, 1994.

Tocci, Salvatore. *Biology Projects for Young Scientists.* New York: Franklin Watts, 1999.

Tremain, Ruthven. *The Animal's Who's Who.* New York: Scribner, 1982.

Tyler-Whittle, Michael Sidney. *The Plant Hunters.* New York: Lyons & Burford, 1997.

Verschuuren, Gerard M. *Life Scientists.* North Andover, Mass.: Genesis Publishing Co., 1995.

Wade, Nicholas. *The Science Times Book of Fish.* New York: Lyons Press, 1997.

Wade, Nicholas. *The Science Times Book of Mammals.* New York: Lyons Press, 1999.

Walters, Martin. *Innovations in Biology.* Santa Barbara, Calf.: ABC-CLIO, 1999.

Watson, James D. *The Double Helix: A Personal Account of the Discover of the Structure of DNA.* New York: Scribner, 1998.

Wilson, Edward O. *The Diversity of Life.* Cambridge, Mass.: Belknap Press of Harvard University Press, 1992.

Videocassettes

Attenborough, David. *Life on Earth.* 13 episodes. BBC in association with Warner Brothers & Reiner Moritz Productions. Distributor, Films Inc. Chicago, Ill.: 1978. Videocassette.

Attenborough, David. *The Living Planet.* 12 episodes. BBC/Time-Life Films. Distributor, Ambrose Video Publishing, Inc., N.Y. Videocassette.

Web Sites

ALA (American Library Association):
Science and Technology: Sites for
Children: Biology.
http://www.ala.org/parentspage/greatsites/
science.html#c
(Accessed August 9, 2000).

Anatomy and Science for Kids.
http://kidscience.about.com/kids/kidscience/
msub53.htm
(Accessed August 9, 2000).

ARS (Agricultural Research Service):
Sci4Kids.
http://www.ars.usda.gov/is/kids/
(Accessed August 9, 2000).

Best Science Links for Kids
(Georgia State University).
http://www.gsu.edu/~chevkk/kids.html
(Accessed August 9, 2000).

Cornell University: Cornell Theory Center
Math and Science Gateway.
http://www.tc.cornell.edu/Edu/
MathSciGateway/
(Accessed August 9, 2000).

Defenders of Wildlife: Kids' Planet.
http://www.kidsplanet.org/
(Accessed August 9, 2000).

DLC-ME (Digital Learning Center for
Microbiology Ecology).
http://commtechlab.msu.edu/sites/dlc-me/
index.html
(Accessed August 9, 2000).

The Electronic Zoo.
http://netvet.wustl.edu/e-zoo.htm
(Accessed August 9, 2000).

Explorer: Natural Science.
http://explorer.scrtec.org/explorer/
explorer-db/browse/static/Natural/\Science/
index.html
(Accessed August 9, 2000).

Federal Resources for Educational
Excellence: Science.
http://www.ed.gov/free/
s-scienc.html
(Accessed August 9, 2000).

Fish Biology Just for Kids: Florida
Museum of Natural History.
http://www.flmnh.ufl.edu/fish/Kids/
kids.htm
(Accessed August 9, 2000).

Franklin Institute Online: Science Fairs.
http://www.fi.edu/qanda/spotlight1/
spotlight1.html
(Accessed August 9, 2000).

GO Network: Biology for Kids.
http://www.go.com/WebDir/Family/Kids/
At_school/Science_and_technology/
Biology_for_kids
(Accessed August 9, 2000).

Howard Hughes Medical Institute:
Cool Science for Curious Kids.
http://www.hhmi.org/coolscience/
(Accessed August 9, 2000).

Internet Public Library: Science Fair
Project Resource Guide.
http://www.ipl.org/youth/projectguide/

Internet School Library Media Center:
Life Science for K-12.
http://falcon.jmu.edu/~ramseyil/
lifescience.htm
(Accessed August 9, 2000).

K-12 Education Links for Teachers and
Students (Pollock School).
http://www.ttl.dsu.edu/hansonwa/k12.htm
(Accessed August 9, 2000).

Kapili.com: Biology4Kids! Your Biology
Web Site!.
http://www.kapili.com/biology4kids/
index.html
(Accessed August 9, 2000).

Lawrence Livermore National Laboratory:
Fun Science for Kids.
http://www.llnl.gov/llnl/03education/
science-list.html
(Accessed August 9, 2000).

LearningVista: Kids Vista: Sciences.
http://www.kidsvista.com/Sciences/
index.html
(Accessed August 9, 2000).

Life Science Lesson Plans: Discovery
Channel School.
http://school.discovery.com/lessonplans/
subjects/lifescience.html
(Accessed August 9, 2000).

Life Sciences: Exploratorium's
10 Cool Sites.
http://www.exploratorium.edu/
learning_studio/cool/life.html
(Accessed August 9, 2000).

Lightspan StudyWeb: Science.
http://www.studyweb.com/Science/
(Accessed August 9, 2000).

Lycos Zone Kids' Almanac.
http://infoplease.kids.lycos.com/
science.html
(Accessed August 9, 2000).

Mr. Biology's High School Bio Web Site.
http://www.sc2000).net/~czaremba/
(Accessed August 9, 2000).

Mr. Warner's Cool Science: Life Links.
http://www3.mwis.net/~science/life.htm
(Accessed August 9, 2000).

Naturespace Science Place.
http://www.naturespace.com/
(Accessed August 9, 2000).

NBII (National Biological Information
Infrastructure): Education.
http://www.nbii.gov/education/index.html
(Accessed August 9, 2000).

PBS Kids: Kratts' Creatures.
http://www.pbs.org/kratts/
(Accessed August 9, 2000).

Perry Public Schools: Educational Web
Sites: Science Related Sites.
http://scnc.perry.k12.mi.us/
edlinks.html#Science
(Accessed August 9, 2000).

QUIA! (Quintessential Instructional
Archive) Create Your Own Learning
Activities.
http://www.quia.com/
(Accessed August 9, 2000).

Ranger Rick's Kid's Zone: National
Wildlife Federation.
http://www.nwf.org/nwf/kids/index.html
(Accessed August 9, 2000).

The Science Spot.
http://www.theramp.net/sciencespot/
index.html
(Accessed August 9, 2000).

South Carolina Statewide Systemic
Initiative (SC SSI): Internet Resources:
Math Science Resources.
http://scssi.scetv.org/mims/ssrch2.htm
(Accessed August 9, 2000).

ThinkQuest: BodyQuest.
http://library.thinkquest.org/10348/
(Accessed August 9, 2000).

United States Department of the Interior
Home Page: Kids on the Web.
http://www.doi.gov/kids/
(Accessed August 9, 2000).

USGS (United States Geological Service)
Learning Web: Biological Resources.
http://www.nbs.gov/features/education.html
(Accessed August 9, 2000).

Washington University School of Medicine
Young Scientist Program.
http://medinfo.wustl.edu/~ysp/
(Accessed August 9, 2000).

Index

Italic type *indicates volume number;* **boldface** *indicates main entries and their page numbers;* (ill.) *indicates photos and illustrations.*

A

Abbe, Ernst *2:* 383

Abdomen *1:* 145

Abiotic/Biotic environment *1:* **1–2,** 180–81

Abscisic acid *3:* 465

Abyssal zone *3:* 425

Acid rain *1:* **4–6**

    effects of, *1:* 6 (ill.)

Acids *1:* 2–4

Acquired immune deficiency syndrome. *See* AIDS (acquired immune deficiency syndrome).

Acquired immunity *2:* 316–17

Acrosome *3:* 547

Adaptation *1:* **7–8,** 207, 403

Adaptive radiation *1:* 209

Adenine *1:* 165, 170

Adenosine triphosphate (ATP) *2:* 389

Adrenal glands *1:* 191, 193; *3:* 531, 553

Aerobic/anaerobic *1:* **8–11**

Aerobic respiration *2:* 346; *3:* 514

Agent Orange *3:* 466

Agglutination *1:* 69

Aging *1:* **11–13**

study of *1:* 12–13

Agricultural revolution *1:* 16

Agriculture *1:* **13–17,** 15 (ill.)

AIDS (acquired immune deficiency syndrome) *1:* **17–21,** 20 (ill.), *2:* 319

Air pollution *3:* 477

Aldrovandi, Ulisse *1:* 195

Algae *1:* **21–24,** 23 (ill.)

Alimentary canal *1:* 158

Alleles *1:* 168; *3:* 499

Alternation of generations *2:* 354; *3:* 550

Alvarez, Luis Walter *1:* 220

Amber *2:* 239

Amino acids *1:* **24–25,** 24 (ill.); *3:* 492

Ammonification *2:* 411

Amoebas *1:* **25–27,** 26 (ill.); *3:* 496

Amoeboid protozoans *1:* 27

Amphibians *1:* **27–30;** *2:* 288; *3:* 586

    life cycle of, *1:* 29 (ill.)

Anabolic metabolism *2:* 374

Anabolism *2:* 374

Anaerobic. *See* Aerobic/anaerobic.

Anaerobic respiration *2:* 346; *3:* 514

Anaphase *1:* 106

Anatomy *1:* **30–33**

The Anatomy of Plants 1: 73

Anaximander *1:* 211

Androgens *3:* 532

Aneuploidy *1:* 125

Angiosperms *3:* 472, 525

Animacules *2:* 380

B

F

W

X

Y

Z